I0593172

# THE EARTH KING'S HEIR

## The Kyprian Prophecy Series

*Beginnings – An Origins Novella*

*The Earth King's Heir – Book 0*

*The Firemaster's Legacy – Book 1*

*The Water Catcher's Rise – Book 2*

*The Air King's Return – Book 3*

*The Ice Queen's Revenge – Book 4*

## Other Series

*Fae of the Crystal Palace*

## Anthologies Featuring Kylie Fennell

*Lighthouse*

*Forbidden Doors*

*Stories of Survival*

*First Peoples Shared Stories*

# THE EARTH KING'S HEIR

### THE KYPRIAN PROPHECY BOOK 0

### A PREQUEL

## KYLIE FENNELL

Lorikeet
inK

Published by Lorikeet Ink, Brisbane (Yuggera and Turrbal Country), Australia. The publisher acknowledges the Aboriginal and Torres Strait Islander peoples – the Traditional Custodians of the lands on which we live and work.

www.lorikeetink.com

First published in Australia in 2022.

ISBN 978-0-6454052-1-7 (eBook)

ISBN 978-0-6454052-2-4 (paperback)

A catalogue record for this book is available from the National Library of Australia.

Cover design by Jo Edgar-Baker

Maps by Dewi Hargreaves

Author photo by Marissa Powell

Ornamental break icon by Freepik via Flaticon.com

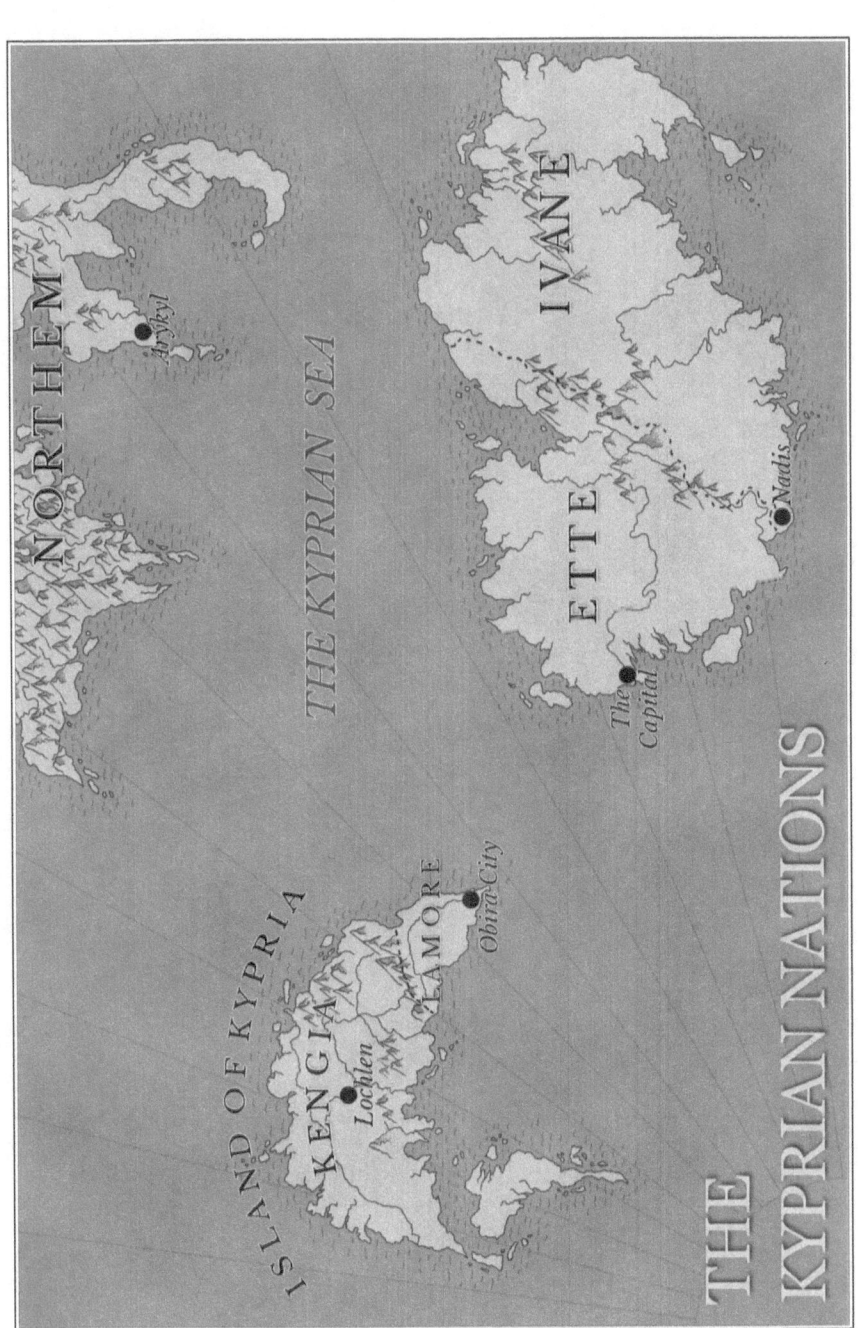

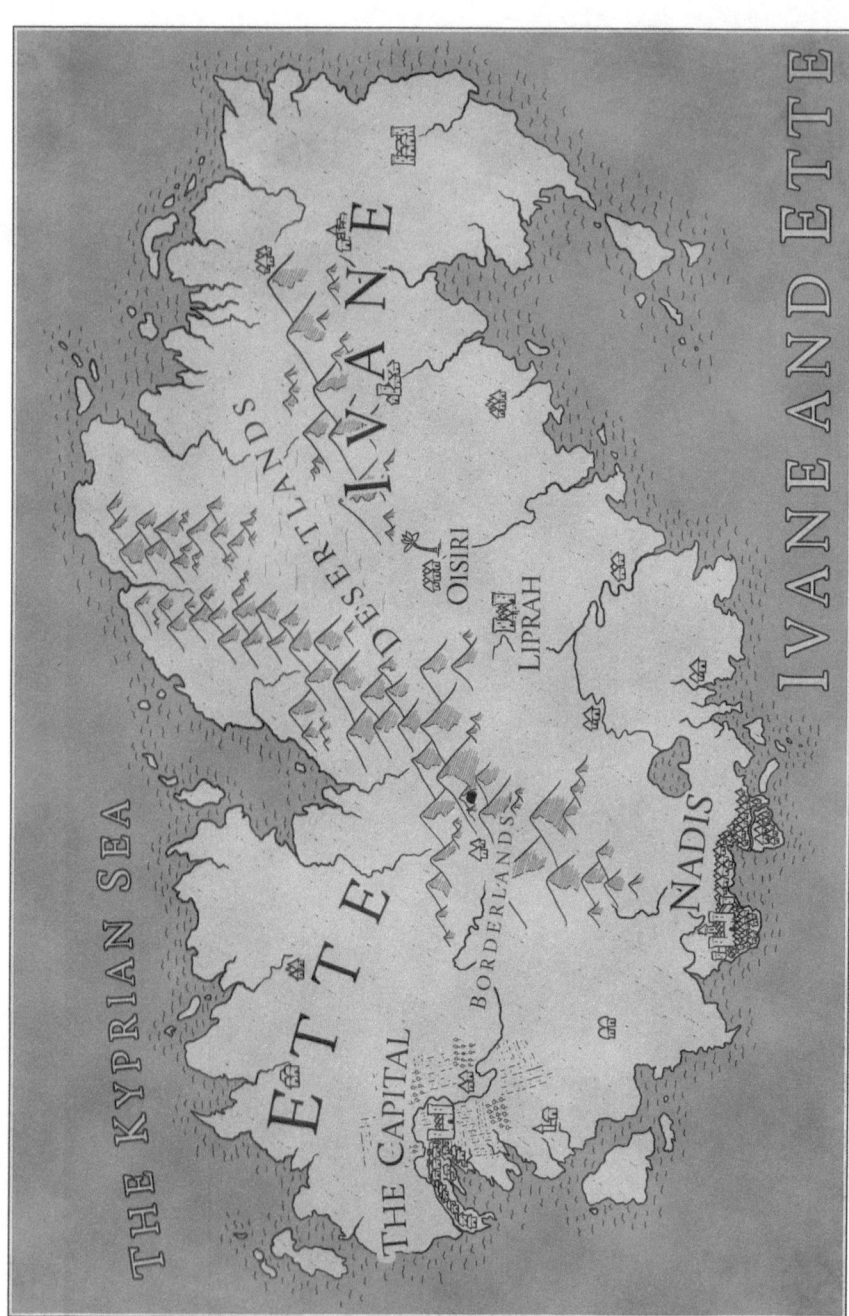

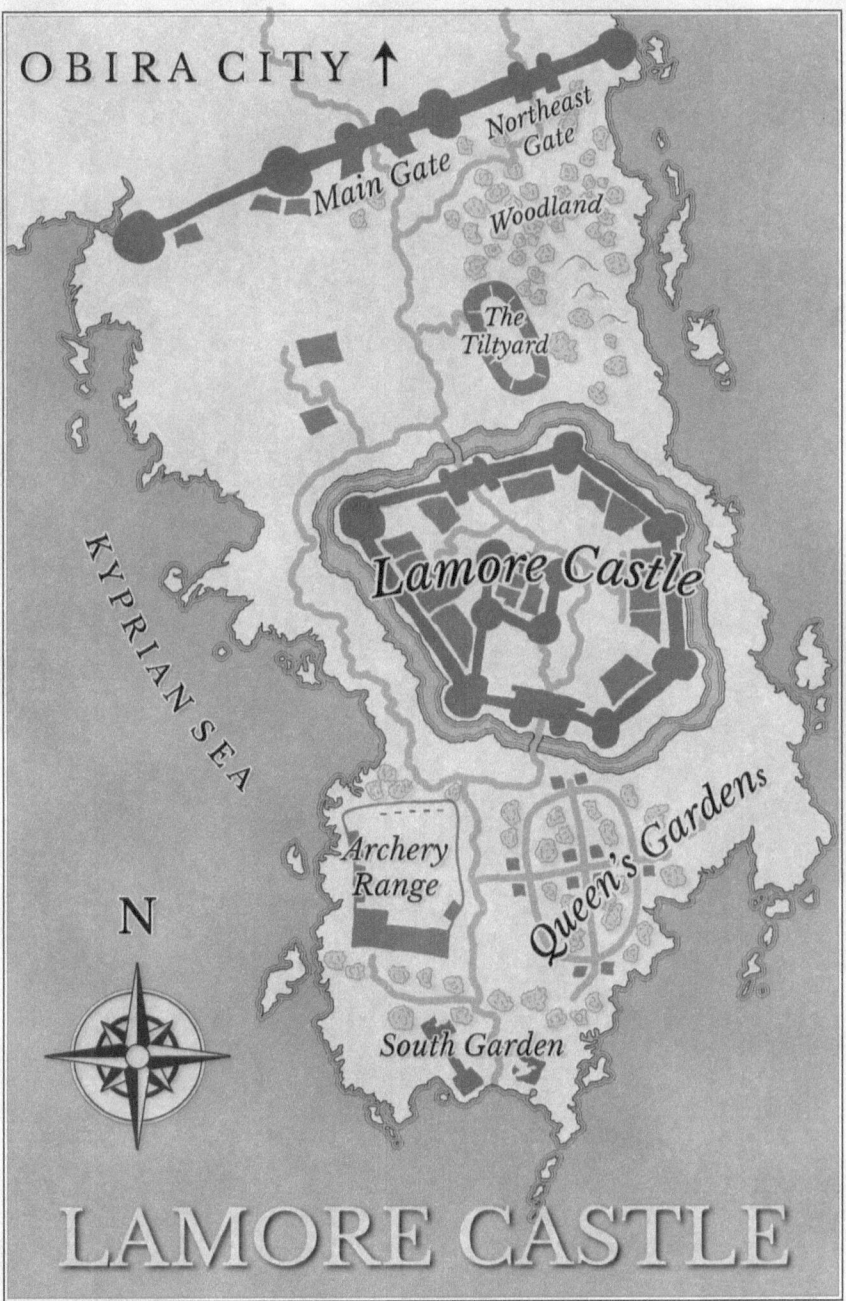

# PROLOGUE

The healer – the witch, as some called her – had seen it.

A reckoning. The means for restoring balance and prosperity to all of Kypria. But the exact path to the final outcome was clouded. Her vision nothing more than a series of interspersing images, like thousands of silk threads that must be woven in a precise manner and order to produce the desired pattern. Even so, she had seen enough to know with certainty what she must do. The first step on the journey was as clear as if it had been illuminated by a thousand Alia crystals.

Blood. Fire. A girl.

To stand a chance of saving the Kyprian nations, and her own kind, she must save the Ettean Princess and get her to safety.

# 1

$\mathcal{N}$avigating the Ettean mountains took an equal amount of care and confidence. One misplaced step or lapse of concentration could spell disaster. But even at ten – nearly eleven – years old, Gwyn could traverse the scree slopes and sheer-faced ridges with the agility of a mountain goat. The Borderlands and its towering jumble of rocky peaks were her home and the only world she knew.

She bounded down the gravelly incline. Every angle, pebble and rock formation was committed to memory, enabling her feet to move in a frantic yet finely tuned and choreographed dance. Her sheepskin pouch, filled with wild berries, slapped furiously against her thigh. Her mother had promised to make berry pie to welcome home her father – the tribal Chief or King of these parts. Gwyn's father had been visiting other villages in the region, helping them to prepare their defences against the Lamorian forces.

For more than a hundred years, Lamore had ruled Ette, but the original inhabitants, particularly those in remote areas like the Borderlands, had been left alone in relative peace, as long as they never challenged the Lamorian regime. But things had changed in recent times. Grumblings of discontent among the people, over rising taxes and the disintegration of Ettean rights, had crescendoed. People like Gwyn's father had started speaking of a revolution – a plan to retake the country and appoint an Ettean King as their leader.

When whispers of an uprising had reached the Capital, the Lamorian-appointed Governor had begun to pick off the nation's regional leaders one by one, putting an end to any potential opposition. The Ettean Kings were given a choice: relinquish their titles and bend the knee to the oppressors or die trying to defend their birthright. Gwyn's father was the last King standing. Many of the women and children had recently fled their village in anticipation of an attack, but Gwyn and her mother had stayed put. The King, of course, had begged his wife and daughter to leave for their safety, but both had refused. Gwyn's mother argued her place was by her husband and their people's sides, and Gwyn was unwilling to be parted from her parents, practically screaming down their stone hut at the prospect of leaving them.

She tried not to think about the danger they were all in, or about whether her father was still alive, but when her mind did unwittingly wander to those thoughts, a hard, spiky lump formed in her throat. Today the lump was overly present. As she raced down the mountainside toward where she hoped to find her father, something felt amiss. The lump suddenly ballooned, threatening to choke her. Gwyn struggled to draw enough air into her lungs and her footing became less sure. Her legs pumped uncontrollably, moving like they had a mind of their own.

A tight corner and a ledge that dropped away to nothing loomed ahead. Gwyn dug her heels into the gravel. Tiny bits of stone sprang up at her, pricking her legs. The passing landscape a blur, she struggled to stay upright as the ledge grew terrifyingly close. She pressed her heels harder into the ground. She was slowing, but the ledge…

Gwyn mustered all of her strength, digging her feet even more forcefully into the gravel, her leg muscles on fire. Heart lodged in her throat, she finally skidded to a halt and came to a shuddering stop just short of the edge.

Doubled over, her eyes closed, Gwyn sucked in chestfuls of air. She told herself to stop panicking. Her father was practically a god – at least in her eyes. He couldn't die…He *couldn't*…

One deliberate inhalation. Another. Her breath slowly regulated. As she opened her eyes, her gaze fell on a lone dandelion, its spherical head a cloud of seeds as light as air. A tentative smile came to Gwyn's lips. The dandelion was a hopeful sign. The plant could survive and thrive almost anywhere.

Gwyn watched the dandelion for several moments, entranced by the delicate arrangement of seeds bending and swaying in the breeze. She recalled a day, a year or so before, when she and her father had been on the mountain trying to track down a stray sheep and had come across a lone dandelion like this one. He'd picked the flower from the ground and shown it to her, explaining how the dandelion's fragility was its strength.

'Each individual seed is filled with the promise of new life,' he'd said. 'Poised for release, they're ready to accept the call to unknown adventures and a new home where they can take root.' Then he'd blown the seeds until nothing was left but a bare stem.

Gwyn had cried, accusing her father of killing the flower.

The King had wrapped his daughter in his giant arms and assured her that everything was well. 'The dandelion is born of the earth, like you and I, and its roots will reshoot again – but its destiny lies in the wind and air.'

Gwyn would help this dandelion fulfil its destiny, but she would ask something of it in return – she would make a wish. She plucked the dandelion from the ground and held it aloft. She didn't dare say her wish out loud in case it wouldn't come true, but what she desired was no secret. Gwyn took a deep breath and wished for the safe return of her father before blowing directly into the dandelion's heart. She grinned as the feather-winged seeds came unstuck and took flight into the clear blue sky. She imagined the seeds reaching all the way to the clouds – the home of the Princess Guardians.

Ettean mythology was another thing the King had taught her, including the tale of the three Princesses. War had come for their father too. Invaders from a far-flung land had arrived to take the Ettean nation as their own. They attacked the Princesses' village and there was a great battle. The King and Queen fought side by side, but the invaders vastly outnumbered the Ettean villagers. The Princesses were only young, not much older than Gwyn, so were put into the care of an elderly couple who tried to take them to safety, but the girls evaded their protectors. They took up their own weapons and followed their parents into battle.

The King, distracted by his daughters' arrival, took an enemy's spear to the chest and perished. The Queen fought on valiantly, trying desperately to keep the girls from harm, but she too was fatally injured. As the Queen drew her last breath, she called on the power within the earth – the Ettean land to which they were forever connected – to save the Princesses.

Wings suddenly sprouted from the Princesses' backs and they rose up into the clouds, where they would remain to watch over the citizens of Ette for eternity. One of the

Princess Guardians became known as Honour. The second was called Justice. And the third was the Ettean Guardian of War.

Mythology, as well as other aspects of Ettean culture, had long been banned by the Lamorians, but it didn't stop the people from believing. All Etteans had a strong connection to the land they lived on, and they had all, at one time or another, called on the Princess Guardians for guidance and protection.

Gwyn drew back her shoulders, confident that her dandelion wish and the Princess Guardians would be enough to secure her father's safety. Taking in a lungful of crisp mountain air and the warming rays of the silver sun, she found herself imagining a different future for her country – a future free of Lamorian rule.

From her vantage point high up in the mountains, she surveyed her homeland. On the horizon, the hint of a river winked back at her as it wound its way through green pastures and orchards all the way to the Capital. Ette's capital city was the reason the Lamorian King Emberto had taken Ette in the first place. It was the largest and most powerful trading port in all the known world – this was why it was known simply as the Capital. Gwyn had never visited the place and never would while she and her family were a threat to Lamorian rule. She sighed, shifting her gaze to the scrubby hills and barren landscape that was the Borderlands – and then she saw it: two distinct clouds of dust to her right, coming from the direction of the village closest to theirs.

The sound of pounding horse hooves reached Gwyn's ears as the outline of a dozen or so riders became clear ahead of the first dust cloud – her father and his men heading toward their village. Some distance behind, a much larger group of riders followed with a flagbearer at its head. Even from this distance, Gwyn immediately recognised the image on the banner. A peregrine falcon – the Lamorian King's insignia.

Gwyn's hands balled into fists, and after one final glance to the sky and a silent appeal to the Princess Guardians, she raced down the mountainside, ready to defend her home.

A BREATHLESS GWYN arrived back in her village amid chaos.

The cries of children and the thunderous approach of horses' hooves filled the air, which was wound so tight there was no room for anything but a sense of rising terror. People sprinted to the village entrance, armed with spears, bows and arrows. A group of older women and children raced toward Gwyn. They barged past her, satchels hung haphazardly over their shoulders, contents spilling to the ground as they rushed toward the trail that led to the neighbouring country, Ivane.

Gwyn grabbed a woman – Trina, the blacksmith's wife – by the arm. 'Have you seen my father?'

Trina shifted her panicked gaze to Gwyn, her eyes struggling to focus. Then there was recognition. She grasped Gwyn's free hand.

'Princess, you have to come with us to safety. The Lamorians are on their way.' She tried to drag Gwyn away from the village.

'No. I can't go.' Gwyn pulled against her, but it was no use; Trina was much stronger than her, having assisted her husband at the forge for years. 'I have to see my father!'

Trina ignored Gwyn's pleas and dragged her further away.

'Father! Mother!' she screamed, but her words were drowned out by growing sobs, wails and calls to battle.

The sound of hooves reverberated in Gwyn's ears. The

riders were close; her father was close. She struggled to break free of her self-appointed saviour, but Trina only tightened her grip.

She would not flee from her home like a coward. She would not give in to the invaders. She had Honour, Justice and the Guardian of War on her side.

Gwyn closed the arm's length distance between herself and the blacksmith's wife and lowered her head. She opened her mouth wide, then bit down hard on Trina's arm.

'Ow!' Trina howled, releasing Gwyn from her hold. 'What did you do that for?' She rubbed the bite mark on her upper arm.

'I have to help Father.' Gwyn stood up to her full height. 'We have to stand up to them.'

A sad look came to Trina's eyes. 'And that is what we tried to do. All of Ette tried, but we failed, child. It's over.'

Gwyn jutted out her chin. 'Not yet it's not.' She spun on her heels and ran full tilt back into the village.

'May the Princess Guardians watch over you,' the woman shouted after her.

Gwyn reached the village entrance and pushed her way to the front of the group assembled there, desperate to catch a glimpse of her father. By now everyone was silent, watching and waiting, just as she was. Their collective gaze was on the bend of the road – the final approach to the village. The only sound was the drumming of hooves on earth. Gwyn held her breath, her fingernails digging into her palms. She wished she had stopped to get a weapon.

'Gwyn!' Her mother's voice, high-pitched, behind her.

She turned slowly to face the Queen.

'What are you doing here? Go back up the mountain or leave with the others.' Her mother's eyes darted to the road and back again. She tightened her grip on the blade-tipped staff in her hands; her knuckles went white. 'You have to go now.'

Gwyn lifted her chin. 'I belong here, fighting for our people. And I have to see if Father...' Her voice broke. She took a deep breath. 'I have to see if Father is alive.'

The Queen's stern expression softened. She bent down so she was eye to eye with her daughter.

'Your father is the greatest warrior ever known. He lives; I know it in my bones. But he will never forgive me if I let harm come to you.' Her serious face returned. 'You have to get to safety.'

A man's scream pierced the air. It came from the same direction as the approaching riders.

Gwyn crossed her arms, partly to show her defiance, partly to still her shaking hands. 'I'm not leaving,' she said with as much courage as she could muster.

Her mother's protest was drowned out by another villager's shout.

'They're here!'

Gwyn swivelled to look for her father and the Ettean riders came into view, their faces and leather chest armour a grimy mix of blood and dust. Several were slumped over in their saddles. The King rode at their lead. A bloody gash arced his upper arm, but otherwise he seemed uninjured.

Gwyn made to run to him, but her mother's firm grasp stopped her.

'Stay alert!' the Queen ordered their group. 'The Lamorians will be close behind.'

The King galloped toward them and leapt from his horse. 'This is it!' he shouted to his people as he took up a position in front of them, along with what was left of his riders. He raised his sword in the air. 'We take our last stand here!'

Gwyn wrenched herself free of her mother's hold and

rushed to the King's side. 'Father!' she cried, throwing her arms around his waist.

The King's eyes widened. 'Daughter? What are you...?' It was the first time she had heard fear, real fear, in her father's voice. Then her mother was there, and the King fixed an accusatory stare on his wife.

'I'll get her to safety.' The Queen yanked Gwyn's arm.

'*No!*' she screeched, pulling hard against her mother. Her ear-splitting scream was second only to the burgeoning roar of the enemy's cavalry. She thrashed around and twisted until she managed to break free and ran back to her father.

She puffed out her chest and looked the King squarely in the eyes. 'I'm no coward. Give me a weapon and I will fight.'

The King reached out with a calloused mitt of a hand and lifted her chin. A smile tugged at the sides of his mouth. 'No one would ever accuse you of being a coward. You have the combined heart of all the Princess Guardians.'

Gwyn's heart billowed with pride, but deflated almost as quickly when her father's smile gave way to a frown.

'But this is not your fight, daughter.' Gwyn made to object, but he held up his palm to silence her. 'The day will come, Gwyn, when you get to fight for what you believe in, but it is not today. Today you must let us defend Ette. It is our responsibility. It is theirs.' He glanced around at the assembled group. 'More than that, it is our honour. An honour we can't be denied.' The King's eyes shone with tears. 'But if you are here in battle, all I will be concerned with is your safety. And it shames me to say that I would forsake my duties to my people to protect you instead. Do you understand?'

Gwyn bit her lip to contain her own tears. She did understand what her father was saying; she just wished it weren't true. 'I will go with Mother,' she said in a tiny voice.

The King nodded and drew her into his arms. Pressed

against her father's chest, uncaring of the film of blood and dust, she felt safe, like nothing could ever separate them.

The King kissed the top of Gwyn's head. 'Remember, Gwyn. You are forever connected to this land. You are the daughter of a King, who was born of this earth, who stands as tall and strong as the Ettean mountains to defend what is right. And as my heir, you will get your chance. I love you.'

'I love…you,' came her muffled, tearful reply, but Gwyn couldn't be sure if he heard her. At that exact moment, amid a cacophony of war cries, the enemy rounded the corner to the village and barrelled toward them.

Dozens of warhorses and their Lamorian riders bore down on the Etteans. Gwyn's father released her and led the charge, sprinting headlong at the enemy with sword and spear raised.

Enemy riders crashed through the Ettean frontline, their sweeping blades carving through the villagers, separating heads and limbs from bodies. In the distance, Gwyn's mother called her name, but it was impossible to see her through the swirling dust kicked up by the horses' hooves. Blood-curdling screams penetrated the murky air along with the whistle of fire arrows, and then the petrifying glow of thatch roofs and huts alight.

Gwyn spun in circles, searching futilely for her parents, her heart hammering in her chest. She blinked rapidly, trying to discern among the chaos anyone who could help her, but everyone was fully occupied fighting for their lives. An Ettean, the blacksmith, crashed into her, a crossbow bolt protruding from his chest. She stumbled backward, only to be skittled by a passing horse.

Gwyn hit the ground hard. Something in her chest cracked. An explosion of pain. She pulled breath through her nostrils, but each inhalation was like a knife slicing through her lungs. She pushed herself into a sitting position and, with sobs stuck in her throat, called on the Princess Guardians. Her prayer was beyond honour, courage or victory in war. It was simply to survive this day.

Running footsteps sounded behind her. Someone grabbed her arm, jolting her and sending waves of pain through her.

Unable to scream, unable to fight, she closed her eyes for death.

'It's me, Gwyn.'

The girl's eyes flung open to see her mother's steely gaze.

The Queen led her daughter back through the village. In her free hand she held her staff at the ready. Gwyn pushed aside her pain, whimpering only when her mother jerked her hard in one direction to avoid a Lamorian soldier.

The Queen steered them to their hut, where the fire arrows were yet to reach. She flung open the heavy wooden door and shepherded Gwyn inside, then pulled a pile of sheepskin rugs from their beds.

'Hide under these until everything is over,' the Queen said. 'Don't come out for anything, no matter what.'

Gwyn nodded, beyond any argument.

The Queen pulled a knife from a sheath at her hip. 'Take this and don't hesitate to use it if anyone comes near.'

Gwyn grasped the bone handle and clenched her fingers into a fist around it.

The Queen fixed her daughter with a drawn-out gaze, eventually giving a strained smile. Then she jutted out her chin and left the hut, pulling the door closed behind her.

GWYN HAD PROMISED her mother she'd stay hidden, but she had to know her parents were alright.

She scrambled to the nearest shuttered window and

angled the louvres open a slit. It was enough to catch snatches of the battle. Lamorians swarmed the village like a plague of hungry locusts. The Etteans floundered in a sea of black and silver – the Lamorian King's colours. Bodies of men and women Gwyn had known since she was a babe lay scattered, lifeless in the dirt. Their deaths captured in grimaces, frozen-eyed surprise and the most gruesome wounds.

Bile surged into her mouth, but she couldn't look away. Her gaze passed over one body, then the next, shifting to the battle itself, searching for her parents. The Ettean numbers were so few it didn't take Gwyn long to spot her mother.

At the centre of the village, just visible through the smoke-filled air, three Lamorians circled the Queen. Gwyn's mother held her staff across her body. Shoulders back, she stepped one way then another, each movement carefully calculated. The Queen's weapon was an Ivanian staff, famous for the uniquely shaped razor-sharp blade on the top. Over the years, sympathisers in Ivane had secretly shared their weapons and trained the most gifted Ettean warriors in their use. The Queen had proven a natural with the weapon, something these smirking Lamorians were about to discover.

One of the group advanced on Gwyn's mother with a rapid series of sword strikes. The Queen side-stepped each with ease, then dropped into a low lunge at the same time as she swung her staff into the soldier's legs, sweeping him from his feet. Splayed flat on his back, the Lamorian didn't get a chance to register his predicament before the Queen plunged the tip of her staff into his chest.

The two remaining Lamorians exchanged a glance, then ran at Gwyn's mother. The Queen ducked and dove, contorting her body to avoid their blades. One must have made contact with her arm, as a trail of blood dripped from the Queen's elbow, but she showed no sign of impairment.

When the Lamorian pair paused to take a breath and one moved to take up position behind the Queen, she switched her stance to attack. She spun and twirled her staff, catching the Lamorian in front of her off guard. She brought her staff to an abrupt stop and leapt toward the enemy. The blade found its target in the man's torso.

The Lamorian behind Gwyn's mother charged. The Queen grabbed her staff halfway down the shaft and yanked it free. She spun to face the other soldier and stabbed him in the neck.

The two Lamorians crumpled to the ground one after another and a triumphant cry escaped Gwyn's lips, followed by a yelp of pain from her injured chest. The Queen's head swivelled in her direction, but her attention was immediately drawn to something else.

A herald's bugle rang out across the village. Gwyn's heart stilled.

It was a victory call. A Lamorian victory.


THE LAMORIAN LEADER, a broad-shouldered man with a bald head and a face that appeared carved from stone, dragged Gwyn's father by his hair to the village centre. He yanked the King's limp head back and held a dagger to his throat, ordering the remaining Etteans to lay down their arms. Gwyn's father was barely recognisable under the bloody mass of flesh that was his face. His eyes were swollen shut. A groan that may have been a protest fell from his mangled lips, but the villagers did as the Lamorian bid.

Gwyn exhaled in relief. They may have lost the battle, but her father was alive. Yes, he and the other Etteans would probably be taken prisoner, but they would live.

The leader glanced back at a Lamorian rider who had

pressed his way to the front of the ranks. Not just any rider; this one wore a crown. Gwyn could barely believe it. The Lamorian King himself had joined his army to witness Ette's final defeat. He nodded at the bald-headed commander, whose mouth curled into a sneer, vanquishing Gwyn's hopes. These were not people known for mercy.

With one smooth movement, the Lamorian slid the blade across the King's throat.

'*Nooo!*' Gwyn screamed, uncaring of the stabbing pain in her chest or whether anyone could hear her. '*No, no, no—*'

It couldn't be true. Her father, the strongest, bravest warrior she knew, a giant of a man in size and heart, a King – he couldn't be dead. Not just like that. Not in such a shameful way. If he had to die, it should have been with a sword in his hand, not while surrendering at the hands of a merciless coward. He should have fought on; he should have done something...but maybe he wasn't dead.

Gwyn forced herself to look at her father's prone body. She searched for any sign of life. There was nothing other than a growing pool of blood.

Her chest shuddered with disbelieving sobs. She wanted to run to him, hold his hand, beg him to come back to her, but one horrifying sight stopped her. The Lamorians must have heard her scream, because two soldiers were racing toward her hiding spot, the Queen following behind.

Gwyn backed away from the window and looked helplessly at the pile of rugs that would be no use now in concealing her. The Lamorians knew she was here and were coming for her.

One of the soldiers kicked open the door and marched menacingly toward Gwyn, his sword pointed at her. She staggered back as far as she could go, coming to a stop against the hut's far wall. Then she remembered the knife her mother had given her.

With trembling hands, she held up the weapon and gritted her teeth. 'Don't come any closer,' she said with feigned authority.

The soldier threw back his head in laughter, oblivious to the Queen's approach.

Gwyn's mother burst through the doorway and grabbed a shepherd's crook propped against the front wall. The Queen smashed the curved end of the crook into the soldier's temple with such force that his legs buckled underneath him and he collapsed to the floor.

'It's alright,' the Queen panted, eyes softening as they locked with Gwyn's. 'I'm he—'

Her assurances were sucked away with her breath.

Gwyn's gaze shot to her mother's chest, where a scarlet patch bloomed around the tip of a Lamorian sword.

A ball of fury exploded in Gwyn's stomach and she launched herself at the soldier, her knife raised. There was a flare of panic in the Lamorian's eyes as he struggled to pull his sword free. The reason soon became apparent: the Queen was using the last of her strength to hold the weapon in position. Blood poured from her hands where the blade bit into them.

Fresh pain ripped through Gwyn. She dared not believe it, but her mother was dying before her, mere moments after her father had been taken from her. Another of Ette's greatest warriors cut down by the hateful Lamorians. Not just any warrior – her *mother*.

But maybe the Queen could still be saved. Maybe Gwyn could save her. She was, after all, an Ettean Princess and the King's heir. It was up to her to fulfil her destiny and be the leader her father had raised her to be. Gwyn knew then that not only were the Princess Guardians with her, filling her with courage, but so were her father and mother.

She jammed the knife hard into the soldier's neck. The man's blood spurted all over her face, but she didn't stop to wipe herself clean. She was already by her mother's side, clasping the Queen's maimed hands and begging for her to live.

'It will be alright, Mother,' she sobbed. 'The soldier's gone now. I did my duty. Now it's up to you. Come back...*please.*'

But all too soon, the glimmer of life in the Queen's eyes faded away to nothing.

'Ready to bend the knee, Princess?' A malignant voice behind her.

Gwyn jumped to her feet and faced the bald-headed leader. She squared her shoulders. 'Never.'

The Lamorian shrugged and struck her in the side of the head with the hilt of his sword.

# 2

---

$\mathscr{F}$ragments of images came to her. Flames licking a tapestry on the wall. Blood – everywhere. Choking on smoke. Searing pain in her chest. A woman with silver eyes leaning over her. The sensation of being dragged from the hut. More pain. Homes on fire. Mortar cracking. Stone walls crumbling.

Her head throbbed. The burning village was getting smaller. She had an urge to stay put. An urge to fight on. A silver-eyed girl was telling her it would be alright. But there was a knowledge that nothing was alright or would ever be again. And then there *was* nothing...

GWYN'S EYELIDS cracked open a sliver and slammed shut immediately against the fiercely bright sunlight. She had no awareness of where she was or what had happened. There was a dull thudding sensation in her head. A tightness in her chest that intensified when she drew breath. Underneath her, rough material that felt like hessian rubbed and scratched her exposed limbs. Beneath that, a hard surface like timber. There was the sense that she was moving. The clatter and crunching of wheels on gravel. Her body rocking and jolting with the motion of what she guessed was a cart.

She clawed her mind for clues – and soon wished she hadn't. Like a lamp suddenly flaring to life, she could see everything. The bodies. The fire. The blood.

Her parents.

Gwyn's eyes flung open and she sat bolt upright. She found herself in the tray of a mule-driven cart. A woman and a child sat at the front, but their features undulated; the scene was a blur. Gwyn's head reeled from sitting up so fast. Her hand went instinctively to her scalp, where she detected a lump and a crusty wound. She glanced down at her fingers, covered in a grey, gritty gunk.

'It's a poultice!' a small voice declared. 'I made it.'

Gwyn struggled to focus on the wavering figure before her. A girl maybe two or three years younger than her, with a mass of brown curls and saucer-like eyes – silver eyes.

Gwyn recalled the image of the silver-eyed woman who'd dragged her from the fire. But none of it made sense. The only people who had silver eyes were of Kengian heritage, and that country had shut itself off from the rest of the world nearly two centuries ago. It was rare to come across anyone of Kengian blood, let alone a silver-eyes. But the girl spoke perfect Ettean, the same dialect and accent as Gwyn.

Realisation hit her with the force of a ram's charge. She jabbed a shaking finger at the woman driving the cart. 'The witch.'

She had heard tales of the line of women with silver eyes who had lived in a cave high up in the Ettean mountains for generations. They were reported to possess magical powers, earning them a reputation as witches. They rarely came down from their mountain home unless called upon to heal someone. Gwyn had always wondered how desperate someone would have to be to make a deal with a sorceress. In every tale she'd heard or read, magic always had a price.

The girl cocked her head and laughed. 'That's not a witch. It's my mother, silly.'

Witch or not, Gwyn wasn't about to stick around to find out what the woman wanted from her. 'Stop the cart! I have to go home.'

The woman gave no indication she had heard.

'*Stop!*' Gwyn attempted to get to her feet and lurch to the front of the cart, but her head spun violently.

'You have to rest.' The girl tugged on the back of Gwyn's tunic, causing a fresh burst of pain in her chest.

Gwyn winced as she lifted her shirt. Her ribs on one whole side were black and blue.

'Mother says you cracked some ribs,' the girl said by way of explanation.

'Where are you taking me?' Gwyn hissed through clenched teeth, gripping the side of the cart as the pain in her head and chest magnified.

'To the Ivanian King,' the girl said matter-of-factly.

Panic tore through Gwyn's body. Ivane, like Ette, was ruled by a Lamorian, a man by the name of Lewin. The difference was the Ivanian Governor had married a Princess of the country's defunct royal line so he could style himself as King. The man's ego was said to be second only to his appetite for power. Gwyn didn't dare think what the Lamorian would have in store for her – heir to an Ettean throne. In any case, she wasn't going to let anyone take her to the enemy.

Gwyn's gaze probed the passing landscape for a means of

escape. Fields of wheat ran either side of the road. They would provide plenty of places to hide if she could get enough of a lead. The sun was starting to set over the mountain range behind them. She could stay hidden until nightfall and then find a way back to Ette. She had to see what was left of her village.

The cart wasn't travelling terribly fast, so Gwyn figured it would be easy enough to jump from it...if she weren't already sporting several debilitating injuries. But she had to risk it. She had to. She just needed some of that courage she'd had back in the hut when she'd killed the Lamorian soldier.

She flinched at the memory, but just as quickly pushed it aside. She would think of that later...She would think of all of it later.

Gwyn stumbled to the rear of the cart and took a deep breath, readying herself to jump.

The child's hand clutched her arm. 'You can't jump. You'll hurt yourself.'

Gwyn turned to face the girl, whose wide eyes were flooded with concern. 'Leave me be.' She batted the girl's hand away.

'Mother!'

Gwyn's fingers curled into fists by her sides and she made to leap—

The cart shuddered to an abrupt stop, throwing her back to the timber floor.

Stabbing pain radiated from her ribs. Her chest heaved, desperate for oxygen, breath evading her. She looked up to the sky, sure she was going to die, angry the Princess Guardians had forsaken her. Hopeful that in death she may see her parents' faces again.

The afternoon sky, sprayed violet and apricot, gave way to darkness. This was it. This was the end.

'I'm coming,' she whispered to her dead father and mother.

Then the darkness took shape. The figure of a woman. Her features slowly came into focus.

Braided brown-black hair. Compressed lips. Piercing silver eyes.

The woman tilted her head and scrutinised Gwyn. She frowned and shook her head.

'You better be worth the trouble,' she muttered.


AFTER GWYN'S FAILED ESCAPE, the woman directed the cart off the road and stopped by a stream to set up camp for the night. She helped clean the blood from Gwyn's body and clothes, giving her a blanket to wrap around herself while her tunic dried. She then handed Gwyn a hunk of bread and some cheese, which Gwyn wolfed down, her appetite winning over the hundred questions that threatened to erupt from her mouth.

The girl plonked herself down on the ground next to Gwyn, grinning stupidly at her between bites of her own bread.

Gwyn took a swig of water from a flask the woman offered her. It did little to quench her thirst. The woman nodded for her to continue drinking. Gwyn guzzled the rest of the water down, one eye on her captor the whole time. The woman returned her stare, silver eyes appraising her — searching for what, Gwyn did not know.

'How are your ribs?' the woman eventually asked.

Gwyn's hand went automatically to her injury and she cringed.

The woman opened a satchel by her side. The scent of dried herbs and plants wafted from the bag filled with small clay jars, vials of coloured liquids and a mortar and pestle. 'I can make you something to ease the pain.'

Gwyn grunted her thanks. She couldn't understand why the woman would want to help her. 'What do you want with me?' she asked.

The woman ignored her question and busied herself pulling items from her satchel. It was the girl who answered.

'We're saving you.'

Gwyn turned to her. 'You have already done that.' She forced a sweet smile. 'And I thank you for it. But now I must go back to my village and help anyone who survived.'

'But...' The girl's bottom lip quivered. 'It's just...'

A rock formed in Gwyn's stomach. 'What is it?'

The girl looked down at her feet.

'There were no other survivors,' the woman said without looking up from her mortar and pestle.

Gwyn's stomach churned violently. She wished she hadn't eaten with such vigour. 'But there are others. Others who fled to safety before the battle. They will return – they will rebuild, and I need to be there...*I need to help my people.*' Her last words sounded like an afterthought, but she was coming to understand that they were, in fact, now *her* people. She was their leader.

The woman shook her head. 'Your destiny isn't in Ette,' she said with certainty.

Anger flared inside Gwyn. She sprang to her feet. 'My destiny isn't with the Ivanian King.'

The woman stopped what she was doing and met Gwyn's gaze. 'That is exactly where your destiny is. I have seen it.'

Gwyn made a scoffing sound. 'And I'm supposed to listen to a witch?'

The girl jumped to her feet and glared at Gwyn. 'Stop calling my mother a witch.'

'If you're not a witch, then who are you?' Gwyn directed her question at the mother.

'I'm a healer and my name is Nima.' She indicated the girl. 'And that is my daughter, Daria, and as she said: we're saving you, Gwyn.'

Gwyn did a double take. 'You know my name.'

'Of course.' Daria giggled. 'You're an Ettean Princess.'

Gwyn lifted her chin. 'Yes, I am, and I demand you take me back where I belong.'

Nima rolled her eyes. 'The sooner you accept your destiny, the better it will be for all of us.'

Gwyn clenched and unclenched her fingers. 'My destiny is not with a Lamorian invader.'

Nima burst into laughter. 'That's who you think we're taking you to?'

Daria was laughing too. Gwyn looked from one to the other. 'I don't understand.'

Nima's laugh petered away, ending in a sigh. She stood up and stepped toward Gwyn. Her silver eyes clouded with sadness, she reached out and tucked a stray wave of hair behind Gwyn's ear.

'You poor child,' she said softly. 'You didn't ask for any of this, but there is a reason this future has been chosen for you.'

Gwyn felt her anger start to wash away with the delicate cadence of the healer's voice.

'What reason?' A wisp of a question.

Nima smiled. 'Because you have the strength to endure it and more.'

Tears pricked Gwyn's eyes. She couldn't imagine having to endure anything worse than what she'd already faced.

Then again, Nima was planning on taking her to Nadis, the capital of Ivane.

'You're sure my future is with the Ivanian King?'

Nima nodded her confirmation.

Daria clasped Gwyn's hand in hers. 'The *real* Ivanian King.'

*G*wyn travelled south with Nima and her daughter, resigning herself to her 'destiny', as the healer called it. It wasn't like she had any choice. Even if she were strong enough to try to escape, where would she go? She knew in her heart and from the images that permeated her sleep that her village was gone, along with her parents.

Sitting between mother and child at the front of the cart, Gwyn interrogated Nima with questions about her future and how and what she had seen. Nima would brush off her queries, saying only that she had had a vision showing that she must save Gwyn and take her to the Ivanian King.

Nima explained that there hadn't been a true Ivanian King on the throne ever since Lamore had taken the nation nearly one hundred and eighty years before, but in secret, the Ivanian people remembered and recognised their royal line. The Princess, Ona, who the Ivanian Governor had married to become King Lewin, was in fact the eldest child of the surviving royal line, but she wasn't the heir. The Lamorians failed to understand – or hadn't bothered to learn about – the thousand-year-old Ivanian custom that didn't allow a female to inherit the throne. As far as the Ivanians were concerned, their actual King was Ona's younger brother, Arlo, the Weapons Master at Nadis Palace. This was the man to whom Nima was taking her.

'This Arlo is a good man?' Gwyn asked, anxious about the nature of the man who was to care for her.

Nima shrugged. 'He must be.' Her eyes didn't leave the road ahead. 'Otherwise, I wouldn't have seen it.'

Gwyn's stomach pitted into tight coils. Nima didn't know the Ivanian King at all.

Sensing her discomfort, Daria squeezed Gwyn's hand. 'You'll be alright. I know it in here.' With her free hand Daria tapped her chest earnestly, but it gave Gwyn little comfort.

Nima clicked her tongue to hurry the mule. 'I may not know the King, but I know an Ivanian healer who serves at the palace. If you are ever in trouble you can go to him – you can trust Ambra with your life.'

Then the tears came.

'Please don't cry,' Daria pleaded. 'You will be alright. Mother said they will take care of you.'

'That's just it.' Gwyn pushed the words out past the lump in her throat. 'Yesterday morning I was up in my mountains, collecting berries for a pie to welcome my father home. I had a mother and a father and a home, a kingdom that one day I would lead, and now…' She choked back a sob. 'Now I'm to live among the enemy, far away from home, and pretend that I'm someone I'm not.'

Nima stopped the mule and turned to her.

'I'm sorry that this is your fate, Gwyn,' she said in a gentle voice. 'But everything that is asked of you is within your power. You have been called on for a great destiny, and you have the strength to see it out. That I am sure of.'

ON THE SECOND night of their journey, they stayed in a ramshackle hut at the base of the mountains. Nima said hunters used it in cooler months when hunting for alpine ibex. The gap-toothed timber walls provided little protection from the elements, but fortunately the night was mild, and there was an assortment of dusty stretchers that they could rest on: a vast improvement on the hard ground they'd slept on the night before. Not that Gwyn had gotten much sleep since the attack on her village.

The first night she had been plagued by nightmares, reliving her parents' deaths over and over. Images of bodies, blood and fire had revolved through her mind, magnifying in gore until she'd woken in a film of sweat.

Tonight, she dreamt she was running through the village, the bald-headed Lamorian chasing her. She was searching for her parents, scanning the faces of the dead, but everybody had the same face...Her own. The heavy footfalls of the Lamorian grew nearer and she tried to run faster, but the harder she tried, the slower her limbs moved. Something was holding her back.

She stole a glance at her feet. A dozen pairs of hands gripped her ankles and calves. Then the hands were hauling her back toward her pursuer, his cruel taunts signalling she would soon follow her parents in death. Then they weren't hands; they were tentacles of flame, circling and spitting at her. She howled in pain as singe marks sprang up on her body, and with an enormous *whoosh*, the fire engulfed her.

Her scream was swallowed up by the flames, and then she was sitting awake on her stretcher. Drenched in sweat, her pounding heart threatening to burst from her chest.

Gwyn took slow gulps of air as she returned to reality.

Her ribs screamed in pain at every contraction. She looked around the hut, her eyes going to Daria next to her. The girl must have pulled her stretcher over to Gwyn's at some stage during the night. There was barely an inch between their beds, but the girl remained fast asleep. Her chest gently rose and fell in a steady rhythm, an endearing snuffling sound emitted each time she inhaled and exhaled. Nima's stretcher was empty.

Glowing light peeked through the cracks of the hut walls. At first, Gwyn thought it was coming from the campfire they'd cooked their dinner on earlier in the night, but a swift glance confirmed nothing remained of the fire except a few dying coals, not enough to produce the light she was seeing. In any case, the glow was a silver colour, unlike anything Gwyn had seen before.

Her gaze went to the source of the light. Nima clutched a vial filled with shimmering liquid. The light pulsed like a beating heart, as if the vial contained the essence of life itself. It was intoxicating, drawing Gwyn to it. She drifted through the hut door, dreamlike.

'What is it?' she asked in a hushed voice.

Nima turned slowly to face her. Her grip tightened around the vial. 'It is Alia.'

'*Ah-lia.*' Gwyn rolled the word around her mouth. It was familiar to her. She realised it was the combination of two Ettean words: *ahha*, meaning *life*, and *lia*, meaning *rock*. She peered closer at the particles floating in the liquid. 'It doesn't look like a rock.'

'Alia is more like a crystal in its true form.' There was a wistful tinge to Nima's voice. 'As strong as it is magical.'

Gwyn seated herself on the sandy ground next to Nima. 'Strong?' She pointed at the Alia. 'But it's little more than dust.'

'This is Alia Water. I used ma—' She bit her lip, presumably to stop herself from talking of spells or the like. 'I used some particular knowledge to ground the Alia crystal into a powder that I could mix with water.'

Mesmerised by the dancing light, Gwyn made to touch the vial, but Nima held it out of her reach.

'I've never seen anything like it,' Gwyn marvelled. 'Where did you get it?'

'It comes from my home in the mountains…' Nima's gaze fixed on a point in the darkness where the end of the Ettean alps would be. 'I don't like to venture far from home. When I leave the mountains, I feel like a part of me is missing.' Her free hand went instinctively to her heart. 'But when I hold the Alia Water…' Nima's chest lifted as she drew a deep breath. 'I feel connected…' Her words trailed away into a sigh and she tucked the vial into her satchel.

Gwyn's stomach knotted. She knew exactly how Nima felt. She had been born to understand and rely on her connection to the earth of the Borderlands. Her home that no longer existed. But there was something that perplexed Gwyn. A question that had tormented her long before she met Nima. Perhaps the healer may have the answer she needed.

'Don't you consider Kengia your homeland as well as Ette?'

Nima jabbed a poker at the dying fire. 'Kengia abandoned my kind a long time ago,' she said without meeting Gwyn's eyes.

'They abandon everyone,' Gwyn muttered, squeezing her hands into fists. 'Why didn't they come to help us? They could have stood with Ette against Lamore and…' Her voice shook, but she pressed on. 'None of this would have happened. Mother and Father would still be...' Her words disintegrated into a sob.

Nima took Gwyn's hand in hers. Her fist naturally unfurled. 'Kengia will never venture beyond the safety of their magical borders,' she said. 'Not until the prophecy comes to pass.'

Gwyn wiped tears from her cheek. 'Prophecy?'

'Yes. It speaks of a catcher of water, from Kengia's first-born line, who will unite all of Kypria and deliver us from darkness.'

Intrigued by such a prophecy, Gwyn sat up straight and turned to face Nima. 'Someone who can catch water?'

'They would have the power to harness and control water.' Nima shrugged. 'But while the Kengian royal family's firstborn is known to inherit power to command natural elements like earth and air, none in history have had an affinity with water.'

The tiny sense of hope that had flared inside Gwyn was immediately extinguished. 'You don't believe in the prophecy?'

Nima retrieved her hand from Gwyn's and looked back toward the fire. 'I believe in many things, but the bigger concern is that the Lamorian Kings have been taught to believe and fear it. The prophecy is the reason why King Emberto, all those years ago, took the throne from his brother, who'd married a Kengian Princess. He was afraid his brother's child – a child of Kengia's firstborn line – would bring about Lamore's downfall. In his mind he had to secure Ette and Ivane before Kengia controlled all of Kypria.'

Gwyn's mind swirled in confusion. She had heard stories of King Emberto, but never an account that painted Kengia in such a manner. 'Kengia wanted more territories?'

Nima shook her head emphatically. 'That is not the

Kengian way. But in Emberto's mind Kengia was the enemy, and he would stop at nothing to make sure the prophecy never eventuated. It is why Kengia has locked itself away from the rest of the world for so long.'

Gwyn scowled. 'Prophecy or not, they should have tried to help.'

Nima got to her feet and brushed sand from her tunic. 'Yes, they should have.' She headed back toward the hut. 'We will reach Nadis by tomorrow afternoon,' she said over her shoulder.

Gwyn jumped up to follow. 'Will I ever see Ette again?'

Nima turned back to her and gave a sad smile. 'I'm afraid your future is elsewhere.'

She made to protest, but Nima held up a hand to silence her.

'You will serve your people, Gwyn. You will serve many, far beyond the reaches of your imagination, but it will not be in Ette.'

'I don't understand,' Gwyn cried after Nima, but the healer was already gone.

# 4

*N*adis Palace emerged from the sand-coloured landscape like a magnificent ship making its launch. At least, that was what Gwyn imagined it looked like, having never seen a ship or a palace. Fresh sea air swelled her lungs. She marvelled at the taste of salt on her lips and sat up tall to get a better view of everything before her.

With its extensive collection of towers and ramparts, and a formidable wall shielding hundreds of buildings across a vast plateau, Nadis Palace was a city in its own right. The Kyprian Sea sparkled like sapphires on the horizon, eliciting gasps of wonder from Daria and Gwyn. At the base of the plateau was a bustling port city marked by clumps of spiring stone buildings resembling a human-made mountain range. People – more people than Gwyn had ever known in her life – scurried like ants along the docks, loading and unloading merchant vessels.

The trio joined a long line of wagons and Ivanians on foot to enter the palace city through a dome-topped archway. Some were carrying wares: pottery, food and other goods.

Some had bundles of belongings tied to their backs or their steeds, as if they intended to stay for an extended period. Then there were the finely painted carriages led by white trotting horses with long necks and tails held high in the air.

Daria bounced up and down in her seat, her head swivelling to take in the waiting line. 'There's so many people,' she said giddily. 'And those horses!'

Gwyn echoed Daria's astonished sentiment. 'I've never seen anything like them.'

'The horses come originally from Ivane's Desertlands in the north. They are prized for their athleticism and beauty.' Nima screwed up her mouth. 'The Lamorian lords, of course, covet them for their ridiculous carriages, built more for status than practicality.'

A quick glance at the surrounding landscape of hot sand scarred by gravel tracks confirmed how ill-equipped the top-heavy carriages were for this environment. Barely nothing was left of their thin rubber tyres designed for city streets. Gwyn visualised a stained trail of melted rubber marking the Lamorians' journeys from towns and cities they had taken as their own. It was a brutal reminder that she was about to live among the same enemy, and for the hundredth time she wished she were back home.

She had to blink back tears, realising she had no home.

'What are all the people doing here?' Daria asked, blissfully unaware of Gwyn's discomfort. 'Is there a celebration planned?'

Nima clicked her tongue, urging their mule forward. 'No celebration I am aware of. This is quite typical of all the times I have visited. The palace city is a beacon not just for trade, but for the finest scholars and craftspeople. Many come here to study and perfect their craft before returning to their homes to put into practice everything they've learned.

Fulfilling a residency in the palace city is one Ivanian custom that has survived Lamore's occupation.'

As the line jostled forward, a pair of guards wearing Lamorian uniforms of black and silver came into view. They flanked the main gateway, stopping each person before allowing access to the city. The brightly shining hilts of their swords burned Gwyn's eyes, and for a moment she didn't see the guards. She saw only the Lamorian King and his bald-headed offsider – the men who'd taken everything from her.

Her hands itched to hold a weapon of her own.

'What are they doing?' Daria asked, squinting at the guards.

'Checking what everyone's business is in Nadis. The Governor lives in perpetual fear that the Ivanians will rise up against him.'

Sweat suddenly slicked Gwyn's palms. 'What are we to tell them? I'm the daughter of an Ettean rebel.' She said the last part in a low voice.

'It is not just you they will be concerned with.' Nima pulled up the hood of her cloak and indicated Daria and Gwyn should do the same. 'My daughter and I are silver-eyes, remember,' she whispered.

Then it hit Gwyn. The risk Nima had taken in bringing her here. She suspected the fear of silver-eyes and their magic wouldn't be limited to her own village. Like the prophecy, Lamorians had probably been taught to fear the mysterious Kengians, and the powerful silver-eyes among their kind.

'I'm scared,' Daria squeaked next to Gwyn, who took the younger girl's hand in her own.

Nima bestowed a reassuring smile on her daughter. 'Everything will be alright, my love. I *know* it will be.'

They moved forward in the line again. They were next to

be questioned. Gwyn could almost feel the guards' sharp eyes drilling into her, willing her to surrender her secrets.

'Don't say a thing,' Nima instructed Gwyn and Daria. 'I'll do all the talking.'

'State your business,' one guard barked in Ivanian while the other inspected the wagon and its contents. Having grown up so close to the Ivanian border, Gwyn had a basic under-standing of the language.

'I'm bringing traditional herbs and medicine to the King's healer,' Nima said from the shadows of her hood, also in Ivanian.

The guard cast a disinterested gaze at the two girls and grunted, seemingly satisfied they posed no danger. He looked to his colleague, who nodded that the wagon passed his check.

'All weapons must be surrendered on entry to the palace city,' he said mechanically, his eyes already trained on the next visitors in line. 'They will be logged and stored in the armoury. You can retrieve them when you leave.'

'We carry no weapons,' Nima said.

The guard jerked his head back in their direction. He peered closer at Nima, eyes narrowed in suspicion. 'You mean to say a woman and two young girls have travelled across the country without any form of protection?'

Anger burred inside Gwyn. She yearned to tell the guard she was perfectly capable of taking care of herself, just like she'd taken care of the Lamorian soldier in her village, but then she remembered she had nearly died in the process.

The other guard raised an inquisitive brow at them, most likely curious why the line wasn't moving. He strode over and scrutinised Gwyn, then Daria, whose eyes were fixed on her sandalled feet. He reached out to lift her chin, but Nima slapped his plate-sized mitt away.

'Keep your hands—'

Her admonishment was cut short as her hood fell away to fully reveal her face.

The guards' eyes doubled in size.

'She's one of them,' one guard said, gaping.

'A silver-eyes,' said the other, cocking his head one way then the other as he stared at Nima, then Daria. 'Two of them.'

'I'd heard of them, but never seen one…Not in the flesh.' The first guard pressed a pudgy finger into Nima's cheek. She flinched and tried to pull away, but his other hand wrapped around her neck.

'Mother!' Daria cried, prompting the other guard to grab her arm and hold her in place.

'Do you suppose they're as powerful as they say?' he muttered to his offsider.

The first guard shrugged. 'Best we take them into custody for questioning…just in case.'

Nima met her captor's mistrustful gaze. 'I have no powers in these lands.' Somehow she sounded confident, authoritative, even, as she pushed the words out from her constricted throat. '*Everyone* knows the source of our magic is in Kengia. You'd be a *fool* to think otherwise. Here, I am nothing more than a healer.'

The guard's face morphed into a blank expression. Slowly he nodded and loosened his grip on Nima's neck. 'It makes sense.'

Nima smiled at the other guard. 'We are no threat. You will let us go on with our business.'

Appearing impassive, the guard released Daria. At the same time, the other guard's fingers dropped away from Nima's neck. The pair waved them through the gate.

Nima urged their mule forward into the palace city. An

imprint of red finger marks on her throat served as an angry reminder of how close they'd come to being arrested. But how had Nima done it? How had she convinced the guards to let them go? Gwyn shot a confused look at Daria, who grinned back at her.

'Kengian suggestive powers,' she said proudly. 'Only those most versed in spells can use them.'

Gwyn shook her head in disbelief. 'You mean to say you can get people to do anything you want?' She directed her question at Nima.

'Only if the subject is willing to believe what you have to say. You must choose your words carefully, but even then, you will only succeed if what you're saying fits within the person's narrative or beliefs.'

Gwyn turned Nima's words to the guards over in her mind. The way Nima had emphasised how 'everyone' knew silver-eyes' magic didn't work here, and how only a 'fool' would believe otherwise. 'Ha!' She slapped her thigh.

Daria and Nima shared an amused look.

'So silver-eyes *can* use their powers here?'

Nima's mouth twitched. 'No...Not exactly—'

'Look! Look! Look!' Daria interrupted, waving frantically at the city before them.

There were hundreds of buildings peppered with pristine courtyards, topiaries and ponds. Grand stucco buildings the colour of sand were decorated with brightly hued tiles laid in geometric patterns. The main road led up a hill through a marketplace bursting with the scent of spices and roasted meat, as well as an intoxicating energy of commerce. Gwyn's mouth watered at the range of fresh vegetables and fruit, many of which she'd never seen before. Some stallholders sold jewellery – gold, silver and sparkling gemstones. A long line had formed at a stall selling jelly sweets and pastries.

Daria asked her mother to stop, but Nima only hurried their mule onward and told them to pull their hoods back up. Gwyn supposed she didn't want to risk the chance of arrest again.

'Do you know where the King is?' Gwyn lowered her voice. 'King Arlo.'

Nima nodded. 'The *Weapons Master* has quarters near the palace. It's been many years since I was last here, but from memory it's just ahead.'

Daria clapped her hands together. 'We'll see the palace?'

'No time for that. We have to get Gwyn to safety.'

Daria's face fell.

'I'm sorry, my love, but we need to leave this place as quickly as possible. On the surface it might look like a peaceful haven where Ivanians can go about their business, but everything and everyone here is under Lamore's eyes.' She looked up to the rooftop of a nearby building, where Lamorian guards were stationed, watching the marketplace.

Nima brought the wagon to a stop outside a saffron-painted wall with an arched gateway at its centre. Twin timber doors lay invitingly open. A vine with sweet-smelling white flowers hung overhead.

Nima led the way through a series of courtyards, dipping her head in greeting at those they passed while remaining careful to keep her face concealed. Fortunately, the few people they encountered appeared quite absorbed in their own business. Dressed as they were in the finery of nobles, Gwyn could picture each of them owning fancy carriages like the ones they'd seen when they arrived. She understood a few Lamorian words here and there, but for the most part didn't know what they were saying. She noticed that some of them were busy marvelling at swords with carved hilts embellished with dazzling jewels.

'All the Lamorian nobility that matter, or at least think they matter, commission at least one sword from Arlo,' Nima explained. 'Having a blade crafted by the King's own Weapons Master is a sign of unmatched status.'

She stepped away from Gwyn and Daria to speak to a woman passing through the courtyard with a basket of oranges resting on her hip. Gwyn recognised the woman's Ivanian features immediately. Unusually tall, with a long, graceful neck and high cheekbones, the woman wore a loose-fitting tunic of maroon and gold.

She cast a questioning look in the girls' direction, but looked back at Nima as the healer pressed a gold coin into her hand. The woman nodded and disappeared through another gateway. Nima followed, beckoning for Gwyn and Daria to do the same.

# 5

The Ivanian woman, who Nima said worked for Arlo and his family, led them through even more court-yards and open rooms, all featuring mosaic walls and floors and elaborately decorated archways. A corridor stretched the length of the main building, completely open on one side to reveal panoramic views of the sea and city. The woman came to a stop outside an arched timber door. Two guards – Ivanian this time, wearing the same colours as their escort – stood on either side of the door.

The woman spoke to the guards in rapid Ivanian that Gwyn couldn't catch. With a final nod to Nima, she returned the way they had come.

'Wait here,' one of the guards instructed before disappearing behind the timber door.

The remaining guard eyed them curiously, his silent gaze faltering on the two silver-eyes before settling on Gwyn. Self-consciously, she patted down her hair, tucking a brown wave behind her ear. She attempted to smooth out her tunic. A stray blood spot had dried a rust colour. She hadn't seen her reflection for days and could only imagine how she appeared.

The timber door swung open and the first Ivanian guard ushered them inside. Feigning confidence, Gwyn lifted her chin and followed Nima and Daria into the room.

The guard led them through an antechamber, its walls lined with Ivanian staffs, swords, shields, longbows and arrows. The sheer number of items and different styles suggested they were on display to provide examples of the Weapons Master's work rather than serve the aesthetics of the room.

The guard opened another door at the far end of the chamber and indicated they should enter. Gwyn found herself in a modestly sized room, no bigger than the living area of the home she'd grown up in. A heavy timber desk sat under a window that framed yet another spectacular view of the Kyprian Sea. An Ivanian man with long black hair tied back in a ponytail and a neatly trimmed beard leant against the desk, running his finger along the blade of a bejewelled gold dagger. A bloody sliver opened up on his fingertip and he nodded in satisfaction. The man, presumably King Arlo, was perhaps the same age as Gwyn's father...or the age her father had been when he—

Gwyn gulped, unable to finish her thought.

'Your visitors, Master Arlo,' the guard announced after what felt like an eternity.

Arlo looked up at them all, his otherwise handsome brow furrowed. He wiped his bloody finger on the bottom of the sleeveless cloak he wore over his long tunic. At first, he looked annoyed at their presence, but when his eyes, the colour of rich earth, fell on Gwyn, his expression softened to one of sadness. It was as if in that small moment he saw everything she had been through. She gritted her teeth and met his gaze with contrived steeliness. She didn't want this man's pity, even if she needed his kindness.

Arlo was the first to look away. He turned the dagger around so the tip faced him and handed the blade to the guard.

'Please compliment the goldsmith on his work.' Arlo spoke in a deep voice that was equally authoritative and warm. 'It is a fine piece and is ready for the client to collect.'

The guard accepted the blade with a bow, then left the room.

Arlo walked slowly back behind his desk and took a seat. He clasped his hands together, fingers intertwined, and rubbed one thumb against the other. He fixed an unwavering gaze on Nima and the girls as if taking their measure. An itch formed on the top of Gwyn's sandalled foot, but she dared not scratch it.

Finally, the Ivanian King spoke. 'I understand you are seeking refuge?'

Nima gave a half-curtsey. 'Yes, Your Maj—'

Arlo held up his hand. 'Master. Master Arlo, as in Weapons Master. Never anything else,' he said firmly.

'Of course, Master Arlo,' Nima corrected herself. 'We seek—'

Arlo waved his hand. 'I'll stop you there. I cannot provide refuge to a pair of silver-eyes. I am already under enough suspicion in this place. Some believe I wish to take Lewin's throne from him.'

'Don't you?' Nima asked plainly.

The slightest curl formed at the corner of Arlo's mouth, but he shook his head. 'I'm sorry, but harbouring silver-eyes is out of the quest—'

His attention was suddenly diverted to the doorway where a striking Ivanian woman had appeared. She was as tall as

Arlo, but the way her shiny black hair was pulled back and arranged in a flawless bun on her head made it look like she could almost touch the stars. The scent of rosewater wafted toward Gwyn, triggering the whisper of a memory. There was something familiar about the woman.

Arlo stood up to address the newcomer. 'Preia. I'll be with you in just a moment.'

*Preia?* Then Gwyn remembered. It was the name of one of the Ivanian women who had come to her village a few years before. She had provided weapons and trained Gwyn's mother and others in hand-to-hand combat.

'I'll meet you in your rooms,' Arlo continued, but Preia was already at his desk, taking up a position next to him.

'Husband, won't you introduce me to your guests?' She offered Nima, Daria and Gwyn a gracious smile.

Arlo's mouth twitched furiously, as if he were trying to discern their names from thin air, for he had never asked for them. Nima came to his rescue.

'My lady. I am a healer from Ette, and this is my daughter.' She put her hand on Daria's shoulder.

Daria gave a clumsy bow, which Preia acknowledged with the kindest of smiles.

'And I was just explaining to your husband that we have brought an *Ettean friend* here to seek refuge.' As Nima stressed the last words, realisation washed over Arlo's face: he had misunderstood their request. 'Her whole village was destroyed a few days ago by the Lamorian army. She is now an orphan.'

A jagged lump formed in Gwyn's throat. *Orphan.* The sound of her heart breaking into a thousand pieces was contained in that one simple word.

Arlo heaved a sigh. 'I had heard that the last of the villages in the Borderlands had fallen.'

Preia bent down to meet Gwyn's eyes. 'You poor child,' she said gently, taking Gwyn's hand in hers. 'What is your name?'

'Gw— Gwyn.' Her name came out of her mouth in a choking sob.

Preia squeezed Gwyn's hand. 'I once met an Ettean girl by that name.' Her eyes flickered over Gwyn's face, then suddenly widened. 'You are she.' Preia released Gwyn's hand, stood back up and turned to face her husband. 'Gwyn is the Mountain King and Queen's daughter.'

Nima nodded her confirmation.

The King shook his head, unconvinced. 'No, no, no.'

'We must offer our protection,' Preia insisted.

Arlo dropped his voice to an ominous grumble. 'We cannot harbour the last standing heir to an Ettean throne.'

Gwyn's stomach clenched so hard she thought she would stop breathing. She hadn't asked to be brought here. She hadn't wanted to come to Nadis, but now that she was here and could see the fear in Arlo's eyes, she realised she needed his protection – whether she wanted it or not. Protection he didn't want to give.

Preia must have read the anxiety in Gwyn's face. She offered her a tentative smile, then grasped her husband's hand. 'She needs us.'

The rise and fall of Arlo's chest appeared to slow, but his jaw remained set hard as he tried to reason with his wife. 'There must be somewhere else she can go. She could find refuge in an Ettean village. No one needs to know her identity.'

'The girl must be here,' Nima spoke up. 'I have seen it.'

Arlo and Preia's eyes shot toward her. 'Seen what?' the King asked.

'Enough,' she said matter-of-factly. 'Enough to know the

girl is key to uniting all of Kypria, but it is only possible if she is under the Ivanian King's protection. The *real* King.'

Preia stood to all of her magnificent height and squared her shoulders. 'Gwyn will have the King's protection. And she will have mine.' In that moment she was every bit the warrior Gwyn remembered.

Arlo snorted. 'You can't make those promises, my love. Not based on the word of a...a...' His face contorted as he searched for the right word.

'A witch?' Nima suggested with no hint of anger. 'I know that is what people think I am. But I am just a healer. A healer who happens to see things at times. Usually nothing more than snippets, but this vision was different.' Her voice rose in excitement. 'I could see it more clearly than I can see you now before me. The girl must be here,' she said with a sense of finality.

Arlo tapped his fingers on the edge of his desk. 'How exactly is she supposed to unite Kypria?'

Nima frowned. 'I don't know exactly, but I do know that if you don't let her stay, it won't only be the fate of your own land and people at stake.'

Preia crossed her arms and directed an uncompromising look at her husband. 'You want that on your conscience?'

'But we have our own concerns,' he countered. 'Our own *plans* that can't be put in jeopardy.'

Preia dismissed her husband with a wave of her hand and turned back to Gwyn. 'How old are you, my child?'

Gwyn shrank into herself as everyone's eyes bored into her at once. 'Ten,' she replied in a mouse-sized squeak.

Preia spun to face her husband again. 'The same age as your own daughter.'

Arlo threw his hands up in the air in surrender. 'Alright.

She can stay. But we must come up with a feasible story. An explanation for her presence.'

Preia tapped her chin thoughtfully. 'The easiest tale to tell is a true one, or at least partly true. So we will say that Gwyn is an Ettean orphan from the Borderlands...but we will say she's a shepherd's daughter, and that she found her way to Ivane after her village was destroyed. There she found passage to Nadis to offer herself to the mercy of King Lewin. He, of course, considers himself a benevolent Governor and much superior to his Ettean counterparts, who are at constant war while he prides himself on the relative peace in Ivane.'

Arlo rubbed his beard. 'Yes...I imagine that would do the trick. But how did she come to be with us?'

Preia tapped her chin again before speaking. 'We will say it was my cousin's village she encountered.' She turned to address Gwyn. 'I have a distant cousin, a farmer who lives near the Ettean border. I will send him a message. I know he will support our story.'

The King followed his wife's train of thought. 'Yes, we can say he brought the girl here, thinking she could serve as a companion for our daughter.'

Gwyn's hands curled into fists. She was tired of being referred to as 'she' or 'the girl'. It was bad enough she was to be demoted from a Princess to a 'companion', but she was still *someone*.

'My name is Gwyn,' she said, this time in a giant's voice – immediately regretting it when Arlo's bushy brows clumped together as he locked eyes with her. Gwyn guessed that Arlo wasn't the type who liked to be challenged, particularly by a child. He stared at her with an intensity that sent her legs wobbling, but she matched his gaze.

After what may have only been seconds but felt like an eternity, he made a mumbling sound that could either indicate he was impressed by Gwyn's fortitude or beginning to regret his decision to offer protection.

'It is settled, then,' Preia said brightly, breaking the tension in the room. 'Why don't I take you all to the kitchen? You must be famished. I hear the cook has made a fresh batch of pastries.'

Gwyn's stomach growled in response. Daria clapped her hands together. They hadn't eaten for hours.

'Please, if you would take my daughter,' Nima said. 'But first I was hoping to speak to your healer. I believe his name is Ambra?'

'Yes. Ambra,' Arlo confirmed. 'Why do you need to see him?'

'Gwyn has injured ribs. I would like him to examine her.'

Gwyn's heart fell. She was starving and had almost forgotten about her ribs, which only hurt when she pressed them to check if they were still sore. Whatever medicine Nima had given her seemed to have worked.

'It's alright. I feel fine,' she assured Nima. 'But I could really eat,' she added with a hopeful look.

'I can take Gwyn to Ambra after she has eaten,' Preia offered.

Nima gave a strained smile. 'Of course. But I would like to see Ambra in any case. I need to restock certain medicines.'

There was nothing out of place in what Nima had said, but there was something in the evenness of her tone that Gwyn couldn't pinpoint. She shook her head to herself. It was most likely nothing but her extreme hunger playing tricks on her.

'I will have one of my guards take you to Ambra,' Arlo said.

Nima bowed her head. 'Thank you.'

Preia took Daria by the hand to lead her to the kitchen. With her free hand, Daria tugged on Gwyn's tunic. 'Can you believe it? Pastries!' she cried.

Nima hurried them out of the room. 'I will come and find you both as soon as I'm done.'

UNDER PREIA'S INSTRUCTION, one of the cooks set up a table for them by a gurgling fountain in the kitchen courtyard. It was piled up with trays and tiered plates overflowing with treats, and chilled jugs of delectably sweet fruit tea. Daria went straight for the fried pastries dripping in rose syrup.

Gwyn had polished off her third orange-flavoured jelly and was licking the sugar dust from her fingers when Nima came to find them. Daria raced to throw her arms around her mother. Her mouth was ringed scarlet from a bright red fruit filled with pearl-like seeds that exploded deliciously when bitten.

'Oh, Mother,' Daria purred, rubbing her belly. 'I have never tasted anything like it before. Like any of it. I've eaten so much I could burst!'

Nima gave her daughter an indulgent smile. 'I hope the girls haven't been too much trouble,' she said to Preia.

Preia gave a carefree wave. 'Not at all. It's been refreshing to see their reactions. My own children don't know how fortunate they are to live in Nadis, and thanks to my husband's position, our home is practically an extension of the palace.' A nervous edge crept into her voice. 'They've never known what it is to be hungry, or seen the horrors of—'

Her words came to an abrupt stop when she met Gwyn's eyes, which, despite the small happiness she'd found in the last few minutes, must still speak of the horrors she had seen.

Preia patted her hand. 'Well, I am just so glad you're here.'

'Say your goodbyes,' Nima told Daria. 'We have to get going.'

Gwyn's face crumpled. 'Already?' she and Daria said in unison.

'I'm afraid so.' Nima looked sideways through the doors into the kitchen, where the head cook was watching them with intense suspicion. 'We don't belong here.'

Daria dropped her gaze to the ground but nodded.

Gwyn's mouth quivered. 'But will I see you again?'

Nima blinked slowly and turned to her daughter. 'Why don't you see if the cook would be kind enough to pack up some of this wonderful food for our journey.'

Preia looked from Nima to Gwyn. 'What a grand idea.' She held out her hand to Daria. 'Come with me.'

Once they were gone, Nima sat down at the table with Gwyn. The light in her eyes undulated like the bubbling fountain nearby. It was as if a strong wind had manifested from nowhere, stirring up the pools of water that were her silver eyes. Gwyn could see the answer to her question before Nima spoke the words, and fresh searing pain ripped through her.

'No. I don't think we will see each other again.'

Gwyn leapt to her feet. 'Then I will come with you.' In the short time she'd spent with the mother and daughter, she'd formed a connection with them. They were also her only connection to the land she loved and the only home she knew.

'Your destiny is here.'

Gwyn scowled. 'Stop saying that. Shouldn't my destiny be wherever I decide it to be?'

Nima sighed. 'If only fate worked that way. But it doesn't, so you must stay here.'

'Then stay here with me,' Gwyn begged.

'We cannot,' Nima said firmly.

'So I am nothing to you?' Gwyn cried. 'Just a part of some vision you've had instead?'

'Please sit,' Nima said gently.

Gwyn folded her arms.

'*Please*, Gwyn.'

Gwyn's stance softened, and with a *hmph* she sat back down.

'No. You are not nothing, Gwyn.' Nima's eyes now shone still and clear. 'You are a very special girl, and…Well, in the short time I've known you,' she laughed to herself, 'you have grown on me.' Nima leant across the table and cupped Gwyn's hands in hers. 'But we cannot stay. You have seen. Silver-eyes are not welcome here, and we can't risk bringing unwanted attention to you. We can't put you in danger. You're too important.'

Gwyn shook her head. She was sick of hearing about how she was key to everything.

'We may not see each other again,' Nima persisted, 'but I do know that you and I will be forever connected.'

Gwyn raised a sceptical brow. 'How?'

'That I don't know, but I know it to be true. I have seen it. It is our destiny.'

Gwyn pulled her hands away to wipe her welling eyes.

'This place is amazing!' Daria's high-pitched voice announced her return. She was clutching a basket of food. 'I wish I could stay here forever. You're so lucky, Gwyn, staying here.'

Gwyn forced a smile.

'It will be like you're a Princess here too.' Daria pouted. 'I wish I could be a Princess.'

Gwyn sniffed back her tears to address the younger girl.

'And perhaps you will be one day. Perhaps that will be *your* destiny.'

'Really? You think I could be?'

Gwyn thought for a long moment about how to answer. The reality that she was about to start her new life at the court of her enemy, where she must hide her true identity, hit her with unexpected force. Suddenly she felt many years older than Daria. Her own innocence may have been torn from her, but she would not take the same from someone else.

She got out of her chair and stood in front of the girl. 'I'm sure whatever you become,' she said with an air of authority, 'you will do many important things.'

Daria squealed and hugged Gwyn tight to her. 'And you will too,' she gushed. 'My mother has seen it.'

# 6

---

*A*fter tearful goodbyes with mother and daughter, Preia took Gwyn to Ambra, an Ivanian with a kind smile and curious eyes. He examined her injuries, murmured his approval of Nima's treatment and gave her more medicine. He was a man of few words, but his all-knowing eyes said everything. He could be trusted.

'Come,' Preia said when Ambra was done. 'I will introduce you to my children.'

She led Gwyn to a nursery where Arlo was listening to his daughter read what sounded like Ivanian poetry, and a young boy sat frowning at an abacus under the watchful glare of a middle-aged man with permanent frown marks.

'Ah, there you are.' Arlo crossed the room in a few strides. All of his previous hardness had disappeared. His demeanour was altogether jolly now that he'd decided Gwyn was to stay. 'I've been telling the children all about you. Gwyn, this is my son, Laskar, and the children's tutor.'

The tutor acknowledged her with a nod. The boy glanced up and took it as an opportunity to escape his lessons. He ran around the room, bursting into riotous laughter as the harried tutor chased him.

'And my daughter, Sofia.'

The girl stood up and gave a shy but friendly smile. Arlo and Preia had mentioned their daughter was the same age as Gwyn, but Sofia was almost a foot taller.

She curtsied. 'It is lovely to meet you,' she said in tentative Ettean.

'And you,' Gwyn replied in Ivanian.

Preia's reassuring hand rested on Gwyn's shoulder. 'We have made arrangements for you to share rooms with Sofia.'

Gwyn tilted her head in question. Rooms. Rooms just for the two of them. She may have been the daughter of a King, but she had never had more than a small room only large enough to house a single cot.

'Yes, a pair of adjoining bedchambers. If that is to your liking?'

'Oh. Yes. That would be…good.'

A wide grin spread across Sofia's face. She had all of her mother's good nature, it seemed.

The rest of the afternoon and evening passed with Sofia taking Gwyn on a dizzying tour of their extensive home and grounds, proudly pointing out that only the Governor's Palace was larger. By the time Gwyn nestled into a four-poster bed big enough to sleep four girls her size, across the room from Sofia's matching bed, she wasn't just exhausted, but overwhelmed.

This was her new life. A life of luxury. She would want for nothing. But she did want for many things. She wanted to be back in her village, tramping up and down her Ettean mountains, where the earth sang to her and only the dande-lions ventured beyond the borders. But most of all, she wanted her parents to be alive. Fat tears rolled down her cheeks.

'Please don't cry.' Sofia's voice. A lit candle placed on a table next to Gwyn's bed. Wide eyes peering down at her. 'Don't be sad.'

Gwyn's sobs only intensified.

'Here.' Sofia offered her doll, a miniature version of herself with shiny black hair and a perfect smile. 'She will make you feel better.'

Gwyn rolled away so her back was facing Sofia and cried harder. She heard the doll fall to the ground with a soft thud.

'Mother, Mother!' Sofia called as she ran from their shared rooms. Her distressed voice echoed up the corridor.

Preia's shadow soon appeared, falling over Gwyn's bed, followed by her voice.

'Sofia, why don't you go to the kitchen and see if Cook has any of those sweet jellies left?'

There was the patter of Sofia's slippered feet on the stone floor.

Preia sat down on the bed, saying nothing until slowly Gwyn's sobs subsided. Gwyn rolled onto her back and eyed Preia, who was holding Sofia's doll and stroking its hair.

'She doesn't understand,' Gwyn said, trying to explain her reaction.

Preia nodded. 'You're right. She hasn't seen what you have. She has been sheltered from the truth.'

Gwyn sat up and propped her back against the wall, curious what Preia meant. 'The truth?'

'Yes, the truth.' Preia's fingers clenched the doll, squeezing it tight. 'Ette is all but destroyed and Ivane is no better. We are not at war like you have been, but the people are not happy. Our people don't want to live under Lamorian rule. We want to determine our own fate. We don't want all of our resources and riches leaving this land to benefit a King in a faraway nation. Our culture is all but gone, or at least bent to the will of Lamore. They take from us what they want and suppress anything they don't like.'

Preia shook her head to herself and put the doll down. She looked Gwyn squarely in the eyes.

'I lived in a village where our people were nothing more than slaves to the Lamorian nobles. Living in poverty on the edges of rich cities built by our people, then forced to work day and night on farms and in mines, never seeing any of the wealth from our toil.' There was a river of tears in her words. 'Everyone was scratching to feed their families. Some weeks we would have nothing but a handful of barley to feed half a dozen or more. All the time we were lining Lamorian pockets, and they got richer and richer.'

A bitter tone invaded Preia's voice. 'We were forced to speak their language and wear their clothes. Our connection to our country and culture was stripped from us. We were banned from practising combat or owning any weaponry. Our warrior ways forgotten. We have generations who don't know how to handle an Ivanian staff. Most have never seen one.'

Gwyn leant in closer to Preia and inclined her head. 'But you came to our village. You taught us how to use weapons.'

Preia dropped her voice to a conspiratorial whisper, although they were entirely alone. 'Some of us have kept our practices alive, sharing them with our allies. Thanks to my husband's position, we are able to access some metals for forging weapons before they're diverted to Lamore.'

Gwyn could feel the pride emanating from Preia as she spoke of their small acts of rebellion.

'Does Sofia know all this?'

Preia took a deep breath. 'I've protected her from everything. She knows only this palace city and Lamorian rule, nothing else.'

'Then stop protecting her.' Gwyn held out her hands, pleading. 'Make her understand.'

Preia lifted her chin. 'When the time is right, she will be told. And there will be a time, because we have plans.'

'Plans?'

Preia's face broke into a victorious grin. 'A greater play at hand. I will share it with you. But you must keep it to yourself. Can I trust you?'

Gwyn nodded vigorously.

Preia patted her hand. 'Of course you can be trusted. So, my husband's sister, Ona—'

'She's married to the Governor?'

'Yes. Ona and Arlo are using their positions to gather support around the country. Smuggling weapons from the armoury, making new ones, recruiting villagers to fight. Those willing to risk everything to reclaim our country. It must be done slowly to avoid raising the Governor's suspicion, but one step at a time we're gathering support and the means to enact our plan. Then one day we will make our move, and Ivane will be returned to its people.'

Something burgeoned inside Gwyn, building like a storm brewing on the horizon at sea. A knowledge. This was her calling. She would help fight the Lamorians. That was why she'd been brought here.

Gwyn crossed her arms. 'Then I shall help you. I will be part of your war.'

Preia appeared momentarily taken aback, but then nodded. 'Yes, you will. You will train as a warrior just like your mother.' With each word her voice strengthened in conviction. Then something that sounded like a realisation: 'And Sofia will join you. You will both train as warriors, and if you choose to take up your weapons when the time comes, I would be honoured to have you both fight by my side.'

Gwyn extended her hand as she had seen the craftspeople and sellers in her village do when making a deal. Preia looked at her hand in confusion for a moment, then took it and shook firmly.

And in that simple handshake, Kypria's future was sealed – but not in the way Gwyn imagined.

# 7

The Kengian Prince, Alik, sat cross-legged under the crystallised branches of the giant yew tree. With his eyes closed, he sucked in lungfuls of air and attempted to clear his mind of everything. The Kengian meditation practice of 'just being' was something that had always eluded him.

'You can do it,' his younger brother, Amund, said in an irritatingly calm voice beside him.

Theoretically, Amund was right. As the firstborn, Alik had inherited vast elemental powers – abilities beyond other Kengians, including his brother – so he should be able to do something as simple as meditate. But no matter how he tried, he couldn't quieten his whirring mind.

'If you just listen to nature,' Amund suggested.

Alik couldn't remember a time when he couldn't hear the whistling voices of the wind, the gurgling words of a waterfall, the mumbling of a stone. Like every Kengian child he had learnt the importance of balance and harmony in all of nature, and how great powers were available to those who dedicated themselves to learning how to harness *kira*: the life-force that existed in every natural element. The ability to listen and converse with nature was key to harnessing the power that resided in every living object. For most, this ability only came from meditation and being fully at one with the natural world, but Alik's powers were innate. Something he'd never had to work for. Something fantastical – but a waste, as far as he was concerned.

Alik yearned to leave his homeland, which was shut away from the rest of the world. He was convinced the only reason he had such powers was to use them to help others – to help Kypria. His mind was filled with impossible dreams and a constant noise that would not be quietened.

Amund knew his brother well enough to recognise his discontent. He had insisted Alik join him after swordfighting practice to attempt meditation.

Alik's eyes flew open. 'I can't do it. I'm not like you, Amund. I'm not a Scholar. I haven't learnt all the things you have at the Institute.'

Amund gave a patient smile, beyond his years. 'You have everything you need to succeed' – he patted his chest over his heart – 'in here.' He lifted his hand to touch his temple. 'And in here.'

The Institute was an academy in the capital, Lochlen, for Kengians who exhibited an affinity with magic. Those who attended typically became Shamans, like Alik and Amund's sister Kairi, or Scholars, like Amund. The former could connect with an animal's mind and ask it to do their bidding. With the right talent and dedication, some Shamans could even catch snatches of past and possible futures – visions, almost. Scholars like Amund studied science and spells that leveraged the essence of *kira*, magnifying lifeforce to heal or manipulate living beings.

It took years and years of study to become an accomplished Scholar, but Amund already exceeded all of his peers and many older than him. He had a curious mind and craved all forms of knowledge, yet never begrudged Alik for being born to his powers, which would always overshadow anything Amund could conjure.

The pair couldn't be more different. Amund would spend his afternoons after classes reading by Lochlen Lake and the sacred yew tree – the source of all Kengian magic. He would pore over spells and formulas, committing them to memory and contriving his own variations. He would stay that way until the silver sun set over the mountains in the distance and the rainbow-hued lake surrendered to darkness. In contrast, Alik would spend his days practising swordcraft or archery, physically exerting himself to overshadow the disharmony that warred within him.

'Just close your eyes and think of nothing,' Amund said.

Alik scrunched his eyes tightly closed, wishing there was a spell he could learn to attain the meditative state he sought.

*You can do it. Just be,* he said to himself. *Be.*

Slowly, his thoughts drifted away like dandelion seeds in the whispering wind.

The sandy ground around him undulated, lifting, morphing and joining the sparkling air, enveloping him in a warming bubble of energy and light.

*I'm doing it.* A tiny whisper of a thought that Alik quickly dismissed, not wanting to destroy his moment of 'being'.

Nothing existed but the bubble, a beating heart of silver light. He was no longer Alik. There was no longer earth, air or water. There was only the pure essence of *kira*. And it was perf—

'Alik! Amund!'

Running footsteps. Their sister Kairi's voice.

Alik's bubble exploded in a kaleidoscope of miniscule coloured dots. His eyelids sprang open and he was on his feet, his stomach gripped with fear at the urgency in their sister's call. Kairi appeared before them, puffing.

'What is it? What happened?' Alik asked.

Kairi doubled over, holding up one hand to indicate she needed to catch her breath.

'Is Father alright? Mother?' Amund said.

Kairi nodded after each question before finally speaking. 'They're fine...both of them.' She sucked in a chestful of air. 'The last Ettean King has fallen.'

It took several moments for the news and the extent of what it meant to wash over Alik, but then he grabbed Amund by his upper arm and shook him.

'It's happened. Finally, it's happened.'

Amund stepped out of his brother's reach and frowned. 'But that's terrible.'

'Yes, yes, it's terrible.' Alik held his hands out placatingly. 'But don't you see? Now Father *must* agree to do something. He has to come to Ette's aid. He'll have to remove the protective barriers over our borders.' He held his hands up to the sky and spun in a circle. 'And we can leave this place.'

When the Lamorian King Emberto had threatened to take Kengia as his own more than a century before, magical barriers had been put in place along the coastline and the Nymoi Alps, the mountain range that marked the Kengian–Lamorian border. The Kengian King at the time commanded the power of earth, like the current King. He put in place spells that would trigger earthquakes along the top of the mountain range and tidal waves along the coast to prevent anyone from entering Kengian territory. The King's firstborn, Princess Mary, who was able to command air, used her magic to create gale-force winds along all the mountain paths to Lamore. These protective measures had been maintained ever since, so Kengia had escaped Lamorian occupation – but it had cost their allies, Ivane and Ette, dearly.

Amund and Kairi shared a horrified look at Alik's words. 'Father can't remove the very things that have kept us safe for nearly two hundred years,' Kairi said.

'I don't understand why you'd want to leave,' Amund tried to reason. 'We have everything we could ever want here.'

Alik rolled his eyes. 'Everything *you* could ever want. You're happy reading your stupid books and sitting under this stupid tree.' He kicked a gnarled waist-high root, then immediately howled in pain.

Amund gave another of his patient smiles. 'I know you don't mean it when you say our sacred tree and my books are stupid.'

Alik raised a brow.

'Alright,' Amund conceded. 'You do mean it about the books, but not the tree.'

Alik shrugged.

'But you must know Father will not open up Kengia…Not yet,' Amund said.

'Not until—' Kairi began.

'Not until the Water Catcher comes,' Alik interrupted in a sing-song voice. 'I'm *so* sick of hearing about that prophecy. It's so stu—'

He cut himself off as Amund's face fell. His brother believed, without question, in the prophecy and its promise that someone from Kengia's firstborn line would have complete command of water – that that person would unite and bring peace to all of Kypria. While none in known history had ever been born with that ability, most Kengians believed it was just a matter of time.

'Fine!' Alik cried. 'Believe in your prophecy, but I'm not going to sit around doing nothing for the rest of my life, when I can be out *there*' – he jabbed a finger at the Nymoi Alps in the east – 'doing something to help.' His hand glowed silver and a whirlwind manifested out of nowhere, springing from his pointed finger. 'Otherwise, what's the point of having these powers?'

His siblings didn't respond, seemingly unsure of what to say to make their brother feel better. But there was no escaping that Alik was as restless as the air that he commanded.

He was born to rule a kingdom that he longed to escape from. That was his destiny.

Alik snapped his fingers into a fist and the whirlwind petered away. 'I'm going to speak to Father.'

ALIK RACED up the pebbled path with his brother and sister in tow. The trio ran past the topiary animals and rock gardens flanked by statues of dragons and other magical creatures. They dodged the throng of people coming and going about their business in the royal palace grounds – a compound of buildings with steepled roofs centred around one main tower or pagoda. They only came to a stop when they reached the tower. There, a pair of guards gave them a cursory glance before stepping aside to let them in.

Alik resumed his frantic pace once inside, nearly knocking a woman carrying a magnificent vase of cherry blossoms off her feet. Finally they reached their destination: the central chambers where the Kengian Council met and the King would hear any petitions.

Alik stopped by a pillar at the edge of the open, high-raftered room to get his breath back. King Leo was sitting at the round table in deep conversation with one of his council-lors. A starling sat on the table in front of them, nibbling at a small pile of seed. A tiny roll of parchment lay nearby. While Kengia was physically shut off from the rest of the world, messages could still be sent and received via starling messen-gers that could fly above any protective barriers.

King Leo looked up at their approach. With an almost imperceptible nod, he dismissed his councillor.

The King eyed Alik up and down, taking in his long silver hair, which was now wildly askew. 'So you've heard.' A state-ment rather than a question.

Garbled words rushed from Alik's lips. 'We have to do something – time to act – open Kengia – challenge Lamore—'

The King rose from his chair. 'This is not the time.' He turned his back on them and strode toward a corridor that led to his private quarters.

'But Father,' Alik pleaded, running to follow him and indicating frantically for his siblings to follow. 'Ette needs us. Ivane needs us. We can help.'

'Whether we can or can't help is irrelevant. The only thing that matters is if we should.'

'Of course we should, Father. The last Ettean King has fallen. We can't leave the country completely to Lamore's mercy.'

Leo appeared to stiffen, but he kept going. 'They were at Lamore's mercy long before this.'

'That's no excuse for cowardice!' Alik shot at his father's back.

The King came to an abrupt stop and spun to face Alik. His nostrils flared. 'You know nothing of cowardice, son. Sometimes it takes courage not to act. And we mustn't act, at least not against Lamore. Not yet. This is in the best interests of Kengia, and Kengia is what I must protect first and foremost.'

'But we could defeat them, Father,' Alik pressed.

'Can we? We have a country of fine warriors that may even outnumber Lamore's army. But Lamore can buy as many mercenaries as they need among the Etteans and Ivanians.'

Alik crossed his arms. 'They would never join Lamore.'

'They would when gold is on the table. Many of them may need to fight to survive. Their livelihoods have been taken from them. The countries' resources, food and materials are all shipped out to Lamore.'

'Which is why they must be stopped!'

The King shook his head and stood up to his full height, but Alik would not be silenced.

'Amund agrees with me.' He nudged his brother hard in the ribs. Amund grimaced.

The King cocked his head and eyeballed Amund. 'Is that true?'

Amund rubbed the back of his neck. 'I think it's important to...help others when we can.'

'So you don't think we should wait for the Water Catcher to come to being?'

Amund bit his lip.

The King's eyes narrowed. 'You don't believe in the prophecy, then?'

Amund looked desperately between his brother and his father, no doubt wishing to please both of them but knowing he would disappoint one.

'Well?' the King prompted.

Amund's voice was a mere sliver. 'I believe in the prophecy.'

The King made a *hmph* sound. *I'm sorry,* Amund mouthed to Alik.

'Kairi…' Alik directed a pleading look at his sister, who looked down at her sandals.

King Leo rested his hand on Alik's shoulder. 'You will come to see that keeping Kengia safe is more important than any notion of pride, and that nothing but danger and heartbreak lies beyond our borders.'

Alik spun on his heels and marched away from his family, stopping only to shout 'Cowards!' back at them.

## 8

*Eight years later*

*G*wyn eyeballed her opponent, tightening her grasp on the staff in her hands.

'Ready?'

The girl scrunched up her face, fierce concentration beyond her years etched into her brow. She blew a stray curl out of her eyes, but it immediately sprang back into place.

A pang registered in Gwyn's chest at the girl's wild curly hair, so like Daria's. She hadn't seen the healer and her daughter who had saved her from the battlefield, not since the first day she'd come here. In more recent years, Gwyn had been in contact with some Ettean survivors from the Borderlands, and she had asked after Nima and Daria. All knew of the silver-eyed healers – Daria, it seemed, had learnt her mother's trade – who would venture down from their mountain home for supplies or to attend to a sick villager. But while they were there, they barely spoke, keeping any conversation to their work. As soon as their business was done they would trek back up the mountain.

There were varying opinions about where in the alps they lived. Gwyn was sure she'd be able to find them if given the chance. The Ettean mountains of her homeland were imprinted like a map in her mind, but the prospect of seeing them again was an impossible one. She couldn't risk anyone discovering her true identity. Even so, she still thought about Ette, Nima and Daria every day. She thought about Nima's vision, letting it drive her to help Ivane, believing it was part of her destiny. It gave her strength in her darkest moments when she remembered her parents and their violent deaths, and everything that had been taken from her. She'd been raised to one day lead a kingdom, but now she was nothing more than the companion of a Weapons Master's daughter. Yet being nobody kept her safe.

As predicted, the Lamorian Governor, Lewin, had righteously accepted her into his court, determined to show the Ivanian people and his Ettean counterpart that he was a benevolent ruler. It hadn't taken long for Gwyn to learn the extent of the man's pride, which went far beyond his insistence at being called King. His quest to be equally respected and loved, and his perception that he had already achieved both, blinkered him to anything that didn't support this theory, even those things right beneath his nose. This gave Gwyn a certain level of protection, boosted by the fact that she had gone to great pains to distance herself from her Ettean heritage.

She was fluent in Lamorian and Ivanian and had mostly suppressed her native accent. A hint of an Ettean lilt or inflection in her voice was only detectable when she was overly tired or safe in the privacy of her rooms with Sofia.

Also in private, under the tutelage of Preia, Gwyn and Sofia had learnt the ways of the Ivanian warrior, mastering the staff, sword, bow and arrow, as well as hand-to-hand combat. Skills that many more throughout Ivane wished to learn, including the girl posturing before Gwyn now.

Gwyn advanced on her, twirling her staff in a style that was more flamboyant than it was effective in bettering an opponent. She made a half-hearted thrust at the girl, who blocked it with gritted teeth. Gwyn then loosened her grip on her staff and waited for the girl to strike. Wood struck against wood and Gwyn's weapon ricocheted from her hands, rattling to the tiled ground.

'Ha!' the girl cried in victory, pressing the tip of her staff to Gwyn's neck.

Gwyn held up her hands. 'I surrender.'

'You're lucky it wasn't a bladed Ivanian staff,' Sofia's light-filled voice rang out through the courtyard.

'Very lucky,' Gwyn conceded.

Sofia approached the girl with a dazzling smile that rivalled her mother's. 'Well done.'

The girl puffed out her chest. 'Thank you.'

'It is time for the next lesson.' Sofia held out her palm and the girl handed her the staff. 'Go with the other children to the nursery. Gwyn and I will be there shortly.'

The girl bowed and ran to join a line of children filing back through a doorway to the main building. Gwyn and Sofia had started a quasi-school, tutoring the sons and daughters of Ivanian stallholders and Master Arlo's retainers. There was a school in the palace city, but it was reserved for the children of Lamorian nobles. This had been the way ever since the beginning of Lamore's occupation, so it was widely accepted that the only education an Ivanian child would receive was vocational training limited to how they could best serve the Lamorian nobility. As kin to the Ivanian Queen, Arlo's children, and Gwyn as an extension of his family, were an exception. They were tutored and well versed in all aspects of languages, history, science and mathematics, and Sofia and Gwyn were determined to give others in Nadis the same opportunity.

There would be a day when Ivane would be returned to its people, and the people must be ready to take on that responsibility. Nurturing young Ivanian minds was one way to prepare them. Training them to fight and awakening their dormant warrior spirit was another.

Sofia turned to face Gwyn, her smile fading. 'You shouldn't have let her win so easily.'

Gwyn shook her head. 'She's only ten years old.'

'The same age we were when we started training with *real* weapons.' She looked at the training staff in her hand with a sniff of distaste. 'The same age you were when you came here.'

Gwyn loved Sofia like a sister – they were inseparable. And while she admired the gusto Sofia had brought to Preia's teachings and her father's plans to retake Ivane, Gwyn was acutely aware that her friend had never experienced battle or seen the bloodshed and death she had seen.

'If given the choice at that age, I would have chosen a childhood and play battles over the real thing.'

Realisation flared in Sofia's dark eyes. 'I'm sorry,' she said in a quiet voice.

Gwyn shrugged. 'It's alright.' It wasn't, but she knew Sofia hadn't meant to upset her.

Sofia exhaled before continuing in an apologetic tone. 'But we all need to be ready for war.'

'Uh-huh,' Gwyn said, busying herself with packing up the

games and toys abandoned by the children so she didn't have to meet Sofia's unwavering gaze.

When Preia had first shared Arlo's plans with her, she had said it would take time. Gwyn had thought she meant months, not years. Years with no sign of her ever fulfilling the destiny Nima had seen. Years of Arlo trekking across the vast nation with Governor Lewin, visiting the mining cities and foundries, pretending to be a loyal subject and the Lamorians' protector. And years of Arlo secretly stockpiling weapons, equipping and training Ivanians on those visits. Yet nothing had changed. Gwyn was starting to believe it never would.

Sofia came to stand in her path, forcing Gwyn to stop under the boughs of an overgrown fig tree.

'It will happen,' Sofia said forcefully. 'It must.' Her shoulders slumped. 'Otherwise…what is the point?'

Gwyn flinched at the quaver in her friend's voice and the dark shadows that had fallen on her face under the tree's canopy. In a way, Sofia had lost her childhood too. She had gone from wanting for nothing and knowing naught but peace and joy, to learning she was owed more. That her fellow Ivanians deserved more, and she must help to ensure they got it. It was a heavy burden for any child, or adult, to carry.

'You're right,' Gwyn said in an overly bright tone, linking her arm through Sofia's. 'Your father's plans will succeed.'

Sofia gave a hopeful smile.

'But in the meantime, we have some very serious business to attend to.'

Sofia tilted her head in thought. 'The children's lessons?'

'No.' Gwyn adopted her most serious voice. 'Something much more important.'

Sofia raised an arched brow in question.

'We must get to the kitchen at once. Cook was working on a fresh batch of cream pastries and I'm starving!'

The darkness suddenly lifted from Sofia's face and she burst out laughing.

'Yes. *Very* important business,' she said. And for a fleeting moment, the carefree Sofia who brought delight to everyone around her was back.

Arm in arm, they made to head toward the kitchen, but an out-of-breath Preia arrived before them, clutching a parchment roll tight, as if her life depended on it.

'It is time,' she puffed.

'Time?' Sofia asked.

Preia gave a face-splitting smile. 'Time.'


PREIA SHARED the contents of the message she had received from Arlo. He was with Governor Lewin in Liprah, one of Ivane's biggest cities, famed for its gold mines. The Governor had wanted to increase outputs to meet the Lamorian King's ever-increasing appetite for precious metals and wealth. As on other visits to mining towns, Arlo had been tasked with checking the foundries and operations to identify any productivity improvements that could be made. And like all of his other visits, he'd met in secret with Ivanian rebel leaders. On this visit he had received the news he had been waiting for: they had enough support to try to take Liprah and several other major cities. But they would need to act fast, and all at once.

With every sentence Sofia stood a little taller, her eyes glistening. By the end of the message Gwyn was sure her friend would burst right out of her skin with excitement.

'Finally!' Sofia declared. 'It's everything we've been waiting for. We will take back what is ours.'

'We will.' Preia turned expectantly to Gwyn.

'Yes. It's wonderful news,' Gwyn said, but the way she wrung her hands must have said otherwise.

Preia gave her a knowing smile. 'I know you well enough to know what you're thinking. You're thinking the rebels will need an extra advantage.'

Gwyn's hands stilled. 'Well, yes. The rebels are untested in battle. Their best hope is to have some kind of distraction.'

Sofia's face fell. 'It would have to be something large-scale, yet within the rebels' capability to carry out in every city.'

'Exactly,' Preia said confidently. 'We didn't tell you earlier, in case the rebels weren't ready, but we have had a distraction in mind for some time – or rather, Ambra suggested one to us.'

'Ambra?' Gwyn knew Ambra was more than a healer to Arlo and often gave counsel to him, but she couldn't imagine he was well versed in military strategy.

Preia's eyes skipped around the courtyard, not for the first time, to make sure they were still alone. They were.

'Ambra has a talented apprentice in his service by the name of Lore, who has confirmed…' She paused to take a big breath. 'When the sun is at its highest tomorrow, there will be an eclipse. The moon will move in front of the sun for several minutes in the middle of the day, and all of Ivane will be in darkness.'

'An eclipse?' Sofia said in wonder.

'Yes. We have not had one in decades, but Ambra is sure of it.'

'On the word of an apprentice?' Gwyn asked.

'The apprentice may have been the one who identified the opportunity, but Ambra has consulted the finest scientific minds and they are all in agreement. An eclipse is happening tomorrow.'

Preia had good reason to be excited. An eclipse would be an equal source of amazement and fear. The perfect distraction. Gwyn daren't believe it, but Arlo's plan could actually work. *Could.*

'So what are we to do while the rebels take the cities?' Gwyn asked.

Preia's lips formed a thin line. 'We must take Nadis and hold it until Arlo returns.'

Gwyn and Sofia exchanged a look that was somewhere between terror and exhilaration.

Preia eyed each of them in turn. 'Are you ready?'

Sofia stood up to her full height, meeting her mother eye to eye. 'Of course we're ready.'

Gwyn jutted out her chin. 'Yes. It is *our* destiny.'


PREIA, Sofia and Gwyn discussed the specifics of their plan late into the night until they were sure of every detail.

Preia would stay at their home, fielding enquiries and orders for custom-made weapons as if it were any other day. Sofia's younger brother, Laskar, would stay with his mother. The regular Ivanian house guards would also stay to protect the pair.

Rebel leaders around the city had been given their instructions and would be strategically placed to make their move at midday. They were to secure the city gates, as well as key watchtowers and Lamorian guard stations throughout Nadis.

Sofia and Gwyn were given the task of taking control of the palace with Lewin's wife, Ona, who hadn't joined her husband on his journey. The palace's core staff and guards were all Lamorians and loyal to Lewin, but Ona had been allowed to maintain a small Ivanian household who were supporters of the rebel cause. Still, the Ivanians were severely outnumbered, so a contingent of Arlo's foundry staff would accompany Sofia and Gwyn on the pretence of delivering a large order of weapons to the palace armoury. It would provide the required excuse for bringing weapons into the palace.

An hour before midday, Gwyn stood before the looking glass in her bedchambers, checking that the outline of the dagger strapped to her thigh wasn't visible through her tunic. She grimaced at the damp spot left by her fingertips. Her hands dripped sweat despite the relatively cool day. In her mirror she caught Sofia's reflection through their adjoining rooms' open doorway. Sofia was tucking a sheathed knife into her boot. She glanced up and their gazes locked.

Gwyn gave her best attempt at a confident smile, hoping Sofia couldn't hear the pounding of her heart. Sofia responded with a hesitant smile that confirmed she was as nervous as Gwyn.

Gwyn closed her eyes. *It will be alright,* she told herself. *You have trained for this. It is everything you have waited for.*

'I'm coming with you!' A boy's voice. The rapid clip-clopping of boots on tiles.

Gwyn's eyes flung open to spot Laskar holding a boy-sized sword aloft as he rushed into Sofia's room.

He skidded to a stop and screwed up his mouth. 'I want to fight the Lamorians!'

'*Shush,*' Sofia hissed, looking toward the main door that opened to the corridor. They never knew who might be spying for the Governor.

Laskar scowled, but dropped his voice. 'I'm coming with you.'

Sofia rolled her eyes. 'You're just a boy. You can't help.'

His thick brows knitted. 'I'm not. I'm thirteen! I can help.' He stepped away from his sister and performed a series of thrusts and stabbing motions with his tiny sword.

Sofia gave a dismissive wave. 'I don't have time for this. Go back to your *nursery* where you won't be in anyone's way.'

Laskar's cheeks flushed red and he made to advance on his sister with his sword raised. Sofia crossed her arms and glared at him in challenge.

Gwyn raced into Sofia's room in time to step between the siblings. She shot Sofia a warning look, then directed herself to her friend's brother.

'Of course you can help,' Gwyn said kindly. 'I have seen your skill with a sword, and you are as formidable as any of us.'

Somewhat mollified, Laskar relaxed his stance a little.

'Which is why,' Gwyn continued, 'we have a special task for you.'

He raised a questioning brow and lowered his sword.

Gwyn dropped her voice to a conspiratorial whisper. 'You see, we need you here to watch over your mother.'

Laskar's mouth twitched. 'Mother doesn't need protection.'

Sofia nodded at Gwyn and gave a wink unseen by her brother. 'That is what Mother would have us believe, but I fear for her. She is only one person, and while she is a master in staff-fighting, she lacks your skill with a blade.'

The boy puffed his chest out, completely unaccustomed to receiving any form of compliment from his older sister.

'So you will stay here to protect her?' Gwyn asked.

Laskar sheathed his sword, but his narrowed eyes never left his sister. 'May you find victory,' he grumbled before stomping from the room.

'Ha!' Sofia said once he was out of sight. 'That will keep him out of trouble.'

Gwyn frowned. 'I'm not so sure. Your brother isn't stupid.'

Sofia scoffed. 'He is for believing that utter drivel we just spun, but thankfully he did, because we have to get moving.'

Gwyn wasn't wholly convinced, but Sofia was right about one thing. It was time to put their plan into action.

THEY ARRIVED at the palace grounds with four of Arlo's most trusted men from the foundry and a wagon filled with swords, staffs, bows and quivers of arrows. The party stopped beside the decorative pool that stretched out before them, ending at the entrance to the palace, where a row of Lamorian guards stared back at them. Lined with thousands of star-shaped gold tiles, the pool dazzled fiercely in the sun.

Gwyn shaded her eyes with her hand and looked up to confirm the sun was about to reach its highest point. 'I hope Ambra and his apprentice are right,' she muttered to herself. Without the distraction of an eclipse, they didn't stand a chance at taking the palace.

'They're right,' Sofia said with certainty, her gaze never leaving the palace entrance. 'Victory awaits,' she asserted, and marched toward the guards.

Gwyn and the foundry staff followed with the wagon. Gwyn attempted to appear as confident as her friend, but inside her stomach bunched into a knot. She had seen battle firsthand. She had seen how easily death came, disregarding which side was right or just. She knew what it felt like to take another's life. Confidence in victory was dangerously irrelevant when you were fighting to survive.

They reached the entrance to the palace and one guard

stepped forward. Gwyn recognised him as one of the men who'd confronted her, Nima and Daria on the day they'd arrived at Nadis. At the city gates he'd pushed and prodded Nima with his pudgy fingers, before grabbing her around the neck.

Gwyn's hand went instinctively to her thigh, where her dagger was concealed.

'State your business,' the guard barked.

Sofia indicated the wagon. 'We're here to deliver new weapons for the palace armoury.'

The guard cast a cursory glance at the weapons and grunted. 'I don't know of any such order.'

'And why would you?' Sofia said with the practised assurance of being daughter of the Governor's most trusted protector and kin to the Governor's wife. 'The order came directly from the Governor.'

The guard narrowed his gaze at the term *Governor*.

'Directly from the *King*,' she corrected herself. 'We have been ordered to deliver them to the armoury.'

The guard looked back at his colleagues, who shrugged.

Sofia put her hands on her hips. 'You dare to make us wait when we are on the *King's* orders?'

The guard's head swivelled to face Sofia. He leant in threateningly toward her, but she didn't flinch. The pair stared at each other for what felt like minutes.

Gwyn looked nervously to the sky. The sun was perilously close to its highest position. They needed to be inside the palace before the eclipse.

She crossed her legs and bounced from one foot to the other. 'Please, could we be admitted?' she addressed the guard. 'I am in dire need of the facilities.'

The guard turned to his peers and chuckled, muttering something about the 'weakness of women', before nodding at

Gwyn and Sofia. 'You two can go inside, but my men will unpack the wagon and accompany you to deliver those weapons. Arlo's men can wait here.'

Sofia opened her mouth to protest, but Gwyn silenced her with a sharp look.

Four guards bundled up the weapons and led them through a pointed archway into the palace. A message was sent to Ona to meet them at the armoury to inspect the new weapons on her husband's behalf.

Gwyn and Sofia had visited the palace on many occasions, so were intimately familiar with the layout. The armoury lay at the end of the next open gallery. There they must overpower not only the guards with them, but those stationed at the armoury. Whoever secured the armoury secured the palace.

Gwyn's hands began to shake, but Sofia caught her eye. *It's our destiny,* she mouthed, and remarkably, Gwyn's trembling stopped.

It was the one hope she could cling to. Nima's vision that she would be key to restoring balance in Kypria. The vision had saved Gwyn's life and brought her here to Nadis. It had to be true. Her hands clenched into fists by her sides.

It had to be.

They passed a courtyard where a fountain modelled after Ivane's thorned Batu-riek tree gurgled joyously. Two birds, starlings with iridescent purple, blue and green wings, bathed in the fountain, warbling and whistling to each other, oblivious to the chaos that was about to unfold.

They continued on until they reached the armoury. Two Lamorian guards flanked the heavy timber door reinforced with impenetrable Ivanian steel. There was a brief exchange where Gwyn and Sofia's escorts explained the delivery of weapons before the door was unlocked. The Lamorian guards filed into the room and, under the instruction of the armoury guards, put the new weapons away in their dedicated spaces.

'Where's Ona?' Gwyn said under her breath. Even with the distraction of the eclipse, they would need help to subdue this many guards.

'She'll be here,' Sofia whispered, but Gwyn detected a slight wobble in her voice.

Her eyes darted from the sky, where the sun declared it was almost noon, to the guards, who had nearly finished putting the weapons away. Once the armoury was locked again their plan would be over. *Everything* would be over.

*Please,* she begged silently. *Please.*

Then a shadow passed over the ground in front of Gwyn and she held her breath, slowly lifting her gaze to the sky. A curved sliver of blackness was edging its way across the sun. It was happening.

The air stilled in anticipation. The starling calls in the distance stopped.

'Look!' Sofia cried, pointing upward and beckoning the guards to come out of the armoury.

One guard emerged to look at the sky. His jaw dropped. Nearly a quarter of the sun was now obscured by the moon. He called to the other guards. One by one they came outside, pushing their way in front of Gwyn and Sofia until all of them were gawping at the eclipse. One began babbling about it being a bad omen, that the world was ending. Another's face had blanched white.

This was it. Ona or not, Gwyn and Sofia had to act.

Gwyn slipped a hand under her tunic to retrieve her dagger.

Sofia reached into her boot and pulled out her knife.

They held their weapons behind their backs, waiting for the moment day would plunge into darkness.

As the insatiable moon continued to swallow the sun, Gwyn turned over all of her training in her mind. She focused on Preia's teachings on how to use an opponent's strength and energy against them. She ran through all of her fighting techniques and moves. And she reminded herself they would only have one chance to harness the element of surprise.

Only the tiniest crescent of sun remained. Gwyn and Sofia looked at each other and nodded. Gwyn drew a giant breath and…

Day submitted to night.

As the stars pierced their way through the sky, Gwyn slid her blade across the neck of the guard directly in front of her. He slumped to the ground next to one Sofia had dispatched at the same time.

Blood covered Gwyn and Sofia's hands. The latter's shook violently. It was the first time Sofia had killed anyone. Gwyn, who'd taken a life before, but so long ago, felt suddenly queasy. The friends looked at the guards and each other in shock, but their horror was soon replaced with a need to survive.

The remaining guards spun toward them, their swords raised. The lit torches in the armoury behind cast enough light for the guards to spot their targets.

Gwyn and Sofia looked around desperately for an escape route, but by now the four guards had ringed around them. They retreated into the armoury, each of them choosing a bladed staff. They positioned themselves back-to-back.

Alarm bells sounded throughout the city. The rebels had launched their attack.

Gwyn gritted her teeth and waited for the guards to make

a move.

Sure enough, the largest thundered toward her. The second largest launched himself at Sofia.

Gwyn's staff had a longer reach than the guard's sword, but he had already closed the gap between them. All she had time to do was block his strike with the shaft of her staff. She stumbled backward and the staff recoiled in her hand from the force, but she was able to recover herself and clutch it tighter.

The other two guards mobilised, and in pairs, they attacked.

Strike after strike came in rapid succession. Gwyn moved sideways, defending against each blow. Never turning her back on her attackers. She watched their every movement, observing their timing and the way one of the guards left his side exposed each time he lunged toward her.

She waited until the next time he came at her. Timing it to perfection, she dropped to her knees to duck his sword, thrust the bladed tip of her staff into his belly and twisted it. She immediately pulled her weapon back toward her and scrambled out of her attackers' reach.

The guard dropped his sword and tried futilely to stem the bleeding before he collapsed to the ground.

Gwyn regained her fighting stance and twirled her staff theatrically. The other guard's lip curled upward. He ran at her with full force, holding his sword like a lance.

It was the mistake she had been waiting for. She held her position until the last moment, then swept her staff under the guard's feet. He landed hard, his head hitting the tiles with a sickening *crack*.

A cry sounded across the room. Sofia's cry.

Gwyn's eyes raked the armoury until they fell on her friend, pinned against a wall on the other side of the room.

Sofia's staff lay useless on the ground in two pieces. She held one hand to her opposite arm. Rivulets of blood ran between her fingers. A guard held a bloodstained sword tip at her chest.

Gwyn reached for her dagger. It wasn't in its sheath. She knew she didn't have time to make it across the room, but she started to run anyway.

The guard watched Gwyn with a satisfied sneer plastered across his face.

'*No!*' she cried.

The guard's eyes widened suddenly. His sword clattered to the ground. Sofia leant over to snatch it.

The guard fell to the ground face-first, a knife protruding from his neck.

Only then did Gwyn register the sound of running footsteps and the presence of Ona, who was already ripping linen from her tunic to bandage her niece's arm. A dozen or more of Ona's staff flooded into the armoury to collect weapons, followed by Arlo's foundry staff.

Gwyn released a strangled breath that she'd been holding without realising. 'You're here,' she said to Ona disbelievingly.

'I'm sorry,' Ona said, tightening the linen around Sofia's arm. 'As soon as the eclipse started, guards were sent to my rooms to keep me there. Something about it being a bad omen. We had to fight our way out.'

'But you did it,' Sofia said, tears welling in her eyes. '*We* did it.'

'Not yet,' Ona said. 'We have secured my quarters and the front entrance, but twenty or so guards have formed a barricade to the King's rooms and presence chamber.' She turned to address her household staff and the foundry staff. 'We have to secure those rooms.'

Understanding their orders, all the newly armed staff left.

Ona turned back to face Sofia and Gwyn and beamed. 'Well done, my girls. This is it. This is our victory.'

'I wouldn't be so sure, Ivanian scum.'

A gruff Lamorian accent. The voice of the pudgy-fingered guard now standing in the doorway to the armoury. One of his eyes was swollen shut and blood oozed from a sizeable wound on his temple, but he held his sword steady across a boy's throat.

Not just any boy. He had Laskar.

'I'm sorry,' Laskar whimpered. 'I wanted to come and help you fight.'

'It's alright, brother,' Sofia said in a strained voice. 'Everything will be alright.'

'Yes, everything will be fine,' Ona said, eyeing the guard. 'It is one against three. The guard will let you go.'

The guard shrugged. 'Think I'll take my chances with this hostage.'

'What do you want?' Ona asked through clenched teeth.

'Guaranteed safe passage from the city to port and onto a ship. Once I've boarded and am about to set sail, I will let the boy go.'

Ona held out her hands, pleading. 'Fine. Whatever you want.'

'See? You'll be fine,' Sofia said assuredly, but Laskar screwed up his mouth.

'I will not be anyone's hostage!' He stamped his foot down hard on the guard's boot and elbowed him in the ribs. The guard yelped in pain and loosened his grip on the boy. Laskar slipped out of his reach and ran into his aunt's arms.

The guard recovered himself quickly and propelled himself at Laskar and Ona, his sword raised.

Gwyn reached for the nearest weapon. The bladed tip of

Sofia's broken staff. She had no time to aim properly, but she threw it. It found its target, penetrating the guard's chest, but not before he reached his mark.

The guard's sword met Ivanian flesh – but it was Ona's, not Laskar's.

Laskar stood wide-eyed and unmoving, staring down at Ona's body. He mouthed his aunt's name over and over.

Sofia and Gwyn fell to their knees by Ona's side. Sofia took the Queen's hand in hers. 'Aunt, I'm here. It's Sofia.' Ona's eyes fluttered open and she groaned. 'She'll be alright,' Sofia cried. 'She'll live.'

As Gwyn checked Ona's wound, a vision of her own dying mother came to her. Bile filled her throat. She couldn't lose someone else she regarded as family. But maybe this would be different. Maybe the sword had missed all of Ona's vital organs. Maybe she would survive.

Gwyn's hope was short-lived. The sword had plunged deep into Ona's chest.

Ona made to speak and blood gurgled from her mouth. Her head lolled to the side…

And she was gone.

'Aunt!' Sofia cried again, to no avail. Gwyn reached for her friend and embraced her.

She wanted to tell Sofia it would be alright. That everything would be fine. But she couldn't bring herself to lie about such things. They had lost another great warrior to Lamore's hands.

Later, it would be described as a hero's death. The Queen had thrown her nephew to safety and met her end at the same moment Ivane had begun to triumph. But death was death, and Gwyn knew too well that how it happened didn't make it any easier.

# 9

The fighting continued in Nadis for more than a day, but ultimately the Ivanians were the victors. Arlo's years of planning, recruitment and secret training had paid off – but any celebration of the restoration of Ivane to its people was overshadowed by Ona's death and the loss of many other Ivanian lives.

Arlo was declared King on his return to Nadis, though it was a hollow acknowledgement. He blamed himself for not being there to protect his sister, as did Preia and Sofia, who wished they'd stopped Laskar from going to the palace. Laskar, of course, knew the part he had played in Ona's death and wandered Nadis like the walking dead, his face a mask of shattered disbelief. But it was Gwyn who believed it was her fault, and her fault alone, that Ona had perished. If she'd just thrown the staff a moment sooner. If she'd trusted her instincts that Laskar wasn't so easily convinced not to join them, Ona would still be alive.

But then she would remind herself at exactly whose hands Ona had died. She had never hated the Lamorians more. Even the news that Governor Lewin had been killed in battle in Liprah, and that the Lamorian nobles were all being deported, did little to satisfy Gwyn. She yearned for further justice against the oppressors who'd taken everything from her and those she loved. And finally, she may have it.

King Arlo had just informed Gwyn, Sofia and Preia that on learning of his country's defeat, the Lamorian King hadn't wasted any time mobilising his forces. He had deployed his entire naval fleet to Ivane, sending them upriver to Liprah under the cover of night, and had taken the city.

Sofia blinked rapidly. 'So soon?' She was still scarred from the lives she had taken, and admittedly Gwyn was also affected, the faces of her victims appearing in her dreams at night. But they both knew that was the price that must be paid. Violence was the means to an end. Necessary to save Ivane and Ette.

Arlo shrugged, a gesture in stark contrast to the grim set of his jaw. 'It is to be expected. So we must go to war again.'

'It does present an opportunity, though,' Gwyn ventured cautiously.

Arlo and Sofia shot puzzled looks at her, but Preia immediately grasped her meaning.

'Ette,' she said, her eyes shining. 'It's practically undefended.'

'It's exactly what we've been planning for,' Gwyn beamed.

Arlo's brows jerked. 'Planning for?'

Preia's chin lifted to a proud tilt. 'All the time you've been mustering the Ivanians, Gwyn and I have been doing the same with the Etteans.'

Arlo's eyes threatened to pop from their sockets. 'You've been doing what behind my back?'

Preia batted her hand in the air. 'It only stands to reason that we can't afford to have the enemy remain on our doorstep. And equally, we can't stand by and watch while our neighbours are oppressed and we are free.'

'Of course I know that is a risk,' Arlo blustered. 'And I was going to get to Ette as soon as we were done here in Ivane.'

Preia placed her hand on her husband's arm. 'I know,' she said gently. 'But with everything else you had to take care of, it was something we could do.'

'Something I *had* to do,' Gwyn added.

'Why didn't you tell me?' Sofia's question was ringed with hurt.

Gwyn's gaze dropped to the floor. 'I wanted to, but we weren't sure it would amount to anything. It still may not.' She looked up to meet Sofia's accusatory stare. 'And I knew how important it was for you – how important it was for all of us to retake Ivane.'

Sofia's lips pressed into a thin line, but she nodded slowly.

Arlo gave a resigned sigh. 'Tell me, then. What exactly have you planned?'

Preia's eyes glistened. 'I cannot take credit for any of it. It has all been Gwyn. She has been sending secret messages to the heir of one of the ousted Kings in the Borderlands.'

'Kris,' Gwyn began excitedly. 'His province wasn't too far from ours and we have known each other since we were children. His father was one of the Kings who capitulated to the Ettean Governor to save himself and his people's lives. But Kris's father regrets his decision and wishes he had fought like mine.' Arlo rubbed his beard in thought as Gwyn continued. 'He and Kris have been meeting with the other Ettean Kings and heirs, formulating how they would mount an attack on the Lamorian forces if the opportunity arose and take back their country.'

'And this is that opportunity,' Preia said.

Arlo stopped rubbing his beard and gave an affirmative grunt. 'Well, you can tell this Kris and his father that it's time. This is their shot while we do our best to occupy the Lamorian forces in Liprah. We leave at first light for the battlefield.' He started to walk away.

'*We?*' Gwyn asked, unbelieving that the King was inviting her to join the battle.

'We,' Arlo replied without turning back. 'It's what *all* of us have been waiting for.'

# 10

---

*A*lik wiped the sweat from his brow and scrutinised the warrior in front of him. Tio was an up-and-coming Weapons Master and Alik's training partner. He may have only been two years older, but his sword skills were far superior to the Kengian Prince's – a fact King Leo took pains to point out on a regular basis, only driving Alik to train harder. It didn't matter that Alik was an accomplished swordsman by anyone's standards; he had to be better than the best.

Tio stood in a defensive stance a dozen or so feet away, his swords disturbingly still but at the ready. Alik knew from experience how quickly Tio could launch a devastating attack from his position. The silver sun sat high above them, a sign they had been practising swordplay for several hours. The muscles in Alik's arms burned. His swords felt as if they were made of lead. Under his leather chest plate, his ribs ached in several spots where he'd taken blows. The swords may have been blunted for training, but they could still injure a person. Alik could picture the angry blue bruises already biting into his flesh.

Tio looked him up and down, then lowered his swords. 'Let's take a break.'

It would have been easy, sensible even, to concede. Alik yearned for a steaming bath to ease his physical pain, but he knew a bath would do nothing for his other wounds. He had to prove to his father that he was worthy of the crown he would inherit. Maybe proving he was superior with a sword would inspire King Leo's confidence. Goodness knew he'd tried everything else.

Alik had volunteered at the Institute, shadowing the Head Scholar, assisting with the most menial tasks since he was not well versed in science or spells. He'd spent hours upon hours studying books of Kengian history and culture. He'd stopped voicing his doubts about the Water Catcher prophecy when it was mentioned, and stopped calling on the King to offer assistance to Ette and Ivane. It didn't mean he no longer believed in these things – more than ever, he wanted to use his position as heir for the good of Kypria. His ambitions lay far beyond Kengia's borders and he dreamt of leaving his homeland and taking some form of action. But while he was an *heir* and not a *King*, he was powerless and utterly dependent on his father's good opinion. So he kept trying to show his worth.

When King Leo had refused Alik a seat on the Kengian Tribal Council, he'd gone to his mother Mira, the Queen and High Shaman. He'd appealed to her to get the King to reconsider, but Mira had given a sad smile. She had placed her hand on his chest and said, 'I know you think you are ready to lead, but your heart says otherwise. I'm afraid your restlessness will be your end, and until that can be tamed, you must be protected.'

Alik had told himself they were the words of a concerned

mother and not a prediction. His anger wouldn't let him think otherwise.

'I'm not a child. I don't need protection,' he'd protested.

'You and the firstborn line need to be protected for the good of all of Kypria.'

She'd been talking about the prophecy. His mother and father cared more about protecting a ridiculous prophecy than about him. Pushing aside the hurt, he'd gritted his teeth, knowing his objections wouldn't further his cause.

'What's that got to do with excluding me from the council and my birthright?'

Mira's hand had gone to her son's cheek, and she'd sighed. 'You cannot think clearly and make the right decisions for yourself and others when your heart and mind are so unsettled.'

There had been no point in arguing. Shamans knew a person's innermost thoughts and feelings, better than the person themself. Alik may never convince his mother that he was ready for the responsibilities of his position, but he hadn't given up on proving himself to his father...yet.

So when Tio suggested they take a break, Alik had only one response. He roared in fury and ran at his opponent, leading with his longsword held high.

Tio crossed his swords to block the attack, then immediately countered by raising his longsword and bringing it down hard on Alik's shoulder. A shuddering wave of pain engulfed Alik's chest and torso, momentarily immobilising the Prince and giving Tio the advantage. The Weapons Master circled around Alik and whacked him behind the knees. Alik's legs buckled and he fell into a kneeling position.

Tio stood before Alik with his shortsword pressed against the Prince's throat. 'Now can we take a break?' he said with a triumphant grin.

Alik's body screamed in the affirmative, but he couldn't bring himself to say the words. He couldn't give in.

'Please,' Tio said. 'For my sake.'

Alik narrowed his gaze at Tio, knowing he could easily go another round. 'Got somewhere you need to be?'

Tio looked away and sheathed his swords. 'No, not exactly.'

It was a badly kept secret that Tio was courting Alik's sister, Kairi, and that the pair had been spending a lot of time together.

Alik got to his feet and put away his own swords. 'I know you're trying to woo my sister.'

Tio swung back to face him. 'I'm just...'

Alik waved his hand. 'None of my business. As long as Kairi's happy – but if she's not, I may have to kick your butt.'

Tio laughed. 'Lucky for you, I have no intention of hurting your sister.' His face reddened to match his auburn hair. 'I care for her...a lot,' he added quietly.

Alik shrugged. 'No accounting for taste.'

Tio sighed. 'You know, you could find yourself a fine lass and settle down.'

Alik's eyes went to the Nymoi Alps in the distance. 'My destiny isn't here. It can't be.'

'It could be here, if you gave it a chance. Finding someone to share your life with might give you some...some...'

Alik rounded on Tio. 'Some what? Purpose?' he spat.

Tio held up his hands in surrender. 'That's not what I meant.'

'It should be. I have no purpose. I'm just some insurance for a prophecy that will never come to being.'

Tio opened his mouth and spoke, but his words were

drowned out by the sound of hooves on gravel. Several horses were rapidly approaching the pagoda.

Alik raced from the training ground to get a view of the visitors. He recognised three travel-worn Tribal Council members dismounting their steeds and rushing inside.

The King had called an emergency council meeting.


ALIK FOLLOWED the councillors to the meeting room at the centre of the pagoda where other members of the council, and the King and Queen, were already seated at the round table.

'Is it true?' demanded one newly arrived councillor: Kayla, the leader of one of the rainforest tribes.

The King nodded. 'The starling message was clear.'

'What's true?' Alik called out, and everyone turned to face him.

King Leo frowned. 'Nothing of your concern, son.'

'I can't believe Nadis has fallen,' another councillor said, shaking his head to himself, earning an angry glare from the King.

'Nadis has fallen!' Alik cried.

Queen Mira gave a weary smile. 'Ivane has taken Nadis and several other cities. The rightful King, Arlo, has returned the country to his people.'

A dozen thoughts flooded Alik's mind. All of them leading to one dizzyingly fantastic conclusion: Kengia would have to act now.

'That's brilliant,' he said, beginning to pace the floor. 'Of course, Lamore will retaliate. They will want to take back one of the major strongholds in Ivane, but they'll need their forces from Ette. So this is Ette's chance. While Lamore is distracted, we can send our army to Ette and help them take their country back too. The sooner the—'

Alik stopped pacing abruptly, suddenly aware that every eye and ear was trained on him. The councillors' gazes ranged from surprise to horror. The King's expression was pure rage.

'Is that your proposal?' Kayla addressed King Leo. 'That we risk our people's lives for a war that isn't of our making?'

Every eye and ear was now on the King.

Leo clenched his jaw. 'I propose no such thing. My son speaks complete nonsense and has proved to me once again that he is not ready for matters of state.'

Alik's hands bunched into fists so tight, his fingernails dug deep into his palms.

'We will congratulate King Arlo on his victory and do what we have always done,' the King continued. 'We have faith in the prophecy to deliver peace and unity to Kypria.'

Affirmative murmurs rolled around the room, and Alik knew he had lost.

Fortunately, or perhaps unfortunately, giving up wasn't in the Prince's nature.

# 11

———

*L*iprah was one of the richest cities in Ivane, making it a logical target for Lamore. A couple of days' ride to the north-east of Nadis, it was surrounded by thriving mines, primarily gold, which also happened to adorn many of the impressive buildings in the city. Impressive, that was, until now.

The locals had tried to hold off the invaders, but had been severely outnumbered. The Lamorian King, it seemed, was intent on making a statement. His forces had brought dozens of trebuchets, which they'd used to decimate not just the municipal buildings, but every second storefront and home.

But this wasn't the first thing Gwyn noticed on arriving in Liprah. The stench of blood and death hung over the city, starting at the province's outskirts, where a score of bodies – Arlo's trusted supporters – had been strung up on makeshift gallows, their eyes already plucked from their heads by vultures.

Gwyn tried to ignore the sound of her friend dry-retching

beside her. Sofia wouldn't want anyone to think she didn't have the stomach for battle. It was everything she had trained for.

But no amount of training was enough for what they were about to encounter.

KING ARLO's scouts reported that the enemy was waiting for them at the northern end of the city. They had set up a stronghold at the former Lamorian Mayor's residence and compound. The compound lay on the other side of the river that ran through Liprah. It was ringed by crenellated stone walls that Arlo said were more decorative than functional, the Lamorians never expecting to be challenged after nearly two centuries of occupation.

'Still,' Preia said, 'we don't have trebuchets like they do to breach the walls, and they will launch projectiles at us the moment we try to cross the river.'

A smile twitched on Arlo's face. 'Who said anything about crossing the river?'

He filled them in on his plan to approach the compound from the west under the darkness of night.

'But it's nothing but desert and ravines,' Preia pointed out.

'Exactly. It's perfect.'

GWYN and the others rode Ivanian horses, the same ones the Lamorian nobles had used for their carriages. Their unique builds and athleticism were put to much better use as they navigated the sandy and rocky terrain through the night. With nothing but the full moon above to guide them, the

Ivanian contingent trusted in the surefootedness of their steeds to make light work of the task.

As planned, they reached the rear of the compound just before dawn. Arlo instructed his warriors to take up positions on either side of the ravine.

'You know the plan?' He directed his question to his wife.

Preia nodded.

'And you will stick to the plan?' Arlo's eyes flickered, probing her face, then Sofia's and Gwyn's, for affirmation.

'For Ivane,' was Preia's response.

'To victory,' Gwyn and Sofia said in unison.

Arlo made a huffing noise. He hugged his daughter, then Gwyn, before kissing his wife goodbye.

On horseback, Arlo and his best commander, Letoi, made their way down the steep incline of the ravine until they reached the bottom of the dry canyon. Letoi raised a white flag and the pair approached the western gate of the compound. The flag served two purposes: to allow Arlo and Letoi to get close to the compound, and to signal the Ivanian forces to take up their positions, hidden among the rocky landscape of the ravine.

The Ivanian cavalry mounted their horses, ready to sweep down into the canyon. The rest of the group were to use bows and arrows to provide cover as the leading forces stormed the compound. Arlo was sure the Lamorians would never expect an attack from this position. Why would they? Riding at breakneck speed down the sheer sides of the ravine was downright reckless at best, and deadly at worst, even with Ivanian horses. But it was the only move that gave them the element of surprise they needed.

Arlo and Letoi were within three hundred yards of the compound when a shout sounded from a guard at the top of the wall.

'Stop where you are!' The warning in Lamorian echoed through the ravine.

Letoi held the white flag higher in the air, but the pair continued forward.

'I've come to discuss terms,' Arlo hollered back.

'And who are you?' the guard asked.

'I am Arlo.' His voice was strong and true. 'Anointed King of Ivane.'

Gwyn saw Sofia and Preia lift their chins a little higher.

The guard spoke to another, who disappeared out of sight. A line of archers appeared on either side of the first guard. 'Stop there!' he ordered.

But Arlo and Letoi rode onward.

'Wait where you are!'

The pair forged ahead.

The guard signalled to the Lamorian archers. A volley of arrows arced through the sky, embedding in the sandy ground not three feet in front of Arlo and Letoi, forcing them to stop.

The sound of bootfalls from within the compound filled the canyon, followed by the rattling of chains. The gate shuddered open to reveal a familiar figure on horseback. Even from this distance, Gwyn recognised the bald head and stony features of the man who had taken her father's life.

Her longbow shook violently in her hand.

'Are you alright?' Sofia whispered.

'It's him.'

Sofia's jaw tightened. She knew exactly who Gwyn meant. 'Remember the plan,' she urged.

Gwyn had agreed to Arlo's plan. That she, Sofia and Preia would stay at a safe distance on top of the ravine, no matter what happened. And if the plan failed they would make their escape. But that was before she saw *him*.

She forced her hands to still. She had to be ready.

The Lamorian leader, flanked by a dozen soldiers, rode out to meet Arlo and Letoi.

'*Wait*,' Preia whispered, as the enemy neared her husband. '*Wait*.'

Every Ivanian eye was on them. Waiting for the signal.

Then Letoi dropped the flag to the ground.

The thunder of hooves and the collective battle cry of hundreds of Ivanians reverberated around the canyon as the cavalry rushed down to meet the enemy. At the same time, Gwyn, Sofia, Preia and the remaining Ivanians launched a volley of arrows at the Lamorian contingent.

The Lamorian leader yelled back to the compound guards to close the gate. His order was barely audible over the screams of his fallen soldiers and the roar of Ivanian fighters who'd made it down the ravine. Then there were the high-pitched cries of pain from Ivanian riders and their horses that had fallen victim to the unforgiving terrain.

Gwyn tried to shut out the sounds as she aimed directly at the leader who was galloping right at Arlo with his sword raised. She shouted in triumph as her arrow struck the man in the shoulder, throwing him back in the saddle. But the Lamorian only stopped for a moment to snap off the arrow shaft. It was enough time though for Arlo and Letoi to close the distance between them and attack the Lamorians face-to-face.

The Ivanian archers had to stop firing to avoid injuring their own, leaving Gwyn with nothing to do but watch apprehensively as the compound gate, and their only means of taking back Liprah, shuddered almost shut.

By now some of the Ivanian cavalry had reached the skirmish and their superior numbers enabled a group, led by Arlo, to break away from the crowd and head toward the gate. Lamorian arrows showered down on them from the compound wall above, taking out one Ivanian then another. But there was nothing Gwyn and the others on top of the ravine could do. The compound was well out of arrow range.

Gwyn silently prayed to the Princess Guardians that Arlo would make it. She guessed there was no more than a couple of feet between the bottom of the gate and the ground.

Another of Arlo's group fell. And another.

*Please let him make it,* Gwyn pleaded. *He has to.*

Arlo reached the gate first and leapt from his horse. He and a dozen other Ivanians rolled under just before it slammed to a close.

For a heart-skittering few moments, nothing happened. And then…the gate jolted open.

The Lamorian leader had called for the gate to be reopened, and he and his soldiers retreated to the compound with the Ivanian cavalry in tow. By now, many of their archers were rushing down the canyon to join the battle.

Gwyn acted on impulse alone. She mounted her horse and began to guide it down the ravine.

'No!' Sofia shouted after her.

'Come back!' Preia called out.

But Gwyn would not be stopped. Not when she was this close to getting justice.

It took every bit of her concentration to stay upright as her horse negotiated the treacherous path. Even so, she knew by the proximity of Sofia and Preia's voices that they had followed her. Once she reached the bottom, Gwyn reached for her staff on her back and urged her steed into a gallop toward the compound.

The scene that greeted her on the other side of the gate was eerily reminiscent of the battlefield in her village. Bloodied bodies from both sides strewn across the ground, but in this case, the enemy's fallen far outnumbered the side Gwyn was fighting on.

In the distance, she spotted her target. The bald-headed man was on foot, fighting Letoi. A Lamorian wearing a crown – their King – stood pressed against a wall behind them. A single young soldier, at least a foot taller than any of them, was blocking Arlo from reaching the King. Arlo swung out with his sword and stabbed at the young man, but the Lamorian deflected every strike with ease.

Gwyn pressed her heels harder into her horse's belly, slicing through any enemy who dared try to stop her from reaching her goal. Her bladed staff was painted with blood.

Finally she reached them. She dropped to the ground and launched herself at the Lamorian leader. Letoi attacked him from the front and Gwyn from the side, but their opponent wasn't to be underestimated. He ducked and weaved, his characteristic sneer giving the impression that he relished the challenge.

Sofia and Preia arrived and joined Arlo in his quest to get to the King, who raised his sword and ran at Sofia.

Fear for her best friend was enough for Gwyn to momentarily lose concentration. Pain shot through her as the bald man's sword slashed her upper arm. Instinct kicked in just in time for her to evade the Lamorian's next, more deadly blow.

A guttural howl and a scream cleaved the air behind Gwyn, and she, Letoi and the Lamorian leader stopped to see what had happened.

The young Lamorian soldier was on his knees, one hand clutching a bloody wound on his abdomen – the other reaching for his King, dead on the ground, Arlo's sword sticking from his chest.

Arlo retrieved his blade and held it aloft. 'The Lamorian King is dead!' he shouted. 'Surrender now!'

A hush rolled over the battlefield, and one by one the Lamorians dropped their weapons.

'Victory to Ivane!' Gwyn shouted, disbelieving that the moment had finally arrived.

'Victory to Ivane!' a laughing Sofia joined in.

Preia flashed a jubilant smile, but it just as quickly froze. Her eyes were fixed on a spot behind Gwyn.

In one swift movement, she shoved Gwyn to the ground and sacrificed herself like Ona before her.

The Lamorian leader plunged his sword into Preia's chest. It may as well have been Gwyn's own, because in that moment her heart shattered, and she was right back in her village on the day her parents were killed.

An ear-piercing scream exploded from her mouth as she arced her staff through the air, her blade traversing the Lamorian's throat mid-sneer.

As Gwyn watched the man who took her father's life collapse to his knees and clutch his gaping throat, she hoped to feel something like satisfaction; a release, of sorts, because justice had been served. But she felt nothing but sadness, a swelling sorrow that threatened to consume her like a ravenous tidal wave. It overpowered the keening in her heart, leaving nowhere for the grief to escape, no sound to express the finality of it all.

She had avenged her parents' and Preia's deaths. She had helped deliver Ivane's victory. Kypria would soon be saved and her calling complete.

But then what?

Gwyn was heir to a kingdom that no longer existed, in a land no longer her own. Without revenge and Nima's vision to drive her, what purpose did she have? And how would she go on without Preia to guide her?

The answers expressed themself in a single tear that slid its way down her cheek.

Ivane had had its final triumph. Gwyn had gained vengeance and victory, but she had lost something far more important. She had lost hope.

# 12

---

*A*lik could hardly believe it. The Lamorian King had been killed in battle, his forces decimated. Ivane had resoundingly taken back its country and Ette was in the process of doing the same. There was no better time for Kengia to mobilise its forces to support Ette, to show they weren't cowards. Not even his peace-loving father could protest now that Lamore was barely a threat and the danger to Kengia was so minimal.

He found King Leo in his private rooms meeting with Kairi and Tio, who wore matching silly grins and flushed cheeks. Alik was happy for the pair, but he could never imagine himself falling so deeply in love with someone. Sure, he'd had his share of flings and flirtations, but he could never allow himself to get so attached to a woman. As the heir to Kengia's throne, his would be a marriage dictated by duty and the best interests of his country. That was what drove him. That was why he needed to speak to his father right away.

'Alik.' King Leo stood up to greet his son. 'I'm glad you're here. Your sister has come to tell me the most wonderful news.'

Alik looked to Kairi, whose cheeks only turned a deeper shade of red. 'Tio and I are to be married.'

'Congratulations!' He wrapped his sister in a bear hug, lifting her from the ground and spinning in circles. He only released her after she claimed she would be sick if he didn't put her down. 'I'm so happy for you,' he said seriously, once they'd stopped spinning.

'Thank you.'

Alik turned to Tio and shook his hand. 'Congratulations, or commiserations.'

Tio simply nodded, but Kairi punched Alik in the arm. 'Hey!'

'Ow!' He rubbed his arm in mock pain. 'You're lucky, sister, I'm in a good mood.'

Kairi crossed her arms. 'And why would that be, brother?'

Alik eyeballed his father before responding. 'We are going to help Ette fight against the Lamorians.'

The King sat back down with a sigh.

'We are?' Kairi asked her father. Tio stood next to her with his head cocked, undoubtedly just as curious about the answer.

'We are not,' King Leo said firmly.

Alik couldn't fathom what he was hearing. 'Please tell me you're kidding, Father.'

But the King's unmoving features said he wasn't joking.

Alik threw his arms into the air. 'Now more than ever, our allies need our help. Lamore's King is dead. Their remaining forces in Ette are under attack, but from untrained farmers and merchants. Not warriors.' His voice rose with every sentence. 'We must come to their assistance to ensure Ette is victorious. Only then can Kypria be united and restored. And we can be free to go beyond our borders, and I for one can leave this place!'

The King shook his head. 'Kypria will be united when—'

Alik jabbed his finger at his father. 'Don't say *when the Water Catcher comes*.'

Kairi gave her brother a reassuring smile. 'But the Water Catcher will come, brother.'

Alik raised a hand toward her. His palm burned hot with the magic that pumped through his veins. 'And you know this? You have seen this?' he roared. A gust of wind sprang from his hand and blasted Kairi in the face.

'That's enough,' Tio warned.

Alik closed his fist to extinguish the wind, but otherwise he wouldn't be stopped. 'Please enlighten me as to when the Water Catcher will come, because I can't stand being stuck here a minute longer!'

'Is that why you beg me to join a war that is not of our making?' the King demanded. 'So you can leave your home-land? This place that has given you everything? This place that keeps you safe and secure, and has given you the gift of magic?'

Alik gritted his teeth. 'I beg you to stop hiding behind a questionable prophecy and actually *do* something that demonstrates you're worthy of calling yourself a leader and a King.'

King Leo closed his eyes for a moment and took a breath. Alik waited for the reprimand that was sure to come. But when the King opened his eyes again, there was no sign of anger. In fact, his father looked completely at peace.

'I have *done something*. I have been in contact with the new Lamorian King, and based on our conversations, I believe that Kypria will become a very different place – a better place.'

Alik did a double take. 'A better place? How?'

'We must wait and see.'

Alik's jaw clenched. His father was infuriating. Never involving him in anything of importance. Never listening to him. Yet he seemed intent on keeping Alik a prisoner here.

He stormed from the room.

'Alik.' Kairi chased after him. 'Alik!'

He turned back to face his sister. Her green eyes were flooded with concern.

'I'm sorry about before. I just got so...' Alik screwed up his face, trying to find the right word. 'So—'

'It's alright.' She gave a serene smile. 'I understand. I love my life here and am content, but it's different for you.'

'Different?'

'Yes. You're meant for greater things, brother. That is something I have seen. You will leave this place. You will find someone who is of like mind and spirit, and together...' Kairi let out a laugh. 'You know, a Shaman's visions are never clear or definitive, but I just have this knowledge that you're going to change...' She paused to take a satisfied breath. '*Everything.*'

It was Alik's turn to laugh. What his sister was saying was plain ridiculous. 'You'd say anything to make me feel better.'

# 13
---

It had been six months since the battle of Liprah. Six months since Preia's death. And Gwyn's days and nights were still haunted by the loss of the woman who'd been a second mother to her.

She couldn't shake the belief that it was her fault the Ivanian Queen had died. If she'd just done as Arlo asked and stayed at the top of the ravine, Preia wouldn't have followed her and died at the hands of the Lamorian leader.

No one else blamed Gwyn. Sofia, while devastated by her mother's death, insisted Preia had followed her own path. That she would never have sat idly by and watched the battle play out. Neither Sofia nor Preia were born to be spectators. Even Arlo had pronounced that Ivane wouldn't have been victorious, that he wouldn't have defeated the Lamorian King, if it hadn't been for his wife's bravery and actions on the battlefield.

The Lamorian soldiers who had surrendered at Liprah accepted Arlo's offer of safe passage back to Lamore. Their trebuchets, other weapons and ammunition were confiscated.

Soon after, Arlo helped rally the Etteans to rise against their oppressors and march on the Capital. In the fighting that had ensued, the undersized Lamorian forces had holed up in the city's fortress.

Under the leadership of their renowned military strategist, the Duke of Lakeford, the Lamorians could have survived many months of siege, and perhaps even prevailed – if their newly crowned monarch, King Delrik, had sent reinforcements. Instead, Delrik had ordered the Lamorian retreat. So for the first time in nearly two hundred years, both Ivane and Ette were back in the hands of their respective peoples. And for the first time in just as long, the Lamorian King had expressed no interest in expanding his territories, or taking back the invaded lands.

While it was difficult to take the new and unknown King at his word, life went on at Nadis Palace, and with each day that passed, Gwyn tried to accept the stability and peace now offered to her, hoping it would lift the darkness of her grief.

As King Arlo went about rebuilding an Ivanian nation run by Ivanians, Gwyn and Sofia were left to fill their days with philanthropic and leisurely pursuits, like relaxing in the grand open baths at Nadis Palace. This was precisely what they were doing the morning after a long evening attending a wedding celebration for Ambra's apprentice, Lore, and his wife, Issy.

'Wasn't Issy's dress just beautiful?' Sofia cupped steaming water in her hands and upended it on her bare shoulders.

The palace baths boasted three pools at different temperatures – hot, warm and cold – in a large, open room that was elaborately decorated with domed arches, marble pillars and intricate geometric tilework. The overt luxury of the palace sat uneasily with Gwyn, as did the transition to a life where there was no enemy to kill and no hunger for justice to drive her.

'The colour of the silk, neither blue nor green,' Sofia continued. 'I've never seen anything like it. And did you see the way Lore looked at her when he first saw her?' She giggled, her laughter echoing around the baths. 'His eyes nearly popped from his head at how stunning she looked.'

Gwyn gave a polite nod, but her attention was fixed on her palms. The skin of her fingertips was shrivelled from the water. It was like her essence had been sucked away and she was somewhere between life and death.

Sofia appeared undeterred. 'Tomorrow, after we've visited the school, why don't we head down to the port and see the latest shipment of silks?'

One of the first things King Arlo had done after their victory was open a new school in Nadis. One that was open to all, regardless of birth or wealth. Sofia and Gwyn had been pivotal in the school's establishment, and visiting the students in their classrooms brought the pair endless plea-sure…usually.

'Sure,' Gwyn replied, giving a forced smile.

Sofia sighed. 'At some point, you have to put the past behind you. We got everything we wanted. We have fulfilled our destinies, and now it's time to savour our triumph.'

'Our triumph?' Gwyn spat. 'At what cost? What about all the lives lost? Your mother and aunt among them? You forget too quickly.'

Sofia clenched her jaw. 'I don't forget any life that was lost, including those at my own hands. And my mother and Ona never leave my thoughts. There is a chasm in here' – she thumped her chest – 'that can never be filled. An indescrib-able ache that wakes me all hours of the night, so unbearable I swear I will die from the pain.'

Her voice broke and Gwyn's heart lurched. How could she have questioned her friend's grief?

Sofia drew a lengthy breath before speaking again. 'But I am here. They are not. So I must honour their lives and sacrifice by welcoming and receiving all the goodness we are offered. Mother and Ona would want me to be happy.' Her dark eyes glistened and a shadow of a smile began to form on her face. 'So I shall be happy. As you should be.'

Gwyn should have said *I am happy* or *I will try to be*, but she wasn't sure she was truly capable of either. Fortunately, she was saved from lying by the arrival of a messenger.

King Arlo wished to see them. Immediately.


THE KING WAS in his presence chamber hearing petitions from a long line of Ivanians, each seeking favours. Some sought positions on Arlo's Assembly or recognition of their noble bloodlines, last acknowledged centuries before, and an allocation of land with it. Others sought permission to operate mines previously owned by Lamore. On Gwyn and Sofia's arrival, the King dismissed the petitioners and Ambra, now his head adviser.

He shifted in his throne. 'I have had news from the Lamorian King,' he said bluntly.

Gwyn and Sofia shared an anxious look. 'Has the peace ended?' Sofia asked hesitantly.

Arlo rubbed his palms along the arms of his throne. 'Not if we are to believe King Delrik.'

Gwyn tilted her head. 'What did he say?'

Arlo's hands stilled. 'He says he wants to form a treaty with us and Ette. He wants to formalise trade agreements that will benefit all parties. He wants to encourage free trade among all Kyprian nations and hold summits where the countries' leaders can come together and share knowledge and experiences.'

Gwyn made a *harrumph* sound. 'And we're supposed to believe him?'

'I have also had word from the Kengian King, Leo, who has been conversing with Delrik for some time, encouraging him to seek diplomacy. Leo is sure the Lamorian's words and intentions are genuine.'

'So you propose to accept the word of the Kengian King?' Gwyn cried in outrage. She couldn't fathom Lamore being anything other than her enemy, and she didn't trust Kengia.

'Gwyn's right, Father,' Sofia said. 'The Kengians never came to our aid when we needed them, despite saying they are our allies.'

Arlo stood up and started pacing the room, all the while mussing his beard. Eventually he came to a stop.

'I do share both of your fears.' Gwyn exhaled audibly, but Arlo held up his hand. 'Yet we must at least hear King Delrik out. If we wish for a different future for Ivane, we must be prepared to do things differently. Delrik is not his father, and if we wish to avoid war, then we must listen.'

Sofia bit her lip but nodded.

Gwyn shook her head. 'This Delrik can't be trusted. He is a *Lamorian*. The need to control and oppress others lives in their blood.'

Arlo's brow formed into deep ridges. 'I hope you are wrong. In any case, we are about to find out. King Delrik is coming here. He is due to arrive the day after next.'


King Arlo gave Gwyn and Sofia clear instructions. They were to entertain King Delrik and his entourage on their visit, and do nothing that may jeopardise the proposed treaty between Lamore and Ivane. Begrudgingly, the pair agreed, but Gwyn in particular was determined to detest every moment of it.

It was the second day of King Delrik's visit, and Ambra had arranged a polo game for the visitors' amusement. Gwyn and Sofia made their way to a stage under a tent reserved for the Ivanian and Lamorian royal parties. The women were the first to arrive, selecting two seats at the end of the front row. Stalls offering sweets and cider were set up near the polo field. Gwyn's stomach growled at the mouth-watering scent of fried pastry and rose syrup in the air.

Spectators were beginning to take up positions along the boundary line of the field, cheering on the players taking practice shots at the goal. There were two teams of four: one led by King Arlo, the other by Commander Letoi, each player riding a magnificent Ivanian horse. Arlo's team wore maroon and gold and Letoi's blue and silver, with the horses outfitted in coloured caparisons that matched their riders.

'So, what do you think of him?' Sofia asked, smoothing down her tunic.

Gwyn knew her friend well enough to detect the overly casual tone in her voice. She also knew exactly who Sofia was referring to.

They had only seen the Lamorian King briefly when he had first arrived at the palace with half a dozen retainers in tow. Delrik was around the same age as Sofia and Gwyn, and was exceedingly handsome by anyone's standards: tall and athletic-looking, with an easy smile. He'd greeted the two women in almost flawless Ivanian, before being whisked away to meet with Arlo's Assembly. But Gwyn had resolved not to like the man.

'He's...*young*.' The way she emphasised the last word was

meant to make it sound like a deficiency in the King's character, but evidently Sofia didn't see it the same way. Instead, she beamed.

'Yes. I always pictured the King to be old, you know, like Father.' A flush of pink rose in her cheeks. 'So it was a pleasant surprise.'

Gwyn readied herself to advise Sofia not to fall for looks over substance and remind her that Delrik was their enemy, but they were interrupted by the very subject of Sofia's interest.

'May I?' King Delrik asked in Ivanian, indicating the chair next to Sofia.

She nodded. Her cheeks grew notably redder.

Two other young men who'd arrived with the King took seats on the other side of Delrik. The one who sat closest to the King was of average height, dressed in black robes. He wore his dark hair long around his face, which had a strangely washed-out pallor. His hawklike eyes constantly darted about, as if absorbing every piece of information and detail. His gaze never stopped long enough for Gwyn to get a proper read on his character.

It was the second man who garnered most of her interest. Exceedingly tall and muscular, with an alertness akin to his companion's. When his gaze landed on Gwyn, light flickered momentarily in his eyes before he bowed his head. He was disturbingly familiar. As Sofia and Delrik made small talk about the weather, Gwyn racked her brain for who he may be.

'My lady.' A deep baritone voice. The mysterious man suddenly stood before her, his eyes downcast. Everything from his stance to his physique testified to the fact he was a warrior, but there was a vulnerability in his manner Gwyn hadn't expected. And then the image came to her.

The same man, injured, kneeling over the dead body of his King. He was the one at Liprah who had held off Arlo with expert swordsmanship. He may have prevailed if Preia and Sofia hadn't arrived. It had taken the three of them to defeat the Lamorian soldier.

Gwyn was caught between a sense of fury and admiration for the man, who now stared directly at her.

'I recognise you,' he said in hesitant Ivanian.

'And I recognise you,' she said tonelessly.

'You and the Princess were formidable on the battlefield,' he said with no hint of malice.

Gwyn tried not to show her surprise at the compliment. 'As were you,' she conceded.

The man winced. 'I failed in my duty to protect my King. I'm just fortunate Delrik is a benevolent man and has forgiven me.'

Anger gnawed in Gwyn's belly. 'You don't require his forgiveness. You fought like a true warrior. You were simply outnumbered.'

The man heaved his giant shoulders in a sigh. 'It is kind of you to say so. I would also like to offer my condolences to you and the Princess.' He'd reverted to Lamorian, but Gwyn was able to follow him. 'Your Queen should never have died. We were already defeated. It was dishonourable, what happened.'

Gwyn swallowed at the memory of Preia's death. 'Yes, but at least justice was served to her killer.'

The man nodded. 'I'm Elos. One of the King's knights.'

Gwyn dipped her head in acknowledgement. 'Sir Elos. I'm Gwyn. Princess Sofia's companion.'

Elos waved his hand. 'Just Elos. Please. May I?' He indicated the empty space next to her at the end of the row.

Before Gwyn could respond, he had dragged a chair into position next to her.

'The only title I answer to these days is "Father" or "*Faaada*",' Elos said in a child's voice, chuckling, and Gwyn was surprised to find herself joining in.

'Your wife and child are back in Lamore?' she asked, allowing his relaxed conversation and kind manner to draw her in.

The light in Elos's eyes flickered as if they were filled with storm clouds. 'My child is. My wife died in childbirth.'

'Oh. I'm so sorry.' Gwyn cringed at the inadequateness of her words.

Elos acknowledged her offer of sympathy with a nod and forced smile.

'A boy or a girl?'

A dimpled grin teased its way onto his face. 'A boy. Sar. He spoke his first words not long before we set sail for here.'

'Is he more like you or his mother?'

Elos rubbed his chin in thought. 'He has his mother's fair hair, and some days all I can see is her in his face and mannerisms, but on other days...' He expelled a puff of air. 'If he ends up taking after me in looks and character, only the Princess Guardians could save him.'

Gwyn did a double take. 'You know of the Princess Guardians?'

Elos shrugged. 'I try to learn about other cultures. Delrik has encouraged us to get to know Ettean and Ivanian history...' He cringed. 'I mean, the history before we...you know.'

'I know,' she said. 'The Princess Guardians were a key part of my culture.'

Elos inclined his head. 'Your culture?'

'I'm originally from Ette,' she explained. 'My father was a King of one of the mountain regions.' An involuntary smile came to Gwyn's face. It was the first time in nearly a decade that she'd been able to speak openly about her heritage and her family.

'Wow! So that makes you a Princess too?'

'Yes, I suppose it does,' she said with a laugh. 'But now that you mention it, I think I'd like to stick to just Gwyn.'

Elos sat back in his chair and stretched out his long legs in front of him. 'Just Gwyn it is.'

Shortly after the polo match began, Sofia, at Delrik's request, explained the rules of the game and how the players' aim was to use their mallets to hit the ball into their opponent's goal. The whole time she spoke, Delrik's twinkling eyes never left her. It was as if he were entranced. And judging by her lowered lashes and flushed cheeks, Gwyn suspected the feeling may be mutual.

At half-time, Delrik leapt from his chair, declaring that he wanted to play too. Despite his hawk-eyed companion's protests, the Lamorian King convinced Arlo to let him join his team.

Delrik tapped his chest three times, then strode out onto the field. Gwyn watched on, expecting him to slip up, but before long it became apparent that the Lamorian King's athletic abilities were equal to his charm.

'He's a natural and master of all sports,' Elos said by way of explanation.

'Until he isn't,' the hawk-eyed Lamorian snapped back. 'He'll break his neck.' With that he stood up and stomped off.

'He's a delight,' Gwyn remarked as he stomped away.

Elos gave a dismissive wave. 'Horace has been Delrik's companion since childhood. He's just worried about him.'

'But he doesn't have to be that rude,' Gwyn countered.

'Horace is more serious than rude. He's the real statesman of Lamore. Delrik is an idealist and philosopher, a romantic, if you will. It's Horace's steady hand that guides him and brings his wishes to reality. It's why he's been appointed as the King's Chancellor.'

It occurred to Gwyn that holding a position like that would be quite a burden for someone as young as Horace – but Delrik's role was just as burdensome, and he managed to be affable. 'Still, it's no excuse for rudeness,' she chastised.

'You're right,' Elos agreed, 'but I will say that he is usually more polite than he is today. He's still afflicted by seasickness from our voyage.'

'He is still ill?'

'He has a fear of sailing that affects his body and mind.' Elos frowned. 'His father was the previous Lamorian King's Master of Horse. He was sailing back from Ette after acquiring some new destriers, but his ship was blown off course toward the Kengian coast and their King mistook them for invaders. King Leo summoned an earthquake that created a tidal wave, killing everyone on board.'

Gwyn's hands instinctively curled into fists and her finger-nails dug into her palms. She could never forgive Kengia for not helping Ette or Ivane. And she hated Lamore, but today had shown her that not all Lamorians were the same, or deserving of her hate. After hearing this tale, perhaps she could even find common ground with someone like Horace.

# 14

*a* spring of dances, feasts and amusements organised for the Lamorian visitors soon soured for Gwyn like a fig left too long in the scorching midday sun.

Nadis may have been located by the sea, but it wasn't exempt from the sweltering desert-like conditions that afflicted much of the rest of the country. In the hottest months, Ivanians took refuge inside or by windows, trying to grasp any hint of a cooling breeze. And as the Ivanian summer bore down on Nadis, Gwyn began to fear the Lamorians would never leave.

While Chancellor Horace would spend much of each day handling missives from Lamore or meeting with Arlo and his advisers about trade agreements, King Delrik became a permanent fixture in Sofia and Gwyn's quarters at the palace. If they were embroidering tunics for the poor, Delrik would sit by Sofia, *ooh*ing and *aah*ing at the 'exquisiteness' of every stitch. If they were reading, he would read with them, or pretend to while he surreptitiously watched Sofia over the top of his book with his chest puffed out like a lovesick pigeon. If they were heading out to visit the markets, the Lamorian King would accompany them, cooing over a new bolt of silk Sofia selected or purchasing a new hair comb or trinket for her, always insisting on carrying her basket.

Sometimes Elos would join the King and make good-natured comments to Gwyn about Delrik's unrequited infatuation. And while Gwyn enjoyed Elos's company and would laugh politely at his commentary, she found it the opposite of amusing, for there was something Elos wasn't privy to. Something none of the Lamorians were privy to. This particular infatuation was reciprocated.

Sofia had the poise and grace to not show her thoughts outwardly, and she hadn't said anything to Gwyn to indicate her feelings for the Lamorian King, but she didn't need to. Gwyn knew her best friend better than anyone. She recognised the signs of affection in the slightest flush of her cheek, the way Sofia sat or stood a little taller the moment Delrik entered the room, the slight lilt of her voice whenever she spoke his name. With each passing day Gwyn felt a little part of her friend slipping away from her as the King progressively infiltrated Sofia's heart and mind.

This was not part of the plan, as far as Gwyn saw it. She understood making peace and trading with Lamore. She understood it was all necessary to unite Kypria for the first time in nearly two hundred years. And she understood Delrik was not his father. But what did Sofia really know of him and his character? What did any of them know of him? Gwyn didn't want to see Sofia hurt, and if she was completely honest with herself, she didn't want to lose her friend.

As far as Gwyn was concerned, the Lamorians needed to leave before any declarations of love from either party. Sofia would get over her crush with time and everything could go back to the way it was supposed to be.

⤳

It was approaching noon and Gwyn and Sofia had just returned from a visit to Nadis School. The visit had been even more enjoyable than usual, partly because Delrik hadn't accompanied them, and partly because they'd attended an enlightening science class taught by Lore. He was teaching the students about why and how solar and lunar eclipses occurred. He'd referenced a particular book in the palace library, which had one of the earliest written records of an eclipse from four centuries earlier; not just any eclipse, but a rare blood moon.

No Ivanian in living memory had seen a blood moon. In fact, the account Lore had referred to was believed to be the last time there had been such an event in Kypria. Lore's description of the full moon turning crimson had fascinated Gwyn, and she headed straight for the library the moment she returned to the palace.

The library was one of the most magnificent structures in Nadis. A domed basilica constructed from blush-coloured granite, it was one of the city's oldest buildings. The way the quartz and mica in the stone caught and shimmered in the light gave the whole building an ethereal appearance. Inside, limestone floors ran for more than three hundred feet in one direction and a hundred and fifty in the other. Hundreds of marble columns supported the domed ceiling creating aisles among the vast open space. The towering bookshelves topped with arches were so tall they could only be fully accessed via ladders on rails. Even more bookshelves ran the perimeter of the building on three levels of mezzanines. Scattered among them were desks and chairs.

Gwyn had been told the library housed more than two hundred thousand manuscripts dating back centuries. In a glass cabinet there was even a scroll dozens of metres long, capturing the words of one of the nation's earliest philosophers in gold ink. The library was a testament to everything Ivanians held dear: knowledge, learning and architecture that celebrated their culture and natural resources. And thanks to Arlo, the library was now open to all Ivanians.

Gwyn sought out one of the librarians, who gave her the catalogue number for the book Lore had referenced and directed her to the far corner of the building. She took her time traversing the ground floor, savouring the earthy scent of thousands of old books that enveloped her with the intoxicating promise of discovery – an enhanced understanding of the world and a person's place in it. She sucked in deep, gratifying breaths, a dreamy smile on her face as her sandals flip-flopped on the stone floor and echoed through the library.

Eventually, Gwyn rounded the corner of the shelf bearing the number she'd been given – but there she came to an awkward stop, her smile vanishing.

Chancellor Horace sat alone at a small table, his hawk eyes interrogating a chessboard before him.

Gwyn held her breath and started to back away, hoping the Lamorian wouldn't notice her, but she walked right into an unattended trolley of books, sending a pile of them crashing to the ground.

Horace's eyes shot toward her and he swiftly got to his feet. Wordlessly, he helped her pick up the fallen books. She couldn't help but notice the care he took as he stacked the books neatly back on the trolley. She was so fixated on the elegant movement of his slender fingers that it took her a moment to realise he was speaking to her.

She lifted her head to meet his gaze. 'Sorry?'

'Are you alright?'

The look he gave her was equally comforting and confusing. It wasn't exactly a look of kindness, but a look of complete knowing, or wanting to know…

'Alright?' she squeaked.

'Have you injured yourself?'

'Oh, right. No. I mean, yes, I'm alright,' she said, inwardly cursing herself for how flustered she sounded.

Horace simply nodded and returned to his seat before the chessboard.

Gwyn could have easily gone back to her business then, but suddenly she had a new thirst for knowledge that must be quenched. Starting with the real person behind the gruff Chancellor exterior, and an explanation as to why he was staring at a chessboard, all set up for a game but without a single piece in play.

Without invitation, she sat down at the table opposite Horace. 'Would you like me to show you how to play?' she offered.

'I already know how to play,' he responded without looking up.

Now that she had set herself the mission of getting to know him, she wouldn't be easily deterred. 'Perhaps we could play together?'

Horace looked up at her this time with a sigh. 'I do not wish to offend you, but I rarely play with anyone.'

She gave a teasing laugh. 'Are you scared you're going to lose?'

A smirk tugged at the corner of his mouth. 'I never lose.'

Gwyn jutted out her chin. 'And neither do I.'

A spark of light flickered in Horace's eyes, the colour of black jade. He rested his elbows on the table and steepled his fingers. After a heart-stilling pause, he replied, 'Yes. I can see that in you.'

Horace stated it like a fact, but there was an unmistakable edge to his words – a challenge.

Gwyn smoothed down her tunic, buying time to formulate an appropriate response. 'So you will play chess with me?' she ventured.

Horace folded his arms and stared again at the chessboard. 'I'm in no need of a partner.'

Anger flared inside Gwyn at the snub, but also at herself for foolishly wanting to get to know the arrogant Lamorian. She jumped out of her chair with such force it toppled over. The sound of the timber meeting stone rattled through the building, earning angry looks from librarians and patrons, but Gwyn wasn't to be stopped.

'And you are at no risk of finding one! I only offered out of pity.'

Horace flinched at the word *pity*, fuelling Gwyn to continue.

'Pity for the miserable wretch you are.' She waved her hand dramatically for effect. 'Pity for all Lamorians for being so pathetic in defeat.'

Horace gripped the table with white-knuckled hands, but said nothing.

'I, for one, can't wait to see the back of you Lamorians.'

'That is where we are in agreement,' he hissed through clenched teeth.

Gwyn checked herself. 'In agreement?'

'I too cannot wait to leave this place.'

Gwyn tilted her head in question as Horace stood up and righted her chair.

'The King needs to be back in Lamore. Now.' He indicated she should sit, which she did – she wanted to hear more about why he was so keen for Delrik to leave Ivane.

'Why?'

'He is a newly crowned King who has spent much of his short reign in another country, chasing ridiculous follies.'

Gwyn crossed her arms. 'You don't wish for peace with us?'

Horace tapped his fingers on the table. 'Peace is advantageous for us. We're a country of limited natural resources and much of our land is unsuitable for farming, and now we have thousands of Lamorians who've returned from Ivane and Ette and must be supported. But we do have some things of value to trade, such as wool. And we have a reasonably healthy treasury, which, if managed well, we can use to buy the goods we need.'

Gwyn scoffed. 'A treasury bolstered by pillaging Ivane and Ette for generations.'

Horace didn't so much as blink at her barb.

'Then what follies do you speak of?' she pressed.

Horace raised his brows. 'Don't pretend you don't know. We have both seen it.'

Gwyn leant forward in her chair. 'Seen what?'

Horace rolled his eyes. 'You and I both know that Delrik and Sofia are in love with each other.'

'Shhh.' Gwyn looked around quickly. Fortunately, no one appeared to be within hearing distance. She turned back to Horace. 'Your King has told you this?'

'He didn't need to, but it is plain to me, as it is to you. No one knows them as well as we do. Has the Princess said anything to you?'

Gwyn slumped in her chair. 'She didn't need to.'

'They don't even know each other.'

She threw her hands up. 'Exactly!'

'And Delrik needs to focus on his own country and duties right now.'

'As does Sofia.'

'So we must leave before anything progresses between them.'

'Agreed.'

'But *if* something is said, you must convince her they can't be together.'

Gwyn shrugged. 'I can try, but once Sofia makes up her mind about something…Couldn't you speak to Delrik?'

Horace gave a bitter laugh. 'I think that is where the pair are well matched. As determined as each other.'

'Then all we can do is hope your business with King Arlo concludes soon and you can set sail.'

Horace looked back toward the library entrance, where a glimpse of the sea could be seen in the distance. 'It is better for many reasons if we sail soon. The winter squalls at sea are unforgiving…'

Gwyn recalled the story Elos had told her about how Horace's father died at sea. Without thinking, she reached for his hand.

His gaze shifted slowly to her hand over his, then to her face.

'I heard how you came to be Delrik's companion, and I'm sorry.'

A softness washed over Horace's otherwise sharp features. 'And I heard how you came to be Sofia's companion,' he murmured. 'I'm sorry too.' He placed his free hand over hers, sending tingles up her arm.

Gwyn swallowed. She hadn't expected such compassion from Horace, but had she heard something else in his voice? Had she felt something else in his touch?

'We found you!'

Sofia's enthusiastic voice shattered the intimate moment, forcing Horace and Gwyn to snatch their hands away from each other.

'Well, it wasn't that hard,' Delrik quipped beside her. 'Horace comes here every day to play chess.'

Gwyn shook her head to herself, still confused by who Horace actually did or would play chess with.

'And Gwyn told me she was coming to find that book,' Sofia added.

Delrik responded with a hearty laugh, followed by a nervous giggle from Sofia. There was something more than a little odd about their behaviour.

'I have been to see King Arlo and I have some news that you will welcome, my dear friend,' Delrik addressed Horace. 'We are to set sail by the end of the week.'

Horace and Gwyn exchanged a look of relief that quickly turned to alarm at Delrik's next words.

'I have to get Lamore Castle ready for my wife.' He moved closer to Sofia and took her hand.

'We're to be married,' Sofia gushed.

'I see,' Horace said carefully. 'Congratulations, then.' He nodded at the King, then Sofia. 'To both of you.'

'Yes. Congratulations,' Gwyn said in a thin voice.

'The arrangements are being made as we speak,' Delrik said. 'Elos will stay here while the formal marriage negotiations are undertaken, then will accompany Sofia and her party to Lamore before winter.'

A terrible realisation hit Gwyn. Not only was her best friend about to marry a virtual stranger and move to their former enemy's land, she too would be expected to go. Nausea swept over her with the force of a tidal wave manifested by the Kengian King himself.

The rest of the day passed in a blur. Well-wishers surrounding the happy couple. Toasts given at dinner. And an all-round air of excitement that left Gwyn with the helpless feeling that everything in her life was turning upside down again, and there was nothing she could do.

BACK IN THEIR rooms at the end of the night, Gwyn was brushing Sofia's hair with an intensity that made the latter flinch in the mirror. It was the first time they'd been alone all day.

Sofia took the brush from Gwyn and looked up at her friend. 'I wish you could be happy for me.' The sadness in her voice ripped through Gwyn.

'I am happy for you. I'm just worried for you.'

Sofia clasped both of Gwyn's hands in hers. 'There is no need to worry. This is the right thing to do.'

'You don't have to do this. We already have made peace with Lamore. You don't need to marry their King.'

Sofia released Gwyn's hands and hung her head. 'I wish I could say I am doing this for my country, knowing it will secure a peace beyond anything a trade agreement could ever do. I wish I could say my motives are unselfish, but they're not. I want to marry him because I love him.'

'You really think you love him?' Gwyn asked.

Sofia looked up again, her eyes glistening earnestly. 'I know I do. I know it with the same certainty that you and I were meant to be best friends. With the certainty that you were destined to help us unite Kypria. And with the certainty that I will never be truly content unless I am by Delrik's side. Do you understand?'

Gwyn bit her lip.

'Please say you understand.' Sofia's voice trembled. 'Yours is the only opinion I will heed and if you don't want me to marry him—' Her voice broke, and Gwyn's heart with it.

Gwyn took her friend in her arms, holding Sofia's head to her chest. 'You should marry him,' she said. And she meant it. Sofia needed to marry Delrik, even if it was a mistake, for it was her mistake to make. And Gwyn knew in the most devastating way what it felt like to have no control over one's future.

# 15

*G*wyn weaved her way through the palace city, her labyrinth-like path reflecting her wandering thoughts about the prospect of having to leave before summer's end. She thought of her adopted home and everything she would miss. Then she thought about what it would be like to live among people she had long viewed as her enemy – and about her own future, and whether her part in uniting Kypria was over.

Now that Sofia was to marry Delrik, cementing peace between their nations, what purpose did Gwyn have? She'd grown up being told she was an Earth King's heir and would one day lead the Ettean people, and while Nima had told her she would never return to Ette, Gwyn had always hoped and dared to believe she would return to her homeland. But now...now she couldn't foster such hope. Her future as a royal companion in Lamore was mapped out for her. A future far removed from her birthright and any destiny she had imagined for herself.

Gwyn wondered what might have been until she couldn't

bear another thought shrouded in grief and loss. She could not change the past. She may have no control over the future. But she could at least enjoy the present and the little time she had left in Ivane.

So now as she wandered, she drank in the rays of the afternoon sun and the warmth radiating from the sandstone buildings, uncaring that her tunic stuck to her skin and her arms shone with a sheen of sweat. She stopped in the market-place, welcoming the explosion of scent and spices that tickled her senses. She purchased a cup of juice flavoured with lemon and sugar, closing her eyes as she savoured every refreshing sip. And eventually she found herself on a terrace at the highest point of the city.

She cast her gaze back toward the north and the moun-tains that led to her true home. Fittingly, she couldn't see the Ettean Borderlands, another reminder that hope was beyond her reach. But when she closed her eyes and felt the kiss of a cooling sea breeze on her face, she fancied for a moment she could hear voices in the wind saying, *Farewell, our Queen.* The voices, perhaps, of the Princess Guardians.

'Farewell,' she whispered in return.

'Yes, farewell.' A different voice. A man's voice, seeking and warm as the Ivanian sun.

Gwyn's eyes flung open to find Horace standing before her, his black robes and stiff-backed stance completely at odds with the voice she'd just heard.

'Horace, I was just…' Gwyn didn't know how to finish the sentence without looking foolish in front of the Lamorian Chancellor.

Horace's black eyes stared back at Gwyn, probing her, something that may have been a nervous smile or a grimace on his face. He cleared his throat.

'I suppose you were saying goodbye to your home.' He

nodded toward the mountains in the distance. 'To Ette.' His brow crinkled into seriousness. 'It must be difficult, having to leave everything behind. Saying goodbye not just to the land you were meant to rule…' He locked eyes with her, and she recognised concern in his features. 'But to your connection to your family. You must miss your mother and father terribly.'

Gwyn's head was awhirl. She didn't understand this man whose manner, for the most part, was the height of rudeness, yet who was capable of the sharpest insights into a person's feelings and could convey empathy when least expected.

'Yes, I do miss them,' she said simply.

'It is why we must find family in other places,' he said matter-of-factly.

'You mean Delrik and Sofia.'

Horace was silent for a beat. Two beats. Unblinking. Then, 'And with others.'

Gwyn's breath caught in her throat. Was he speaking of her? Did he want to be close to her? Did *she* want the same thing?

She searched his eyes and face for the answer, but he gave her nothing.

'I wished to say farewell to you,' he said after another excruciating pause.

'You knew I was here?' she asked.

'I did not. I intended on coming to find you at the palace. I came here for another reason.' Horace walked over to a carved stone balustrade at the edge of the terrace and leant against the railing. He looked out to the west, where the sun was beginning to set. 'I come here almost every day.' His voice was warm again with a hint of wistfulness. He took a deep breath of the sea air and gave a satisfied sigh.

'You come here for the sunset?' Gwyn couldn't disguise

her bewilderment that the gruff Chancellor would seek out something so seemingly frivolous each day.

He turned back toward her and gave a languid smile. 'You don't think I have a liking for beautiful things? Of course beauty appeals to me.' Gwyn thought she may faint under the intensity of his gaze. 'When it is accompanied by substance.'

He went back to looking at the sunset, leaving Gwyn to wonder whether he thought her beautiful, and hoping he did if only he also thought she had substance.

'When I see the sunset,' he continued, speaking formally as if he were reciting an oath, 'I see more than its beauty. I see the glowing promise of my own home and I'm reminded of all the great things I will do when I return. How I will help Delrik bring Lamore into a new age of prosperity.'

'What is Lamore like?' she asked, her voice hesitant.

Horace faced her again, with neither a smile nor a frown. 'Well, it's cooler than Ivane, but like here, the castle sits by the sea. I expect you will find the fashions a little different, as well as some customs, but all that you can get used to.'

'But what of the people? Are they…?' She bit her lip, stopping short of asking whether Lamorians hated Ivanians and Etteans, and whether they were as bloodthirsty as those who'd attacked her village.

Horace rested a hand on her upper arm and gave Gwyn what felt like his most serious look. 'You have nothing to fear. Because you have me.'

Before she could interrogate what Horace had said, or what he may be trying to say, he had removed his hand.

'And you never know – perhaps Sofia and Delrik will realise their mistake and the marriage may never take place, meaning you won't have to come to Lamore at all.'

'Do you think that may happen?' she asked, unsure now of which scenario she really wanted.

Horace frowned. 'I don't know. I don't know anything anymore.' He bowed his head. 'But I do hope we meet again. Farewell, Gwyn.' And he walked away.

# 16

*A*lik stared at the ceramic cup filled with rice wine. In the dim light of the drinking house, tucked away in one of Lochlen's less frequented alleyways, the clear liquor was barely visible. The promise of forgetting, even just for a few short hours, lay within reach – the only salvation within his grasp, since he was a prisoner in this place. His sister's premonition that he was destined to leave Kengia seemed more laughable than ever.

The Lamorian King had been in Ivane for months, heeding King Leo's advice to form an alliance with the Kyprian nations in the east. There seemed little chance of war, and while Alik knew he should celebrate the prospect of universal peace, it meant Kengia wouldn't need to mobilise any forces, which in turn meant Alik had no reason to believe he'd be able to leave his homeland.

Initially, he had thought a united Kypria would mean his father would reopen Kengia's borders, but King Leo had quashed his hopes there as well. Alik's father was cautiously optimistic about being at permanent peace with Lamore, but wanted to take an indefinite 'wait and see' approach. Even if he was convinced it was safe for Kengia to join the rest of the world again, he would only allow restricted travel between the two countries. That was to say, the magical protection borders would stay in place.

Even so, Alik had felt a spark of hope, since he was needed to control the mountain passageway – but again this spark was extinguished. Leo had heard that King Delrik's trusted adviser, Chancellor Horace, disliked Kengians, blaming the Kengian King for his father's death. While Delrik had given Leo no indication he felt the same way as his adviser, it was enough for the King to declare that Alik mustn't leave. Ever.

'It is the only way to ensure the prophecy comes to pass,' he had said, sealing Alik's fate as the future King of a land he yearned to leave and the holder of magnificent powers that no one needed.

With physical escape denied to him, he sought a different escape at the bottom of a wine cup. Alik lifted the cup to his lips and downed it, cringing at the burning sensation in his throat before tapping his fingers on the bar to signal a refill.

The drinking house door swung open, allowing unwelcome sunshine and the harsh reality of day to flood the building interior. Alik didn't bother to look up. He merely waved his right hand in the air and summoned a gust of wind to slam the door shut, then lifted his refilled cup to his lips.

'Enough, brother.' Amund's voice beside him.

Alik downed the liquor in one gulp and waited for Amund to chastise him. Both his brother and sister had voiced their concerns over recent weeks. They'd tried distracting him with his favourite pursuits like swordplay and archery, but their feigned enthusiasm and clumsy attempts with the weaponry gave him little pleasure. Alik's mother had tried to get him to teach a class at the Institute, but it had ended sourly when a student had questioned his role as the firstborn Prince, because of course Alik didn't have an answer. He didn't have a role or a purpose, other than to stay alive, it seemed, for the sake of a fantastical prophecy.

'You'll want to be sober to hear this news,' Amund said matter-of-factly.

Alik tapped his fingers on the bar, but Amund laid his hand over the cup to prevent further topping up.

Alik wobbled on his stool as he turned to face his brother. 'Leave me be,' he snarled, expecting Amund to back away, but he was unmoving.

'You'll want to hear what I have to say.'

Alik forced his eyes to try to focus on his brother and the inevitable lecture he was about to receive. 'Say what you have to say, then leave.'

'The Lamorian King is to marry the Ivanian Princess.'

Alik scoffed. 'I do not know the pair,' he slurred, 'and I'm…unlikely to ever know them.' He swept an unsteady arm across the room. 'Or anyone outside of this forsaken country.' He stopped to hiccup and grabbed his cup from under his brother's hand. 'But I am happy…they give me something to toast to.'

'There is more, if you'd just sober up enough to listen.'

There was an urgency in Amund's voice that made Alik put his cup back down on the bar. 'I'm listening.'

'The Ivanian King has asked Father to send an envoy to Lamore to help with the final marriage negotiations. He daren't leave his own country while the peace is so new, but he wants someone he can trust to go to the Lamorian court to make sure King Delrik meets his obligations and Ivane's interests are protected.'

A host of possibilities whirled in Alik's mind, and the hope that he had long given up began to rekindle. But…

'What has Father said?'

'Nothing. Yet. But I thought of what Kairi has seen, how you are meant for something great. And while I don't want you to leave, and I share some of Father's fears…' Amund's brows bunched together. 'I see what this is doing to you. So I will go with you to see Father.'

Alik leapt from his stool, immediately regretting it when his head spun. He dropped back onto his seat.

'Once you're sober,' Amund added.

'You won't regret this, brother,' Alik declared loudly, directing his wine-soaked words at Amund's face.

Amund grimaced. 'I'm afraid I already am.'


SEVERAL HOURS and a dozen cups of tea later, Alik was recovered enough to meet his father. He and Amund found the King alone in his rooms, his quill poised over a blank piece of parchment. He looked up at their arrival, narrowing his gaze at Alik's unkempt hair and stained tunic. Alik stood up taller and patted down his hair.

'Father,' Amund began, 'we've come to speak to you about King Arlo's request.'

Amund spoke with a confidence Alik had never heard before. He gave his brother an admiring nod.

King Leo laid down his quill. 'Yes. I was about to write my reply to the Ivanian King.'

Alik stepped forward. 'Of course you're going to agree to his request,' he said excitedly, earning a warning look from Amund.

Leo's eyes, tired and dulled like worn silver, scrutinised Alik's face. 'I don't know how I will reply.'

'Let me reply for you.' Another warning look from Amund, which Alik ignored. 'I will go to Lamore.'

Leo shook his head. 'If anyone is to go, it won't be you, Alik. You are the firstborn of our line. The Water Catcher prophecy must be protected.'

'But why, Father?' Alik held his hands out imploringly. 'The *point* of the prophecy is to bring about a united Kypria, and the marriage between the Lamorian King and Ivanian Princess will do that.'

'If the marriage goes ahead, perhaps the prophecy is redundant,' the King said slowly. Alik's hopes were buoyed until his father held up his hand. 'But for how long? We don't know whether this peace will last. We can't risk the prophecy being lost. We can't risk losing *you*.'

Alik cocked his head to the side. Had his father expressed a genuine concern for his welfare because he cared for him, or was he driven by his care for the prophecy? In any case, Leo had made his position clear. Alik wasn't going anywhere.

'Father, if I may?' Amund ventured. 'By your own account from your correspondence with King Delrik, he is not like his father.'

Leo sat back in his chair. 'That is my assessment. But I don't really know—'

'Of course,' Amund interrupted. 'But we must also consider our historical alliance and duty to Ivane, which we've neglected for too long. If we have the power to help them now, when peace can be ensured, shouldn't we do what we can? They aren't asking for much.'

Leo looked from Amund to Alik, his heavy gaze resting on the latter for a protracted pause before returning his attention to the former.

'You're right. We should help.' Leo picked up his quill and started writing. 'I shall send Tio to support the negotiations in Lamore.'

Fury erupted within Alik like a whirlwind roaring to life. 'I'm going, Father, and you can't stop me!' he exploded.

Leo dropped his quill and met Alik's angry glare, but Alik wouldn't be stopped.

'I'm not a boy any longer. I'm a man who should get to decide his own fate, and as the future King, I want to be part of these negotiations. I want to form a lasting peace between all of the Kyprian nations, for Kengia's sake as much as Ivane's and Ette's.'

Leo stood up so he now met his son eye to eye. 'I thought you wanted war? Not too long ago you were begging me to help fight against Lamore.'

'I was begging you to come to Ivane and Ette's aid!'

'That is true, Father,' Amund said. 'While I know there's part of my brother that relishes adventure, and the idea of battle may have appealed to him, his motives are pure at heart. He has always wanted to help Ivane and Ette.'

Alik gave his brother a nod of thanks. 'And the best way I can help them now, help *us*, is to go to Lamore and secure this peace. We shouldn't have to sit around waiting for a prophecy that may never come to being. With this peace, we won't have to rely on magic to protect our homeland.'

Leo frowned. 'I'm afraid your idealism may be your downfall, son.'

'Well, Father, you can be afraid for both of us, because I'm going with or without your blessing.'

Leo took three long, drawn-out breaths, his gaze fixed on Alik the whole time. Alik was surprised to see what he thought was the glimmer of a tear in his father's eyes, but before he could be sure, King Leo turned his back on him and looked out the window in the direction of the Nymoi Alps and Lamorian border.

'Then you shall have it.'

But the King's blessing sounded more like a warning.

# 17

---

*G*wyn had been hopeful that once the Lamorian King returned home, Sofia's affection would wane. With time and distance she would realise it had been nothing but a silly crush, and that she had never really known Delrik. However, the King's absence only served to magnify Sofia's feelings. She counted down the days until they would meet again and penned letters every second day to her fiancé. She gushed about her wedding plans and urged her father to hasten the negotiations, while Gwyn secretly hoped they'd fail.

Gwyn had been surprised by the complexity of the negotiations, which had very little to do with the marriage itself. She had quizzed both Lore and Elos, who had explained each party's perspective. Ivane needed assurances that Lamore would not mount an attack on them, or on Ette. Delrik could not have any military presence outside Lamore and must agree to restrictions and screening of any Lamorians coming to Ivane or Ette. Lamore's biggest need was an iron-clad trade agreement for all of the food and resources they lacked. There was also the matter of the dowry, which was to be paid in a number of instalments. These were just a few of the points to be negotiated and agreed upon before Sofia would set sail to Lamore.

After several months, agreements were signed off in principle by both sides with only the finer details to be finalised, giving King Arlo enough confidence to allow Sofia to leave.

THERE WAS a time in Gwyn's life when she couldn't have imagined Ivane being her home, but that was what it was to her now. Some days she could barely remember what it was like living in her old village, unable to recall the feeling of crisp mountain air filling her lungs as she rambled up and down the scree slopes, or the feeling of earth being pressed into her hand by her father as he reminded her that, as his heir, she was one with the land.

Leaving behind her life in Ette had broken her. Living among Sofia's family in Ivane had restored her. Leaving Ivane now threatened to rip her apart again. The only thing that stopped her from crumbling was the indisputable happiness of her friend, who couldn't wait to start the next chapter of her life.

There were tearful goodbyes with friends and family, and promises from both sides to visit soon. King Arlo, in a very un-Arlo-like way, wrapped Gwyn in a bear hug. He sniffed back tears and told her how proud of her he was. By the time he had finished saying goodbye to Sofia, he was a sobbing mess.

Prince Laskar begged Gwyn to take him with them, saying he longed to visit Lamore to see what their sweets tasted like, but really meaning that he wanted to make sure they were both protected. It was an understandable sentiment given what had happened to his mother and aunt. Gwyn explained to him that it was his duty as the future King to stay and lead his country, and that Ivane needed him more than they did.

Laskar puffed out his chest and told Elos to protect both of his sisters with his life, 'or you'll have to deal with me'. Elos, who was a good foot taller than Laskar, had the grace to nod his head sagely and confirm he would give his life for his charges.

And on the last day of summer, Sofia, Gwyn, Lore and his wife, Issy, with Elos as their escort, boarded a ship bound for Lamore.

GWYN WASN'T sure what to expect when she arrived in Lamore, other than the little Horace had told her. She'd not allowed herself to think about it too much, as the only thing she knew for sure about Lamore was that it was full of Lamorians, and her experience with Lamorians to date didn't bode well. So when she disembarked at Obira Port to be greeted by rain and a bone-chilling wind that stabbed like needles, she regretted not having done more research.

Elos came to the rescue, offering her his own cloak. 'Not even proper winter yet,' he chuckled.

Gwyn glanced around to make sure Sofia was alright and found her retrieving a full-length fur coat from one of their trunks. 'Delrik sent it as a gift,' she explained.

Gwyn gave a strained smile in return.

Before long, Elos had bundled them up into a plain-looking carriage. It wound its way through a city as grey as Ivane was colourful. There was street after cobblestone street of narrow stone buildings wedged up against each other, with people darting between them like wet rats. Signs of wealth were evident in the silks some women wore and the gold jewellery adorning many a Lamorian. Silks and gold that, of course, had come from Ivane, yet brought with them none of the vibrancy and life Gwyn associated with her adopted homeland.

She wasn't sure if it was just the drab and dreary weather, but the air felt heavy with defeat. Yes, Lamore had lost the war, but wasn't it now time to celebrate? Peace was about to be properly secured and they were soon to have a new Queen, Delrik's mother having passed away from Lamorian fever when he was just a child. Gwyn was suddenly curious to know why the King hadn't met them at port, or why he hadn't sent a carriage bearing his own insignia. Didn't he want his people to know Sofia had arrived? With all the fuss he'd been making about his love for her, it had never occurred to Gwyn that Lamorians may not welcome the match.

Gwyn cast a concerned glance at Sofia, but her friend appeared oblivious, her attention out the window toward Lamore Castle, barely visible through the rain.

Soon they had passed through a set of city gates and were making their way up the headland. The grey stone castle loomed bigger on the horizon, like a dark shadow drawing closer beneath the surface of the sea.

The carriage passed through the castle's main gate, set into a thick stone wall. The wall extended either side across a peninsula all the way to the sea. They passed over a draw-bridge and moat before reaching the main keep and then a courtyard. On one side were what looked like stables; on the other, a set of marble stairs opened up to a grand breezeway that ran the length of the main building. Even from this distance, Gwyn could see hints of gold fretwork topping the marble columns and archways. It may not have been colourful like Nadis, but it was beautiful.

As footmen appeared to help them from the carriage, the rain magically stopped and the sun appeared through a break in the clouds. Sofia screeched – not because the rain had stopped, but because the footman helping her had flung his hat to the ground to reveal he was actually King Delrik.

Before anyone could protest, Delrik scooped Sofia up in his arms and spun her around in circles. An involuntary smile crept over Gwyn's face as the pair broke into uncontrollable laughter. Who was she to argue with love?

Suddenly she ached for something, something she hadn't been willing to admit to herself. She wanted to see Horace. Ever since their last encounter in Nadis she had wondered whether she'd felt something for him, and vice versa.

But it was probably nothing. Just her imagination. Horace was likely still the gruff Chancellor she'd originally thought he was. She hadn't heard from him since he'd left Ivane. She would have to put any notion of them meaning anything to each other from her mind.

She looked over instead at Elos, who was running up the stairs toward a blond-haired boy. He lifted the boy high into the air, eliciting a squeal of delight from his son.

'May I escort you?'

Gwyn's breath hitched in her throat at the authoritative voice behind her. Slowly she turned to face him, taking her time to compose herself.

Horace stared back at her. His sharp eyes and expression were still, giving away nothing, but his steady presence and proffered arm said everything.

# 18

If Gwyn had been asked to describe her experience living at Lamore Castle in one word, she would have said 'tedious' or 'freezing'. She would favour the latter if it was a particularly cold day (and there were many of them in Lamore), when the unforgiving winter wind howled through the gaps in the window shutters, shaking the timber slats along with Gwyn's resolve.

Gwyn wanted to support Sofia and her decision to marry Delrik. She tried to be happy in their new surroundings and in the opulent apartments that the Lamorian King had gone to great pains to make comfortable. But no amount of fine tapestries, fur rugs or the perpetually lit fires in each room did anything to thaw the chill in Gwyn's bones and heart.

Each day Sofia would take her place in a gilded throne-like chair in her presence chamber, smiling sweetly and exchanging niceties with the simpering wives and daughters of Lamorian nobles. She was ignorant of, or pretended not to notice, the condescending looks directed at her and Gwyn's accents and occasional mispronunciation of Lamorian words.

The women's smirks and snickers were only partially masked by their lace handkerchiefs.

One young Lamorian woman named Countess Datanya, the granddaughter of a late Duke who was as pretty as she was rich, was either too dim or confident enough in her own position to not bother hiding her distaste of the Ivanian inter-lopers. Datanya had openly mocked their tunics and unstructured dresses, which she'd described as 'charming little sacks'. The next day Sofia had presented Gwyn and Issy with several Lamorian-style gowns complete with mountains of petticoats, suffocating corsets and unwieldy hoop skirts. The only saving grace was that they were made for the Lamorian climate, with wool, velvet and fur trims favoured over silk. And while Gwyn savoured the warmth of her new gowns, she resented the fact she was surrendering another part of her old life and identity.

Initially, for Sofia's sake, Gwyn tried to make friends with the Lamorian women, but her efforts were rebuffed. Their rejection became clear in snippets of overheard conversations about the King's 'ridiculous folly' and how he was marrying 'a foreigner and enemy'. Some women claimed Delrik had brought shame on Lamore by not fighting to regain Ivane and Ette. Others bewailed being indebted to Ivane for critical materials and resources. It was clear that the planned union was not popular among the Lamorian people, but Gwyn couldn't bring herself to tell Sofia, knowing it would crush her.

At least once a day, King Delrik would come to the Queen's apartments, bestowing his intended with all manner of gifts. He'd recite poetry he'd written in her name and report on the progress of the negotiations, kissing her hand and claiming they would be married 'any day now'.

When the King visited, Gwyn would find an excuse to

leave them alone. She'd wander the castle and, more often than not, find herself in the library, seeking out the chess table, hoping to find Horace, whom she'd barely seen since the day they'd arrived. She wanted to speak to him about the planned marriage and the Lamorians' concerns she'd heard, hoping he'd be able to help – but she had other motivations for seeing Horace too. Something told her that in Horace she could find someone who understood her and her sense of unbelonging. And in that understanding, perhaps they could find belonging with each other.

Unfortunately, she had been bitterly disappointed each time she visited the library, and today was no different. Gwyn stared at the untouched chess set and the vacant chairs on either side, reflecting the emptiness in her chest that ballooned with each day.

*Enough!* She had experienced all kinds of loss and desolation before, but she had never just sat by and done nothing. She had picked herself up. She had picked up her weapons. She had gone to war.

She packed the chess set into its box and marched out of the library, through the castle's maze of stone corridors, stopping only when she came to the Chancellor's rooms.

Tightening her grip around the chess set, she announced herself to the guards flanking the door to Horace's study. Without deigning to meet her gaze, they barked at her to go away, saying the Chancellor was busy.

A thorny knot of anger burred inside her and she readied herself to challenge the guards, but just as she opened her mouth, the door flung open to reveal Horace, a harried expression on his face.

'Gwyn? I was just leav—' Horace's eyes fell on the chess set in her hands and his lips lifted on one side in a hint of a smile.

He stepped back from the door and indicated for her to follow him into his study.

'Thank you, *Chancellor*,' she said, giving the guards a pointed look before sashaying through the doorway.

'Please.' Horace indicated a seat on one side of a table strewn with parchment and scrolls. He sat next to her.

'I could come back later,' she offered, realising she'd probably interrupted something important.

Horace shook his head. 'It can wait.' He steepled his fingers and studied her with no indication of whether he liked or disliked what he saw.

All of a sudden, Gwyn's mouth felt dry and she was incapable of words.

His brow furrowed into deep ridges. 'Is there something I can help you with?'

*Do something. Say something.* Gwyn thumped the chess set onto the table. 'It occurred to me that we never got to play that game of chess.'

Horace lowered his hands and busied himself tidying up the paperwork on the table. 'I believe I told you I have no need of a partner.'

'It wasn't clear what kind of partner you were referring to,' she said boldly.

Colour bloomed on Horace's cheeks. 'I should have clarified,' he said carefully, 'that I don't tend to play nicely with others.'

'I believe that,' she scoffed.

His face fell, as if she'd genuinely hurt him. 'Have I not been nice to you?'

'I suppose you need to see someone to be nice to them.'

A stillness washed over Horace's face, and the room was silent except for the faint crackle of flames in the fireplace.

When Horace did speak, his voice was precise and clear. 'I see you.'

Gwyn's heartbeat hammered in her eardrums.

'I see what no one else sees,' he continued. 'Past your fine features and the way your hair shines like newly polished mahogany. The way your eyes dance when you bite into a favourite sweet.'

Her heart fluttered to a stop. No one had ever described her in such a way. What could Horace possibly say next?

'I see past all of that to your sharpness and curiosity of mind. I see the wariness, a sense that something bad could happen at any moment. I see how fiercely loyal you are to those you love, but you don't love or trust easily, which is why you're an outsider.'

Gwyn's heartbeat returned with a vengeance. 'You make me sound horrible!'

'Not at all. You're a realist. Like me.'

He did understand her. But she wasn't sure she fully understood him.

'You're hardly an outsider. You're the King's right-hand man, the *Chancellor*.'

'Exactly! The King made me – a nobody, his childhood friend, a commoner – his Chancellor. In the eyes of the court, I'll never be good enough. But it doesn't matter, because I make my own power.'

Then Gwyn realised what fascinated her so much about Horace. His ambition and determination to take or make his rightful place. She'd always mourned losing her own position as an Ettean leader, but Horace had shown her what was possible. She didn't need to let go of the part of her identity linked to power. He made her feel that it was acceptable, normal, in fact, to expect something more.

Horace continued. 'The problem is, the higher I rise, the

more they want to keep me in my place.' His fingertips dug into the table's surface. 'But the harder they push me, the harder I work to prove *not* that I'm as good as them…' His black eyes glistened. 'But that I'm *better* than them.'

The incongruous pieces of who Horace was fell into place.

'You don't play chess,' she began, 'because no one is a match for you.'

Horace clasped his hands together. 'I do play chess. I play myself. I see every move and countermove play out in my mind, challenging myself alone. I have no need to prove myself to anyone else in a *game* when I can do that in real life. Do you think that makes me arrogant?'

*Arrogant? Yes. Even more fascinating? Definitely.*

'Arrogance is hardly relevant if you are, in fact, the best.' She ran her fingers seductively along the top of the chess box. 'Maybe you've finally met your match.'

Horace's smile went all the way to his eyes. 'We'll see.' Then, to Gwyn's disappointment, he stood up. 'Another day. I must see the King. I have just heard he has done the most preposterous thing, and I'm hoping I'm not too late to stop him.'

Gwyn too stood up. 'What has he done?'

Horace screwed up his mouth. 'Delrik has invited the Kengian King to send a delegate to represent King Arlo in person in the final marriage negotiations.'

'But…' She didn't need to spell out either her or Horace's feelings about the Kengians and their King.

'Delrik's cousin, the Duke of Lakeford, has been working against me, encouraging him to make peace with the Kengians as well. Behind my back, arrangements have been made for the Kengian King's eldest son to come here.'

'Speak to the King now,' she urged. 'He will listen to you.'

'I used to think that was the case, but Delrik will do anything to hasten his marriage to Sofia.' Horace's expression darkened now, his gaze going distant. 'Love is a powerful thing, and not even I am a match for it.'

# 19

'There are no winners in war. Even if you win, you have to be prepared to prove your strength and fight again and again to keep your enemies at bay.'

Amund spoke with a wisdom far beyond his years. It was why he was one of the only people Alik would truly listen to, and why Amund had been tasked with preparing the elder Prince for his diplomatic mission to Lamore.

'It takes greater courage to seek peace than to fight,' Amund continued, quoting from one of the many manuscripts dedicated to Kengian philosophy that Alik had studied over the last couple of weeks.

'I understand that, brother. War is always a last resort. But you do know the purpose of me going to Lamore is to support peace negotiations, and King Delrik has made it clear he has no appetite for war.'

Amund pushed his spectacles up the bridge of his nose. 'That appears to be the case, but there are those close to the King whose position isn't as clear, and who won't welcome your presence at court.'

Alik slouched a little in his chair. Word had reached Kengia that King Delrik's Chancellor had tried to stop Alik's visit to Lamore, citing Kengian magic as a threat. But Delrik, wishing to forge ahead with his wedding plans, had ignored his chief adviser. When King Leo had received the news, he'd begun to waver on whether the visit should go ahead. Again, Amund had come to Alik's defence, saying he was needed to secure lasting peace for all of Kypria. It was heartening to have his support, but also a considerable burden on Alik's shoulders.

Alik leant across the table and closed the book in front of Amund. 'Thank you, brother. I am ready.'

Amund rubbed his nose vigorously, a telltale sign he was nervous. Alik reached out to place a hand on his brother's forearm, stilling his movement.

'I am ready,' he repeated.

Amund took off his spectacles slowly. 'I'm not sure any of us can ever be truly ready for what lies ahead.'

'And that's the beauty of it. It's an adventure!'

Amund's brow transformed into valleys of deep ridges. He looked awfully like King Leo at that moment. 'No, brother. It is a diplomatic mission with potentially disastrous consequences if you fail.'

'Why can't it be both?' Alik laughed. 'A diplomatic adventure!'

Amund sighed. 'Please just be careful. And no magic. Lamorians don't understand it and could fear it. You don't need to give that Chancellor any ammunition to use against you.'

'Yes, yes to careful. No, no to magic,' Alik said in a sing-song voice.

Amund shook his head to himself.

Alik gave a wistful smile. 'I'm going to miss you and your worrying, brother.'

Amund made a *harrumph* sound. 'And I will miss you and your *adventures*.'

THE TIME CAME for Alik to farewell his family in Lochlen. Amund held out a book, a collection of ancient Kyprian tales.

Alik shook his head. 'I can't accept it. It's your favourite.'

'It is, which is why I got you your very own copy,' Amund said, and pressed the book into his hands. 'When you read it, think of us.'

'Thank you.' Alik accepted the book. 'But I'm not sure I will have much time for reading.'

Amund gave his signature serene smile. 'There's always time for improving your mind, brother.'

Kairi hugged Alik in a tight embrace. 'You better be back for my wedding.' She sniffed back tears.

He kissed the top of her head. 'It would take an apocalyptic disaster to stop me.'

Kairi pulled out of the embrace abruptly and batted him in the chest. 'Don't say that,' she admonished.

'Your brother will be fine,' Queen Mira assured her daughter. 'A great destiny lies in Lamore, and Alik will be central to it, I am sure of it. But I will still miss him.'

'Thank you, Mother.' Alik kissed her on the cheek.

King Leo, who'd been completely silent, lifted his chin and grunted. 'With honour and courage, son.'

It was as close as Alik's father would ever get to saying he would miss him.

Alik bowed his head. 'With honour and courage.'

⟋⋀⋎

HE RODE SOUTH-EAST with a handful of guards toward the Nymoi Alps and Lamorian border. Along the way they stayed at several villages, where other Kengians joined them. As a show of faith, King Leo had offered Kengian expertise to transform some of Lamore's most barren estates into fertile farming lands.

Kengian farmers were adept at harnessing balance and harmony in nature, and without overtly using magic they could bring life to the most challenging landscapes. An agreement had been made for a number of families to settle in Lamore to assist the local farmers. These families were travelling with Alik, along with a Shaman who would provide spiritual support to the Kengian settlers. By the time they reached the border, the Kengian contingent numbered fifty or more.

It was the first time Alik had ever been this close to the alps. The perilous rocky range towered above them, blanketed in snow. Clouds high above swallowed the peaks whole. The group had navigated winding uphill paths until they came to the point where they would make their crossing into Lamore. Any higher up and they wouldn't survive the icy conditions, near-vertical incline and lack of oxygen. They stood at the only gap in the range where the elevation wouldn't kill them. Here two mountain bases merged, but their summits stood apart from each other, forming an opening at the centre – a path protected by air magic.

Eddies continually sprung from the path, ricocheting off the mountain walls and crashing into each other. There was a steady percussion of exploding snow accompanied by shrieking wind that pierced its way right into Alik's bones.

Shivering at the prospect of the task ahead, he pulled his fur coat closer to him. He had never used his powers for anything but trivial tricks and demonstrations. There was nothing trivial about this. He would need to be able to control the wind and blizzards long enough for all of them to make it safely along the path that extended for several hundred yards. There was much more than his pride at stake if he failed.

All of the farmers looked at him expectantly. His horse, Meteor, whinnied encouragement.

A guard from Tio's household nodded at him. 'We're ready when you are, Your Highness.'

But Alik stood as frozen as the icy path ahead.

'This is everything you've been waiting for.' A female voice. A steady whisper. 'Everything you've trained for.'

Alik spun around to face the owner of the voice. The Shaman. Her eyes, a dark blue-black, the colour of the sky as it transitions from twilight to night, fixed on his. Probing yet reassuring. Questioning, yet with a knowingness to them. He could lose himself for a lifetime in their depths, yet never come close to uncovering her secrets.

He led the Shaman out of the group's earshot.

'You know what to do,' she said with a smile as gentle as the flutter of butterfly wings. 'It is your calling.'

'What, exactly? What is my calling?'

That intoxicatingly serene smile again. 'Your calling is your calling.' She nodded toward the path. 'All you need to do is take the first step.'

'What if I let everyone down? What if my destiny is to fail everyone?'

'Have no doubt. You will fail. But your failure will be your greatest success.'

Alik's gloved fingers curled into fists. Shamans were maddingly imprecise in their predictions, but at least his sister's vision had appeal to it. She had said he was meant for greater things and that he would change everything. This Shaman spoke in riddles – and predicted that he would *fail*.

Fury engulfed him. Heat coursed through his veins.

He would not fail.

His hands burned so hot they threatened to combust. He shook his gloves to the ground. The palms of his hands glowed silver.

He turned back to the group and marched to the start of the path. The silver light had extended all over his hands and up his wrists. His whole body buzzed with energy. He lifted his arms and pointed his palms at the swirling wind and snow. Arcs of light erupted from his hands, connecting with an eddy.

Alik gritted his jaw and summoned the reaches of his power. The light pulsed brighter, and the whirlwind slowed and shrank until it was only a foot high. He led the group along the path, containing the eddies one by one. It was painstakingly slow and Alik struggled to keep his hands aloft, but eventually they made it to the end.

As the last Kengian stepped to safety through to the Lamorian side of the alps, Alik's eyes sought out the Shaman. He wanted her to acknowledge his triumph. But when their gazes met, she merely gave him a knowing smile, as if it were her victory as much as his.

Alik let his attention be drawn to the panoramic view of Lamore. To their right, a magnificent waterfall roared down the mountainside into a sparkling clear lake, which lapped the edges of a forest. The immediate countryside was dotted with green hills and more lakes, but beyond that, Lamore was a patchwork of every shade of brown. The Kengian farmers would have their work cut out for them.

The group trudged down a rocky mountain path that required dismounting and all of their concentration to stay upright. No one noticed the Lamorian party waiting near the base of the mountain until they were upon them.

A dozen armed men in black-and-silver regalia blocked the only path. At their lead stood two exceedingly tall men: an older man with a square jaw and steely gaze, the other with an air of highly trained alertness, even when perfectly still. And each of them was still. Their hands rested by their sides, but Alik was under no illusion as to how quickly they could reach for their swords. Had Chancellor Horace convinced the King that Kengia meant Lamore harm? Had he sent these men to dispatch them?

Tio's guard indicated for Alik and the others to stay back. But Alik strode to the head of his group, mustering every last bit of strength.

'I am Alik. Prince of Kengia.' He bowed to the Lamorians. 'We are at your King's service.'

'I am the Duke of Lakeford,' the older Lamorian leader said formally, in a tone that indicated neither friend nor foe.

'I am Elos,' the younger Lamorian said, and a grin spread across his face. He closed the distance between himself and Alik in a few easy strides, holding out his hand. 'And we are at your service.'

Alik took Elos's hand, knowing instantly from the man's enthusiastic handshake, firm and true, that this was a Lamorian whose word could be counted on.


THE DUKE LED the group down the mountain and through what he explained was the King's Forest. They followed a gravel road east as the sun rapidly slipped out of sight behind the Nymoi Alps.

After riding for an hour or so, Alik shifted in his saddle, feeling suddenly vulnerable at the prospect of travelling in the dark through unfamiliar lands with nothing but the Lamorians as their guide. He prayed he hadn't done the wrong thing in convincing his father to let him come, because it wasn't just his own life at risk. His only solace was that he could draw on his magic as protection – the same magic he'd promised Amund and their father he wouldn't use in Lamore.

Elos, who rode beside him, jovially pointing out various landmarks, must have sensed his unease. He pointed ahead and said they would reach their destination before nightfall.

The plan was for the group to stay the night at the Duke of Lakeford's property, Talbot. The Kengian farmers would stay on with the Duke under his keeping. Lakeford would introduce the Kengians to his tenant farmers initially, before connecting them with neighbouring counties. He would provide food and lodgings at Talbot until they were established, with the long-term plan being to allocate land leases to the Kengians…if the Lamorian Duke could be trusted.

'Your Duke is exceedingly generous.' It was more of a question than a comment, and Alik made no effort to hide the suspicious edge to his voice.

Elos made a pensive humming sound. 'Despite his brusque manner, the Duke is a fair man, respected by those under his charge. He's faultlessly loyal to the crown and will do anything to ensure the King's wishes are met – and the King wishes for his marriage to take place. So you can trust the Duke.'

The crescendoing buzz of crickets reverberated in Alik's ears as the carpet of night draped the green hills around them. It was difficult to sort his newfound fears from reality.

'From what you say, I understand that while my services are needed in the marriage negotiations, we have nothing to fear. But beyond that…?'

Elos shook his head firmly. 'King Delrik genuinely seeks

peace with Kengia, just as he wants peace with Ivane and Ette. And he is smart enough to know we need your people's help.' He nudged his chin toward the dark landscape. 'We need to learn as a nation how to make the most of our resources and stand on our own two feet.'

Alik thumbed the pommel of his saddle. What Elos said made sense, and there was something intrinsically honest in the Lamorian's demeanour. Elos had also explained how he had taken a knight's oath, which meant he was bound to always act with honour. He'd recited the oath to Alik; it was in Old Kengian, dating back to the time of King Alfred, who'd married a Kengian Princess before being ousted by his brother Emberto. While Alfred's rule hadn't lasted, the knight's oath inspired by Kengia's warrior code had endured. Elos spoke of the code with such reverence that Alik felt almost ready to dismiss his concerns...*almost*.

'What of Chancellor Horace?' he asked. 'I understand he advised against us coming to Lamore.'

Elos nodded slowly. 'He did. But I fear he acted based on personal bias, rather than the good of the kingdom.'

'But the King usually listens to him?'

'The King always *listens* to him. This was just the first time Delrik didn't take his advice.' Elos said the second part in a faraway voice, as if it were the first time this fact had occurred to him.

The pair fell into silence. Neither needed to state that Horace posed a risk to the Kengians. The only way Alik figured he could mitigate that risk was to befriend the King himself.

ALIK'S OPPORTUNITY TO establish friendly terms with King Delrik presented itself much earlier than expected.

After spending the night at Talbot, Elos and Alik, with their respective guards, set out for Lamore Castle. Arriving travel-worn and weary after being on the road for a near week, Alik was looking forward to being shown to his quarters. Instead, he found himself being escorted by a groomsman to meet the King immediately.

Again Alik was surprised, finding himself not in the King's presence chamber but in a training yard set up below the main keep. Two men in visors, mail shirts and plate armour were engaged in swordplay. The taller of the two, who wore a peregrine falcon insignia on his chest, was presumably the King, as the other man's armour was plain. They took positions to start another bout. The King tapped his chest three times, then rushed at his opponent, sword raised.

Alik watched the pair with interest, knowing you could tell a lot about a person from the way they fought.

Each man was clearly adept with a broadsword, and the two were well matched. The King's opponent struck with precision and economy. Every movement had a purpose, no energy wasted. He always waited for the King to come to him. Side-stepping, ducking and falling back when needed, but with little fanfare.

In comparison, King Delrik never stopped moving. He continually changed his stance and kept his blade in motion. He thrust his sword and parried with theatrical flair and effectiveness. His technique was simultaneously flawless and poetic. It was clear that the King was a natural sportsperson and loved the thrill of the game itself. But it didn't escape Alik's notice that he also acted with urgency, rarely stopping to consider his next move. He was someone who wanted to be admired – but he also wanted to win.

The bout ended when the King raised his sword high and

brought it down hard toward his opponent's exposed fore-arm, just above his leather wrist guard but below where the mail sleeve ended. Alik held his breath, sure the King was about to sever the man's arm, but the blade merely kissed the skin. It was enough to leave a thin line of blood as a mark of contact, but not enough to injure the man.

Alik exhaled with a laugh and started clapping. The King removed his visor and turned to him with a wild grin. Delrik performed a mock bow before striding over to his guest.

Alik bowed at his approach. 'Your Majesty, it is I who should be bowing to you,' he said carefully in Lamorian. Ever since he'd first called on his father years ago to intercede in the Kyprian wars, Alik had started learning Lamorian, sure that one day he would need to speak it.

Delrik gave a dismissive wave, sword still in hand, forcing Alik to leap backward. After recovering himself, he met the King's inquisitive gaze. Twinkling brown eyes set in a hand-some face flitted up and down.

Delrik stroked an imaginary beard. 'Extraordinary,' he declared.

'Sorry?'

'Silver eyes,' he said pleasantly. 'Of course, we've heard of the famed Kengian silver-eyes...' He narrowed his gaze. 'And their magic. How great are your powers, exactly?'

Alik wished he could shrink back into himself and appear small and unthreatening somehow. But there was no escaping that he was as tall as Delrik and shared his athletic build. And there was no hiding who he was – or his capa-bilities.

'As you have probably guessed, I'm Prince Alik, the first-born son of Kengia's King – so yes, I have some abilities to harness nature's power. In my case I can control the air and wind, but I have never used that magic for anything other than simple tricks until I needed to open the passageway through the Nymoi Alps.'

The twinkle in Delrik's eyes hardened. 'Show me what you can do.' It sounded like an order, but also a challenge.

Alik considered his family's warnings, but also the potential value in impressing the King. Showing his magic could go a long way toward befriending Delrik, but it could also give the Lamorian court reason to fear him and his fellow Kengians.

'I'm afraid, Your Majesty,' he began carefully, 'that Kengian magic is a sacred thing, a gift and an honour.' It was something Alik had been told many times by his family and tutors, not that he'd paid much attention to it. 'It is not a toy.'

Delrik's lip twitched in interest or frustration, perhaps both. Alik would need to try another tack.

'My father taught me that great responsibility comes with my powers, and that I must only use them when absolutely necessary.'

Delrik rolled his eyes. 'And what do fathers know? Mine spent his whole life fighting to keep two nations under his rule, only to lose them. When all the time it would have been easier and smarter to make peace.'

'And mine has spent his whole life on the sidelines, waiting for some prophesied Water Catcher to turn up and unite all of Kypria.'

Delrik tilted his head. 'You don't believe in the prophecy?'

Alik shrugged. 'I've got no idea if there will ever be a Water Catcher, but I do know that there's no point sitting around waiting to find out. We need to act now.' His voice began to rise. 'And if you and I do things right, Kypria will be united and we won't ever need a saviour.'

The King sheathed his sword and moved in closer to Alik, as if hanging off his words.

'You can make your trade agreements with Ivane and Ette,' Alik continued with enthusiasm. 'And we can help make all of your land fruitful. There won't be any need to conquer other nations, because Lamore will independently thrive.' Delrik's eyes shone, encouraging Alik to go on. 'And we can permanently open the borders between Kengia and your country. We can share each other's culture and technology for the betterment of all.' Brazenly, Alik rested his palms on the King's shoulders and looked him squarely in the eyes. 'Together, we can deliver a peace and prosperity that neither of our fathers could.'

Delrik mirrored Alik's pose, putting his hands on Alik's shoulders, locking the pair together.

'Exactly! This is our time. Our chance.' Delrik released his grip and stepped out of Alik's reach. His expression was suddenly serious. 'But there's something you must do first.'

'What is it?'

The twinkle returned to Delrik's eyes and he gave a face-splitting smile. 'Get me married, of course.'

He broke into raucous laughter and Alik joined in. The King slapped the Kengian good-naturedly on the back, and Alik took his biggest intake of the crisp Lamorian air yet. Relief flooded his body, along with the satisfaction that he'd been right.

Everything was going to turn out exactly as it should.


THE LAMORIAN KING couldn't wait to introduce Alik to his betrothed. After pages had removed Delrik's armour down to his gambeson, he led Alik into the castle, down stone corridors, past tapestries depicting great victories and paintings of former monarchs. Delrik took the stairs two at a time, eager to introduce 'the most magnificent woman ever born'.

They passed an anteroom of large proportions, which the King identified as the entrance to his chambers. They stopped at chambers almost as impressive next to the King's. At their appearance, guards stepped aside from a pair of timber doors that Delrik flung open with a dramatic gesture.

Alik found himself in a presence chamber buzzing with laughter, music and chatter. Men and women sat at tables, playing cards. A particularly pretty woman was attempting to show a young man a series of dance steps while spouting orders at a group of musicians. At the end of the room, two women sat reading. Delrik's gaze was locked on the taller of the two. He emitted a contented sigh and beamed as she registered his presence. Her eyes met his and skipped to life.

Princess Sofia was altogether striking, from her high cheekbones to her welcoming smile that was equally graceful and full of joy. She broke her straight-backed poise to leap from her chair, but on noticing Alik she appeared to check herself. She curtsied at the same moment the others in the room realised they had visitors and scrambled to curtsey or bow themselves.

Delrik threw his arm around Alik's shoulder. 'Introducing the Kengian Prince, Alik,' he declared to a murmur of excitement. Delrik then indicated Sofia. 'Alik, my Queen…Sofia,' he grinned.

Alik bowed, taking a moment to gauge his first impressions. One thing was abundantly clear: the King and Ivanian Princess were genuinely in love, and it hadn't escaped Alik's notice that Delrik already referred to Sofia as Queen. Ensuring Ivane's interests were protected in the marriage and peace negotiations should be easy, for a man so in love would surely defer to his wife's happiness in all things.

A giggle and a high-pitched voice came from beside Alik. 'Would you like to dance?'

He turned to face the young woman who'd been dancing before. Her cat's eyes raked his face and body. She appeared as if she were about to lick her lips.

'I'm Countess Datanya.' She giggled again and offered a gloved hand. Alik had met women like Datanya before, those whose interest was fuelled by a man's status, yet he enjoyed the attention.

He would have taken Datanya's hand, but Delrik dismissed the Countess and all the other Lamorians. The King escorted Alik across the room to Sofia and her companion, Gwyn, who curiously did not appear to be Ivanian.

The future Queen clasped both of Alik's hands in her own. 'I'm so pleased you're here.' Her assured voice wrapped around Alik like a warm hug. 'We're indebted to Kengia.'

Gwyn, who'd acknowledged Alik with a polite smile and the slightest incline of her head, bit her lip at Sofia's last remark and looked away. Alik didn't have a chance to question her reaction before the King began a detailed overview of his and Sofia's plans.

'My Queen is the most brilliant of women,' Delrik raved. 'Sofia had the idea to build a school in Obira City that will be open to all children regardless of birth, wealth or gender. "Education is key to our nation's prosperity," she says.'

'What a fine idea,' Alik remarked, raising an inquisitive brow. Sofia's philosophy was similar to Kengia's approach to education. Perhaps he could share other Kengian ideas with her and the King.

Sofia batted her future husband's arm. 'Delrik is too generous in his praise. I merely have an idea or two, but it is he who will make them happen.'

Delrik gave the Princess a fond smile. 'And Sofia is too modest. She is helping plan sewers for the city based on those in Nadis. They will better dispose of waste and lower the spread of disease.'

'You must both take the credit you deserve. I can see that together you will steer Lamore into a new age of excellence.' Alik meant what he said, believing Delrik and Sofia's enthusiasm. 'And I hope Kengia can be part of that journey.'

'You are already part of it,' the King said, and Sofia nodded her confirmation. Bolstered by their support, Alik was already bubbling with ideas for how else Lamore could be enhanced.

He looked to Gwyn, expecting her support as well, but her attention was on another. A man in black robes who'd arrived in silence, but whose sharp eyes now probed Alik with a burning intensity that sent the Kengian Prince's blood cold.

He could only assume that this was Horace – and from the Chancellor's expression, he still wanted Alik nowhere near the castle, or the King.

# 20

---

*E*arly the next morning the King arrived at Alik's rooms, his twinkling eyes promising an adventure, his hunting attire indicating its nature.

Delrik informed a bleary-eyed Alik that they were to go fox hunting. Blinking rapidly, Alik was immediately alert. Kengians abhorred hunting for any reason other than obtaining food; when an animal was killed, it was done with a conscious respect and solemn acknowledgement of honouring the creature's life. Fox hunting didn't typically fit that description.

'Fox hunting? Where?' he asked.

'In the castle woodland,' the King said, suggesting with frantic hand gestures that Alik should hurry to get organised and join him. Alik recalled the rolling hills he'd seen in the north-east of the castle grounds when he'd first arrived. 'The cook tells me that a wily fox has been stealing chickens from the kitchen's coop. On one night alone, they lost half a dozen.'

'Oh,' Alik replied as he pulled on his coat. He supposed it

made sense that the fox had to be dealt with, though the enthusiasm in the King's manner unsettled him. But Alik reasoned that the hunt would at least give him some time to talk to Delrik about both of their ideas for Kypria.

He picked up his longbow, and with a slap on the back from the King and a fervent 'Tally-ho', they set off for their expedition.

ALIK FOUND himself riding on Meteor with a hunting party composed of nobles, whom Delrik pointed out by name but didn't introduce. The King appeared intent on having the Kengian Prince to himself. The royal huntsman and his team had been sent ahead with foxhounds to track down their target, confirming for Alik that this expedition was more about sport than preservation of food sources.

'Will the Chancellor join us?' Alik asked as they passed the tiltyard and headed toward the fields that led to the woodland.

Delrik gave a throaty laugh. 'Horace does not have time for *such frivolities.*' He said the last part in a mock stern voice that Alik gathered was meant to imitate Horace.

From the little Alik had seen of the unsmiling Chancellor, he was certain Horace would be no ally of his, so he was relieved by his absence. It gave him an even better chance to get Delrik's attention, and it occurred to him that *frivolities* may present an ongoing opportunity to obtain the King's ear.

Delrik glanced over at Meteor, taking in her shimmering caramel coat. He gave a mischievous grin. 'Want to show me what your Kengian horse can do?' Not waiting for a response, he dug his heels into his stallion's belly and set off at a fast gallop.

Meteor, recognising the challenge, pulled at her bit. Alik

patted her neck. 'Alright, girl. We know you could beat that nag in your sleep, but for the King's pride, I'll need you to hold back a little.'

Meteor snorted. Alik knew her mind as clearly as his own. She would acquiesce, but only because it was he who asked.

He leant over and murmured in her ear, 'Make it look convincing.'

It didn't take Meteor long to close the distance. The stallion was several hands taller than her and a fine steed, but had nothing of the Kengian mare's athleticism.

They raced neck-and-neck across the fields, passing the rest of the hunting party with ease. Delrik, at first, seemed pleasantly surprised by the challenge, but soon looked agitated. Alik let the King get ahead a couple of times, signalling Meteor with a tap on her neck to pull back. And when the woodland loomed closer, Alik didn't need to tell her what to do. The mare diminished her efforts enough to give the King a clear win. Delrik pulled up just short of the woodland, and Alik stopped soon after.

'Well done, Your Majesty,' he said, and Meteor capitulated with a whinny.

The King grinned and waggled his finger. 'Delrik, please. Lamorian steeds are fine, are they not?'

'They are indeed, Delrik.'

The King nodded his approval and directed his stallion at an easy walk into the forest of oak and pine, with Alik following suit.

As they dipped into the darkness of the woodland, Delrik turned in his saddle to address Alik. His voice was unnecessarily low, as their fellow hunters were still far behind them.

'I've always been fascinated by Kengian magic,' he said. It was hard to tell in the dim light, but the King seemed to wear an almost hungry expression.

Alik shifted in his saddle. 'Oh,' was all he could manage.

'My father versed me in the prophecy and was sure that any day some powerful Kengian would destroy Lamore with their water magic. He was terrified.'

'There's nothing to be scared—'

Delrik gave a dismissive wave. 'Oh, I'm not scared of the prophecy. As you said, it probably won't ever come to being.'

Alik allowed himself to exhale, realising he'd been holding his breath.

'But if it did…'

Alik's heart stilled in his chest. 'The prophecy won't come to pass. None from the firstborn line have ever had the gift of controlling water, and in any case, you have nothing to fear from Kengian magic.'

Delrik rubbed his chin in thought. 'Help or hinder. It strikes me that Kengian magic can do either, or both. I wonder just how much it can help Lamore.'

A chill ran through Alik, which he prayed was from the drop in temperature in the woodland and not the slightly sinister tinge to Delrik's voice. He needed to change the subject.

'We don't need magic to help Lamore,' he said with forced confidence. 'There's much else that can be done. I was only thinking last night of how farmers who work infertile lands could be offered land titles.'

Delrik cocked his head. 'Go on,' he said slowly.

'This would be land that no one else wants, but with the help of my people, can become fertile. With the right incentive, the farmers would put their all into working the land and harvesting it, which means more resources for all of Lamore, income for the poor who may previously have been a burden on the state, and more revenue for the state. It's a win-win-win.'

There was an uncomfortable pause before Delrik clapped his hands together. 'Brilliant! Sofia will love this. We must discuss more of your ideas.'

And like that the King's demeanour completely switched. He no longer wished to talk of magic, only his plans for Lamore, how Alik could help, and how it would please his 'wonderful Queen'.

Alik's hopes for succeeding in his mission were restored, but he couldn't kid himself. The Chancellor wasn't the only person who had to be handled carefully. Friendship with the King would also require a fine balance.

A hunting horn blasted ahead of them. The barking of hounds echoed around the forest.

'The hunt is on!' the King declared, and galloped toward the sound.

THE PACK of snarling hounds had the fox cornered against a large boulder. The fox bared its teeth and growled, but it was an act of final defiance. Its arched back and darting yellow eyes spoke of the creature's terror and its knowledge that it was about to die.

The rest of the hunting party had dismounted to watch the King take his trophy. Delrik stood at an easy distance from the fox, his bow and arrow poised. It was a straightforward shot, but the King appeared to be taking his time. Eyes fixed on the animal, he seemed relaxed. A self-assured smile played at the corner of his mouth. It was as if he were enjoying the position of power he held over the hapless creature. As if he were feeding off the fact he held the fox's fate in his hands.

Alik couldn't look any longer. He scrunched his eyes closed, shutting out the sight and sound of the dogs and the fox, and the earthy scent of the forest undergrowth – a reminder of death and decay.

It was the cheers of the hunting nobles that alerted Alik that the deed had been done.

Alik opened his eyes to see the Baron of Iveness pull the arrow from the dead animal's body and hand it to the King. 'Your trophy,' he said.

The King accepted the arrow with a satisfied grunt and shoved it back in his quiver, which was lying on the ground, the bloody end sticking out to signal his victory to all.

Delrik looked to Alik for congratulations, which the Kengian Prince couldn't give. Fortunately he didn't need to, as everyone soon became distracted by the sound of running footsteps. A young boy, perhaps twelve years of age, appeared before them, red-cheeked and puffed.

'A whole family...' he addressed the huntsman between gasps of breath. 'I counted six of 'em...A mother and five kits...Their den is half a mile away.' The boy pointed back the way he'd come.

Shouts of excitement erupted among the hunting party, but the King remained unmoving, his complexion suddenly pale. Delrik tapped his chest three times. 'Seeing a family of foxes is bad luck.' His voice was wound tight. 'Anyone who sees such a sight brings misfortune upon the castle.'

Everyone looked toward the boy, whose face blanched. 'I only saw 'em for a second,' he argued.

Delrik pointed a shaking finger at the boy. 'You. You must go back and kill them all. Slit each of their throats, and then you must leave the castle...forever.'

The huntsman scrambled toward the King. 'Please, Your Majesty, the boy is my son. He won't survive away from 'is mother and me.'

Delrik lifted his chin, refusing to make eye contact with the man. 'You have heard my orders.'

The King turned his back on all of them. Without stopping to pick up his longbow or quiver, he mounted his stallion and galloped away. The nobles immediately followed their King – but Alik had to do something.

He picked up the King's longbow and quiver and told the huntsman his plan, then asked the boy to take him to the fox den. There, he bundled the animals up into a saddle bag.

'I thought you were goin' to kill 'em,' the boy said between hiccupping sobs.

'They don't deserve death. And you don't deserve any punishment.' He gave the boy the name of one of the Kengian farming families and their location in Lakeford. 'Go there. They will take care of you.'

The boy nodded. Alik handed him the saddle bag. 'Release the foxes in the King's Forest. It's not far from Talbot.'

He wouldn't take the bag. 'A family of foxes is bad luck,' he sniffed. 'The King said so.'

Alik crouched down so he was at eye level with the boy. 'It is a silly superstition. I for one have seen many foxes in my time, and you see that I am fine. And *you* will be fine. You have my word.'

The boy screwed up his mouth. 'Why should I believe you?'

'Because for a Kengian, there is nothing more important than honour and courage. Dishonour would bring shame onto me and all of my people.'

The boy sniffed back the last of his tears and took the saddle bag. 'I'll miss my family.'

'Don't worry. I'm sure the King will relent.'

Alik believed what he said – or at least hoped he did,

since he'd just claimed that he wouldn't lie. And if what he said wasn't true, the task ahead was more dangerous than he had ever expected.

BY THE TIME Alik made it back to the castle, he was mentally exhausted and looking forward to a hot bath. He trudged up the marble stairs and headed toward the King's rooms. He planned on leaving Delrik's longbow and quiver with a guard, as he wasn't ready to face the mercurial King again.

He was outside the future Queen's apartments when Gwyn ran headlong into him.

'I'm sorr—' she started to say, but stopped short on recognising him.

'My apologies, Lady Gwyn.' He inclined his head, even though it was she who had run into him.

Gwyn looked him up and down as if assessing his worth or level of threat – maybe both. Her eyes landed on the bloody arrow sticking from the King's quiver. She pursed her lips as if she'd just eaten something sour. 'You've been hunting.'

'Do you hunt, Lady Gwyn?' he asked pleasantly, wishing to establish friendly terms with Sofia's closest friend.

Gwyn jutted out her chin and spoke in a tone as sharp as the finest Kengian blade. 'No, I do not partake in the killing of innocent animals for sport.'

But before Alik could respond with 'neither do I', she was already walking away.

# 21

---

'So, what do you think?' Gwyn asked Horace, who was hunched over the chessboard, his brow bunched in concentration.

'I think that *you* think you've won,' Horace muttered.

Gwyn was one move away from putting him in check. All he needed to do was admit defeat, something she knew wasn't in the Chancellor's nature. Fortunately for Horace, he was nearly always the victor in their games, but tonight he seemed distracted.

'But there is always an escape,' he said without lifting his gaze. 'Another move to make.'

'I was asking what you thought about the Kengian Prince's latest scheme,' she said.

In the few weeks since Alik had been at court, the Kengian had failed to impress Gwyn. As far as she could tell, he spent most of his days in leisurely pursuits with the King. If it wasn't swordplay, it was tennis. If it wasn't archery, it was flirting with the women at court. And when Delrik and Alik weren't at leisure, they were discussing philosophy and even bigger altruistic endeavours beyond their abilities and purses. All the while, Horace was left with the burden of the day-to-day running of the kingdom.

Gwyn hated seeing Horace being taken for granted and his position usurped by a Kengian Prince who appeared to have the political nous of a child. She also hated that it meant she could only see Horace when he wasn't consumed by his work.

She would sometimes sit in his study, reading while he finished his paperwork. More often than not she'd fall asleep with a book on her chest and be woken by Horace's gentle prodding and an invitation to play chess. Gwyn had come to yearn for those chess matches, thrilled she had someone she could speak to openly. Someone whose intelligence was unmatched and whose all-knowing gaze never failed to send a ripple of excitement through her. Horace was the complete antithesis of the Kengian Prince.

So far Alik had convinced the Lamorian King to lower taxes on the poor and offer land titles to farmers who worked previously infertile lands. The Prince's latest grand idea was to close all of Lamore's prisons and introduce Kengia's approach to punishment, which was based on mediation between criminals and victims to agree on amends.

Horace looked up, the furrow in his brow deepening. 'The King will never close the prisons. Where else would he put or threaten to put his detractors?'

'Detractors? I thought he was popular.'

'Perhaps with the poor, but many of the nobles and merchants aren't too happy about their reduced income from taxes, or the fact he's marrying an Ivanian. No amount of bolts of premium silk gifted to their wives by Sofia will appease them.'

'Oh.' Gwyn leant back in her chair. She had thought that

Sofia, and herself for that matter, were becoming accepted among the Lamorians. Certainly the snide remarks and condescending stares were less frequent.

Horace raised a brow at her. 'There are bigger things to worry about than popularity.'

Gwyn sat up straight. 'I know that,' she snapped.

A smile teased at the corners of Horace's mouth. 'Then I suppose you know that thanks to all this benevolence and the fact that the majority of Sofia's dowry hasn't been paid, the treasury is almost empty.'

Gwyn dismissed his concern with a wave of her hand. 'King Arlo is a true ally. He will pay the dowry as soon as the wedding date is set.'

Horace's brow reformed into a series of deep ridges. 'What if he doesn't?'

'You worry too much,' she said, wanting to reach for his hand but hesitating in fear of messing up the chess pieces in front of them.

'But it is my job to worry, especially while everyone else is focused on a wedding.' He gave her a pointed look. He knew she had allowed herself to get wrapped up in the excitement of the wedding plans, having finally seen how devoted Delrik was to Sofia and accepting how happy he made her. 'It's alright, though. I know that when everyone's attention is else-where, I can make my move.'

With that he picked up his king and moved it two spaces to the right, then moved the rook from that side to the left of the king. He was effectively moving two pieces in one turn and shielding his king in the process. Gwyn's first instinct was to protest, but then she realised he'd used a move called castling. It could only be used once in a game and under a certain set of conditions. It wasn't a move she or Horace had employed in their games before. It was like he'd been biding his time to use it.

Gwyn shook her head. 'Of course you had another move up your sleeve.'

Horace shrugged.

'Always protecting your king,' she said, not bothering to conceal her admiration.

Horace leant his elbows on the table and steepled his fingers, as he often did when wanted to speak about something serious. 'Was I protecting my king or moving my rook into a position of power?'

Gwyn tilted her head, sensing it was a rhetorical question.

'You see, whoever controls the castle' – he glanced down at the rook – 'controls the crown.'

Gwyn's heart faltered in her chest. Horace wasn't talking about chess anymore. It scared her a little…and thrilled her.

He pushed the chessboard aside and took her hands in his, sending tingles up her arms.

'People think you and I are pawns. Nothing more than royal companions. But we're rooks. We're the real power behind the crowns. Together we can run all of Lamore. It is our calling.'

Gwyn hadn't thought about her destiny for some time. Not since they had defeated Lamore at battle. It had been the catalyst for uniting the Kyprian nations. As predicted, Kypria was on the eve of being formally at peace. Hadn't her destiny been fulfilled? Or was there something else in store for her? Did she have another future, one with Horace by her side and the power of a crown – a crown she had been denied all these years? She may never have the title that went with it, but she would have everything else. The thought was intoxicating.

'Delrik and Sofia need us,' Horace pressed. 'They need us

to lead them. The pair of them are too soft-hearted to know what *really* needs to be done.'

'And what needs to be done?' she asked in a tiny voice, unsure if she wanted to know the answer.

'We must be rid of the Kengian Prince.' Horace's fingers tightened around Gwyn's. 'When the time is right, I shall move against him.'

When he said 'be rid of', Gwyn told herself he meant nothing more sinister than having Alik sent away from court. But she couldn't help fearing that Horace's crushing grip said otherwise.

## 22

*I*n the weeks that followed there was no more talk from Horace about being rid of Alik, and Gwyn assumed the Chancellor's fleeting whim had been forgotten. So the Kengian Prince was able to do exactly what he'd been asked to do. He negotiated the final points of the alliance between Lamore and Ivane. He was able to assure King Arlo of the fidelity of Delrik's promises. Agreements were duly signed by both parties, and a wedding date was set.

GWYN CRACKED open the door to the Great Hall and gasped.

'What is it? Is everything alright?' Sofia asked nervously as she patted her hair for the umpteenth time.

'You're…beautiful.' It was the only word Gwyn could find – it was vastly inadequate.

Nudging in beside Gwyn, Sofia peeked over her head and gasped too.

They had been in Lamore Castle's Great Hall many times

before, and while they had always marvelled at the room's grand proportions, they had never seen it transformed for such an important occasion. The walls had been hung with countless elaborate tapestries. The gold-tiled ceiling overhead sparkled in the candlelight from hundreds of triple-tiered candelabras standing to attention along rows of trestle tables dressed with gold cloth, flowers and greenery. Silver plates and cutlery lined the tables, awaiting the feast that was to come. Musicians played a traditional Ivanian folk song from a gallery above.

Guests from every noble house, city officials and merchants dressed in all their finery stood on either side of an aisle leading to a dais at the end of the room. King Delrik stood at the centre of the dais, wearing an ermine-trimmed red cape with a gold doublet and matching breeches. He shuffled from one foot to the other, only stopping to tap his chest three times.

'Does he think he's going into battle?' Gwyn knew Delrik had inherited the battlefield ritual from his superstitious father.

Sofia gleaned her meaning and swatted her arm. 'Leave him be. Getting to this point for him has been a battle.'

Gwyn's attention then went to Horace in his signature black robes, standing to the King's immediate left. Her heart swelled, but stopped just as quickly when she noticed that Alik was also on the dais, standing right behind Delrik.

'What is he doing up there?' she hissed.

'Prince Alik is conducting the marriage blessing,' Sofia said simply.

'Why him? Shouldn't it be Horace? Or the Duke? Or anyone else?' Gwyn spat, feeling all of Horace's humiliation.

Sofia sighed. 'Not today, Gwyn. You know Alik is a good

friend to the King and ensured this day could happen, which makes him a good friend of mine.'

Sofia was right. This was her day. 'I'm sorry,' Gwyn said. She took Sofia's hands in hers, stepped back and admired her friend.

The Ivanian Princess – soon to be Lamore's Queen – wore a maroon velvet gown with gold embroidery. The dress was in the Lamorian fashion, but its colours and geometric pattern traced in gold were a nod to her homeland. King Arlo, who was still too cautious to leave his post, had sent his daughter a gift of a garnet necklace and earrings. They matched Sofia's dress perfectly.

Gwyn nodded her head in approval. 'You look every part the Queen.'

'I agree,' came Lore's voice behind them. He had arrived to escort Sofia down the aisle. He offered her his arm. 'Shall we?'


A WEDDING FEAST and entertainment followed the ceremony, with troubadours singing and reciting poetry dedicated to their new Queen. Acrobats and conjurers performed mind-boggling feats for a crowd plied with never-ending jugs of wine and ale.

After the last dish was served, most took up dancing. Elos asked Gwyn to join him for a quadrille, but for all of his enthusiasm, it soon became apparent his coordination in sport and swordplay didn't translate to the dance floor. His boot found her shin and her slippered toes several times. She limped off the floor with the assistance of a sheepish Elos at the end of the song. He escorted her back to her empty table with a dozen apologies and enquiries after her wellbeing.

Once she was seated, he left in search of a heat pack for her injuries.

Gwyn rubbed her shin in earnest as she watched the dancers enjoy a pavane. Delrik and Sofia stayed close together, wearing identical lovesick smiles. Near them, Prince Alik danced with a giggling Countess Datanya.

Gwyn made a scoffing sound. 'They really are perfect for each other.'

'Do you think so?' Horace had appeared in a seat beside her.

'They're as ridiculous as each other. He lives with his head in the clouds and she's a giggly fool. I would have taken him, though, for someone motivated by more than looks.'

Horace frowned. 'I'm sure he's motivated by much more. She is the richest heiress in all of Lamore.'

'Does Alik strike you as ambitious?"

'Everyone is ambitious.' Horace stabbed a piece of apple on a wooden board with his knife, skewering it with excessive force. 'But not everyone is willing to admit it.'

A chill ran up Gwyn's spine, but she ignored it, wanting to move the conversation away from Alik.

'Why don't we dance?' Dancing was the last thing she felt like doing, but she'd do anything to forget the image of Horace's stabbing knife and his earlier words about how he wanted 'to be rid of' the Prince.

Horace scowled. 'I don't dance.'

'You also don't play chess with anyone…except me.'

His expression softened and a smile crept across his face. 'Chess, then?'

Gwyn returned his smile. Everything was back to the way it should be, she told herself. For now.

## 23

The starling landed on Alik's window in a flurry of shimmering violet, blue and green feathers. A tiny parchment scroll was tied to the bird's leg. Starling messages went back and forth between Alik and Kengia on a regular basis, with the Prince providing regular updates on his progress.

Amund had been sending his own updates about what he'd been learning at the Institute and how their sister was planning her own nuptials with Tio. He'd always end with a warning for Alik to keep his head down and stay safe. King Leo was more explicit, reminding his son not to use any form of Kengian magic.

This was advice Alik had heeded. He'd resisted calls at court to demonstrate his powers like it was some form of mummery. He was well aware of Horace's dislike of him and knew he couldn't give the Chancellor any ammunition to use against him. While Alik was in the King's good graces he was safe – but he'd also noted a mercurial side to Delrik's nature.

Just today he'd seen the King rip shreds off the Baron of

Iveness for not cheering loud enough when Delrik had won at jousting. This was despite the fact that Delrik had used an illegal move to unseat his opponent and strike him in the head. The opponent, who was the Baron's younger brother, had been rendered unconscious. This changeable nature, coupled with Delrik's superstitiousness, could see him turn against Alik if given good enough reason. Alik would have to be sure not to provide one.

Now that Delrik's wedding had taken place, King Leo had been urging Alik to return home. But as far as Alik was concerned, there was much still to be done in Lamore. The Kengian farmers were making headway in transforming some of the most barren land, but it would take time to see crops come to fruition. Alik couldn't abandon Lamore – or Delrik, someone he'd come to regard as a friend, albeit an unpredictable one.

He'd expected today's message would be more of the same from his father, but he was wrong. It was a hastily scrawled message from Amund.

*Dear brother,*
*You must come home. Our sister has had a vision.*
*All of Kypria is in imminent danger and not even you can stop what's coming.*

ALIK RESISTED ROLLING HIS EYES. He knew what Kairi's visions were like. Snatches of images, never enough to know what would happen for sure. Never enough to know if anything would happen at all.

Then again...Kairi had predicted him coming to

Lamore. She'd said Alik would find someone 'like of mind and spirit', and together they'd change everything. He and Delrik *could* change everything, given time.

Alik scanned Amund's note for any specifics about Kairi's vision, but all it said was that she'd seen 'a horizon of fire and blood', and that the only thing that could save them all now was the Water Catcher. The note ended with another desperate plea for Alik to return home.

He may have taken some notice, if the vision hadn't been so far-fetched. 'A horizon of fire and blood' was far too dramatic, even for Kairi's visions, and the notion of relying on the Water Catcher prophecy sounded like something their father had put in their heads. The whole thing was some sort of elaborate ruse concocted by their father to get Alik to come home.

He screwed up the message and threw it into the fire. It wasn't worthy of a reply, which would take time he didn't have. Right now, Delrik needed him.

THE LAMORIAN KING had summoned Alik to the archery oval. Soon after arriving in Lamore, the Prince had discovered that Delrik appeared to think clearest when he was engaged in some form of sport. With a sword or bow in his hand, his focus sharpened beyond anything Alik had seen when Delrik was sitting on his throne or in his council chambers. It was Alik who suggested they participate in various recreational activities. More often than not, Sofia and her ladies would be invited to come and watch, which of course gave the King the added benefit of proving his superiority in all things in front of an appreciative crowd.

Alik arrived to find Delrik in an archery match against

Elos. Sofia, Gwyn and Datanya stood off to the side at a distance. Horace hovered behind the King. A clerk and two groomsmen were beside him, setting up a table with parchment, a quill and ink. Presumably Delrik had told the Chancellor he'd be carrying out his day's business at the archery oval.

From what Alik could tell, Elos was winning the match, by quite a bit. Elos was indeed an excellent archer, but he was also smart enough not to embarrass the King. It was widely accepted that when you played the King in anything you must lose, without making it obvious that was what you'd done. Fortunately Delrik was excellent at most pursuits, so his opponents often lost naturally.

Not so today. Delrik's mouth twitched in irritation as he tried to line up his shot. He put down the arrow and tapped his chest three times. Elos had explained to Alik that it was something Delrik's father had done for good luck before heading into any battle. No one dared to point out that it hadn't helped the previous Lamorian King in the end.

Delrik picked up the arrow again, reset his bow, then released it. He muttered something about the 'blasted wind' – there wasn't so much as a wisp of a breeze – as the arrow wobbled its way through the air and landed in the target's outer ring. Then he looked over in Alik's direction and frowned before waving him over to where Horace stood.

'What's this about Kengian farmers destroying our wool trade?' Delrik demanded, his eyes glinting like a sharpened blade.

Alik racked his brain for what the King could be talking about, acutely aware of Delrik's accusatory glare. Finally he remembered.

'I understand that some of the farmers are working on

common land – previously only suitable for sheep. They have developed a remarkable technique to drain the land, leaving behind incredibly fertile peat soils.' Alik's voice rose with excitement. 'Now they can grow all sorts of crops – potatoes, cereals, greens. They hope to transform all of Lamore's marshlands, and then there will be plenty to meet the nation's needs plus more.'

Delrik rounded on Horace. 'Is this true? Were they common lands?'

Horace's face contorted. 'Yes, they were common lands, but the noble landowners have always used them for sheep to support our wool trade – and at the moment, wool is the only thing we *have* to trade.'

Alik shook his head earnestly. 'The nobles have plenty of private land for their sheep. Give it time and you won't be so reliant on the wool trade. Trust me.'

Delrik rubbed his chin in thought.

Horace made a scoffing sound. 'You can't trust—' he began, but Delrik grabbed him by the front of his robes.

'Don't presume to tell me what I can and can't do,' he spat. 'I am the King.'

'Forgive me, Your Majesty,' Horace said quickly.

The King released him, clenching and unclenching his fingers as he marched past Alik to return to his archery game. Horace met Alik's gaze and screwed up his mouth, as if he were still choking on the bitterness of his apology and blamed the Prince for having to say the words.

Alik retreated to the archery game. Delrik's cheeks flushed a deeper shade of red as each of his shots became more erratic than the last. Alik watched as Elos prepared to take his next shot. He noticed Elos make a slight and unnecessary adjustment, which he knew would send his arrow awry.

Delrik must have seen the same thing. 'If I catch you

deliberately throwing this match, Elos,' he hissed, 'your next position at court will be as Groom of the Stool…*if* I decide to let you keep your head.' His tone indicated that he wasn't joking.

'He's angry that the dowry hasn't been paid.' A whispered voice in Alik's ear.

Alik found Datanya standing next to him, smiling like the cat who got the cream. She was a beautiful woman by anyone's standards, but her love of gossip brought out an ugliness in her. Most of the time Alik could overlook her behaviour, putting it down to something she'd grow out of, and in truth he enjoyed her attentions. But today her presence and her words grated on him. When the King was in a mood like this it was like dancing with a wild tiger, one that didn't need further antagonising.

'The treasury is nearly empty,' Datanya continued gleefully. 'Apparently the Ivanian King will not pay the rest of the dowry until there's a child. But *I* think he'll never pay it.'

'Thank goodness no one cares what you think,' Alik said, more forcefully than he intended.

Datanya's bottom lip quivered.

'I'm sorry…I didn't mean…' Alik hadn't wanted to hurt her. But it was too late. Tears welled in Datanya's eyes, and before he could stop her, she was running.

Running straight across the archery oval in the path of an errant arrow from the King.

There wasn't a moment to consider the consequences. He did what he had to do. He did what he was born to do.

Silver-hot light burst from Alik's hands. A swirling whirlwind erupted from his palms. With a sweeping *whoosh* he directed the column of wind at the arrow, stopping it within two feet of striking Datanya.

The startled look on Datanya's face was matched by the

onlookers – all except Delrik, who raised his hand as if to tap his chest but stopped, and Horace, who smirked as if he were the victor of the day's match.

## 24

$\mathcal{I}$t had been two full days since Alik had seen the King, and with each hour the Prince's anxiety grew. It was impossible not to hear the whispers at court and see the fear in many a noble's eyes. In saving Datanya, he had shown a mere sliver of his abilities, but it had been enough to ignite angst among the Lamorians.

It was unclear how Delrik felt and whether he thought Alik posed a threat, because Alik hadn't managed to gain an audience with the King despite several attempts. The only way to gauge the precariousness of his situation was from the triumphant look Horace had given him at the archery field. This alone was enough for Alik to consider leaving – but that would mean turning his back on his duties.

He and Delrik were destined to unite Kypria and secure its future. Alik just needed a chance to see the King and convince him he wasn't a danger to Lamore.

His chance finally arrived when he was summoned to meet the King at suppertime.

'Your Majesty,' he ventured hesitantly after being escorted into Delrik's private chambers.

Delrik sat in the dark in front of his fireplace, his eyes fixed on the gyrating flames. The shadows cast from the fire-light gave a nefarious look to the King's features, sending a shiver up Alik's spine. *Beware*, the fire crackled. It was the first time since being in Lamore that nature's voices had spoken so directly to him.

The King turned slowly toward Alik and appraised him for a moment, then broke into a wide grin. Delrik leapt from his chair and strode across the room.

'How many times must I tell you to call me Delrik?' the King chided as he embraced him, pinning Alik's arms to his sides.

'Of course, Delrik,' Alik muttered in confusion.

Delrik released him and clapped his hands together. A door to their right swung open and a parade of servants appeared with trays of pies, roasted pheasant and steaming fish, followed by bowls of fruit, loaves of bread and cheese wheels. A pair of gold plates were laid on the table with bejewelled goblets and eating utensils. A servant filled the goblets with wine.

Meals at Lamore Castle were always generous, even those served and taken alone in one's rooms, but Alik hadn't seen the likes of such a supper since the King's wedding. He couldn't imagine the occasion for such a meal. His senses sprang to immediate alert.

The King indicated for Alik to take a seat. 'Please.'

Alik did as he was bid, but only after checking his exits.

Delrik offered the tray of pheasant to Alik before taking anything himself. The Prince's mouth watered at the rich scent of the roasted meat and its crisp skin, but he was too nervous to eat. Regardless, he didn't want to offend the King, so he helped himself to a few slices.

The Lamorian King had no such qualms, picking up a pheasant leg with his hands. He bit into the flesh with relish. 'I'm so glad to see you again, friend,' he said between bites.

'And I you.'

'That was quite a show you put on for us the other day,' Delrik remarked as he polished off the first leg and reached for another.

Alik took a deep breath, having rehearsed in his mind what he would say. 'I apologise and deeply regret any fear I may have caused with my actions. I only did what was necessary to save the Countess's life. I can assure you it will never happen again.'

Delrik put the pheasant leg carefully back on his plate and wiped his face and hands with slow, deliberate movements.

'Never again?' he said evenly.

'Never. I will never give you or your people any reason to be afraid of me.'

Delrik gave a hearty laugh. 'I'm not afraid of you. If anything, I found the whole display *fascinating*.' The King's eyes gleamed. 'In fact, I was hoping we may see such a display again.'

Alik felt as if the missing pieces of a giant puzzle had just dropped into his mind, but he couldn't figure out how to place them.

'I'm not sure using my powers again would be a good idea,' he suggested quietly. 'I've heard people talking at court, and…well…the Chancellor—'

Delrik sat back in his chair and gave a dismissive wave. 'Don't worry about Horace. He's just upset he's no longer my favourite.'

'Oh.' Alik didn't know how else to respond.

Delrik slammed his palms on the table, which Alik rushed to steady so as not to lose the contents of their goblets. 'Ha! You think you've replaced Horace as my favourite.' He chuckled. 'I mean, you are a dear friend, but no one comes before Sofia.'

'Yes…of course,' Alik said awkwardly, reaching for his wine.

Delrik shook his head, chuckling some more, then picked up one of the pies. He bit a big chunk out of it and began talking again, spraying flakes of pastry in Alik's direction. 'Of course, I do value your friendship, and in recognition of that, I'd like to offer you Datanya's hand in marriage.'

Alik spluttered his wine all over the table. 'Datanya? Marriage?'

Delrik cocked his head. 'Don't you find her handsome enough?'

'She is very handsome.'

The King's brows knitted in puzzlement. 'You cannot claim she's not rich enough. She is the richest woman in all of Lamore.'

'I have no need of riches.'

'Hmm. What of her position? After the Duke of Lakeford, she is closest to the crown. Her children would be in line after mine and Lakeford's.'

'I have a position,' Alik said simply. 'In Kengia.'

Delrik swallowed the last of the pie. 'What if I wanted you to stay here? To…' He waggled his fingers in the air, looking for his next words. 'Advise me…and so forth.'

'I will stay here as long as I'm needed.'

'Then marry Datanya.'

'Please don't misunderstand me. The Countess is a fine woman, but I have come to believe in marriages of love.'

'Pfft. Datanya won't stop speaking of how much she is in love with you.'

Alik winced. 'I'm also talking of a love match for myself. I see how you are with the Queen, and I want that for myself.'

'Yes. I am a very fortunate man. Often love and a kingdom's interests don't coincide...' The King's words trailed away as if a thought had just occurred to him. 'Perhaps they never coincide.'

'You can't mean that you're not in love?'

'Of course I'm in love with Sofia.' Delrik moved his plate to the side and brushed crumbs from the table in front of him. 'But I do wonder sometimes whether the alliance with Ivane and Ette is the best strategy for Lamore.'

Alik gulped down a mouthful of wine and tried to collect his thoughts. It was the first time the King had ever voiced doubt over the alliance. 'What makes you say that?'

Delrik sighed. 'I don't know. There's the matter of the dowry and Horace telling me the treasury is empty. But Sofia and I have such big plans for Lamore – plans that need money. Just today she came up with the idea of building a hospital in Obira, but how will we pay for it?'

'Soon, Delrik, your treasury will be replenished. With all of the work of the Kengian farmers, your people and nation will be prosperous again. Soon, I promise.'

'You're probably right,' the King said unconvincingly, and Alik could taste his wine rising with bile in this throat. 'It was just a thought.'

'Delrik, I *am* right. You have to trust me.'

The King sat back in his chair again and crossed his arms. 'Of course I trust you. You trust me, don't you?'

'Of course,' Alik hurried to respond, knowing it was the only acceptable answer, whether it was true or not.

'Good. So when the time comes that I need something from you, you *will* be there for me?'

'I'll be there for you whenever you need me.' Alik did at least mean that. He would be there for his friend.

Delrik gave a satisfied grunt. 'And if you change your mind about Datanya, you have my blessing. I'd be proud to have you as family.'

Alik nodded his thanks, certain he would never change his mind.

## 25

*A* few days after Alik used his magic to save Datanya, Delrik visited Sofia in her apartments, as he would any other day. But unlike any other day, Gwyn noticed, he was aloof and miserly in his attentions. He didn't join in on the relaying of gossip from court about how the Lamorians were equally delighted and terrified of the Kengian Prince's powers. Instead the King tapped his foot incessantly before asking Sofia directly when her father would pay her dowry.

Sofia, of course, had no answer to give, other than the one everyone embarrassingly knew. King Arlo maintained that the rest of the dowry would be paid when there was an heir. Privately, Sofia and Gwyn had started to share their concerns that Arlo was postponing the payment because he had no money to pay with. He was rebuilding his country and needed to reward those who had supported him. The Lamorians had stripped Ivane bare, and it would take time for the nation's industry and finances to recover.

Delrik's narrowed eyes then shifted to the Queen's flat stomach, staring intensely as if his kingly gaze alone could manifest a child. It was bad enough that the entire court now looked upon Sofia as a broodmare, but Gwyn knew her husband compounding this expectation was like a dagger to the Queen's devoted heart.

Sofia lifted her head, pretending to be unaffected by Delrik's cruelty, but the slight wobble of her chin betrayed her devastation. Gwyn gripped the book in her hands so tightly she bent the cover. She had never imagined Delrik could be so unkind to anyone, let alone Sofia, or that there was such a fine line between the King's favour and disfavour. But just as Gwyn abandoned any hope in their love being enough to transcend the kingdom's troubles, Delrik looked up at his wife and his demeanour softened. He reached out and took Sofia's hand, pressing it to his lips.

'I shall not allow anything to ever come between us, my love,' he murmured. 'Not your father, not money, nothing. *Whatever it takes* to keep you and our dreams for this kingdom alive, I will do it.'

Sofia sniffed back tears and smiled.

Gwyn excused herself to give the pair privacy, but she couldn't shake the billowing sense of unease in her stomach. She hadn't liked the way Delrik had said *whatever it takes*. It sounded like a threat as much as a promise.

How far would the Lamorian King go to get what he wanted?

LATER, Gwyn went to visit Horace for their usual chess match. She found Horace pacing his room. The chessboard and pieces he would normally have set up in anticipation of their game were still in their box.

'Is everything alright?'

Horace's head swivelled in her direction. His black eyes

bored into her like a hawk assessing whether she was a threat…or perhaps prey, causing the hairs on the back of her neck to stand on end.

'Is everything alright?' she repeated.

'Nothing is alright,' he snapped.

Gwyn backed away at the vicious edge to his voice. 'I'm sorry for disturbing you,' she said, and turned to hurry from the room. She didn't want Horace to detect the tears threatening to come.

In that moment she came to a shocking realisation. Horace wasn't the person she thought he was – and she could never love him.

He had been a friend when she needed one, and she'd been attracted to his determination and ambition, which had appealed to her because she'd lost a future that had promised her so much more. But they weren't as alike as she had first thought. He hungered for power for power's sake, whereas Gwyn wanted power over her own future. It had never been about personal gain for her, but about knowing who she was and her place in the world. She may have still been finding her purpose, but she would never go after what she wanted with the ruthless single-mindedness Horace had shown – and she couldn't condone some of his behaviour.

'Wait.' Horace's concern-filled voice. His hand on her arm. 'Please.' A desperate, childlike plea.

Gwyn's tears suddenly evaporated. She was beyond the initial shock of his behaviour, now angry she'd let him upset her. She rounded on the Chancellor.

'Don't ever speak to me like that again,' she said through clenched teeth. 'I am not your subject, or pawn, for that matter.'

Horace nodded rapidly. 'You're right. I'm so sorry.' He put his fingers to his temples. 'I'm just so frustrated that no one will listen to me. I no longer have the King's ear. Instead he listens to that Kengian charlatan, even after what he did.' Horace's eyes widened. 'Did you see what that man is capable of? He is a threat to all of us.'

Gwyn's anger started to seep away. While she wasn't scared of the Kengian Prince, she still hated how he had usurped Horace, whom she believed did have the kingdom's best interests at heart.

'I don't think Alik means any harm.'

Her words were meant to placate him, but had the opposite effect. Horace threw his arms up in the air. 'Any harm! He's proved to us what he's capable of, what he would do if we − *I* − don't do his bidding. I had thought that when the King saw Alik's powers, his superstitious nature would kick in and he'd act against Alik, but he hasn't. Have you noticed that Delrik doesn't even tap his chest anymore? It's as if he has nothing to fear any longer.'

The Chancellor began pacing the room again, this time with more fervour.

'Instead of being scared of the Prince, Delrik seems determined to keep him closer than ever. He's meeting with Alik as we speak and has agreed to the Kengian's harebrained scheme to build a hospital, with money we don't have. Mark my words − there won't be any hospital. I will make sure it never happens.'

'The hospital was actually Sofia's idea, and I think it's marvellous,' Gwyn countered, but Horace didn't appear to hear her. He only picked up his frantic pace.

'I swear the Kengian has put a spell or something on the King.' Horace was talking to himself now. 'Yet Delrik seems to have something in mind for Alik. I can understand wanting to keep someone with those powers on his side, but the Kengian can't be trusted.'

He came to an abrupt stop and stood poised like a snake about to strike.

'I will use Alik's magic against him. I will end him.'

The conviction with which the Chancellor spoke, the same conviction that had once invigorated Gwyn, now filled her with dread. She had to temper Horace somehow.

'You don't need to act against the Prince,' she said with confidence. 'Soon the Kengian farmers will deliver and the treasury will be full, and all your worries will be over.'

'Over?' Horace scoffed. 'They're just beginning. I'm the only one who can see the truth. Kengia can't be trusted. King Arlo will never pay the dowry. The alliance with Ivane and Ette is a sham. I've alerted the King to the fact that we're surrounded by enemies who must be dealt with.'

Gwyn couldn't believe Horace was seriously thinking about breaking the alliance. 'What about me? I'm Ettean by blood and Ivanian by choice. Am I your enemy too?'

Horace pressed his lips together into a thin line. 'Choose me and you don't have to be.'

She stared at him, the words making her feel hollow inside. 'Don't ever ask me to make that choice.'

Gwyn spun on her heels and marched out of Horace's rooms. She had stomped halfway across the castle before calming down enough to interrogate what had happened.

The Chancellor was acting crazed, threatening to 'end' the Prince and 'deal with' Kengia, Ivane and Ette. He couldn't be serious, she reasoned. He was talking out of frustration. He would never act on it. Would he...?

By the time Gwyn made it back to the Queen's apartments she was determined to speak to Horace again in the morning. She would make him see sense. Or better still, he would realise he'd been wrong and apologise. Everything would be alright again.

But the look on Sofia's face when Gwyn walked into the Queen's presence chamber told a completely different story.

Lore was there, relaying at great speed that his wife was gravely ill. Issy, who was in the final stages of pregnancy, had taken to bed a few days earlier with what everyone had thought was overexertion and tiredness. Lore, who was skilled in Ivanian medicine, had been tending to her, but her condition had worsened. He mentioned the words *Lamorian fever*, which Gwyn knew was practically a death sentence.

'I've done everything I can,' he said. 'But nothing works. I'm so scared she and the baby are going to…' He put his fist to his mouth, muffling a sob.

Sofia rested her hand on Lore's shoulder. 'They will be alright.' Then she addressed Gwyn with a calmness not reflected in her eyes. 'Go to my husband and get help.'

# 26

*A*fter several goblets of wine too many, Alik was about to beg leave of Delrik when the doors to the King's rooms flung open, despite the protests of several guards, to admit Gwyn. Her cheeks were as red as her scarlet gown.

Delrik jumped from his chair, albeit a little unsteadily. 'Sofia! Is she alright?'

Gwyn nodded. 'She is well...but Issy, Lore's wife, and her baby...Issy has Lamorian fever and Lore can't save them.'

Delrik immediately called for his guards, ordering one of them to fetch his personal physicians. Alik poured Gwyn a cup of wine and offered it to her. Initially she seemed taken aback; perhaps it was the first time she'd noticed his presence, or maybe it was because she didn't much care for him – Alik had certainly gotten the impression that she had little time for him.

Gwyn accepted the wine and sat, at the King's urging, in Delrik's chair.

'Lady Issy and her babe will be well again in no time,'

Delrik declared. 'I have fetched the most accomplished physicians in the land.'

'Thank you, Your Majesty,' she said in a flat voice, staring into her cup of wine.

'What is it?' Alik asked.

Gwyn looked at him, then at the King, and took a large gulp of wine before she spoke. 'With the most respect and gratitude, Your Majesty, I hold out little hope for them. Lore is the finest scholar of Ivanian medicine, which, from what I have seen, is much…'

Delrik, catching her meaning, frowned. 'You mean to say that Ivanian medicine is superior to Lamore's, and from what *I've* seen, you're right.' The King turned to Alik. 'I witnessed it myself in Ivane. Lore brought one of my men back from the brink of death. He'd been plagued with a weakness and phlegm in his chest for years, and now he's my swordmaster. But no one has ever cured Lamorian fever once it's set in.' Delrik slumped down in a chair next to Gwyn and poured himself another cup of wine.

A thought occurred to Alik. A dangerous thought, given his current situation, but he couldn't stand by and witness so much pain if he could help stop it.

'I could send for a Kengian Shaman I know in Lakeford,' he suggested. 'There might be another treatment or medicine that Lore or the King's physicians aren't aware of.'

Gwyn sat up straight and blinked rapidly.

Alik started to regret saying anything. 'I don't mean to say that Kengian medicine is—'

She held up her hand. 'I'm familiar with Kengian medicine, and it is indeed powerful. It's certainly worth a chance. Could you please send for the Shaman?'

'If the King will allow it?' Alik said, noticing a suspicious glint in Delrik's eyes.

Before the King could answer, they were interrupted by Horace's harried arrival.

'Sire—' He paused to catch his breath. 'I heard your physicians…were sent for.'

Horace was known to have spies throughout the kingdom, but he must have even had them in the King's rooms for the news to have reached him so quickly.

The Chancellor paused again to take a lungful of air. 'Are you well?'

The King assured Horace he was well, explaining about Lore's wife and the possibility of sending for a Kengian Shaman.

Horace's mouth twisted into a sneer. 'You can't let a Shaman come here. Not with their powers.'

'Powers?' the King asked.

'Suggestive powers. They're capable of making anyone do anything.'

'That's not quite—'

'That's not how they—'

Gwyn and Alik spoke at the same time, both earning a filthy glare from Horace.

'Do Shamans possess these suggestive powers?' Delrik asked Alik.

'The way they work—'

'Yes or no, Alik.'

'Yes.' He shot Gwyn an apologetic look. 'Shamans typically possess these powers.'

Delrik rubbed his chin in thought. 'I shall allow the Shaman to come to the castle…'

'What?' Horace bellowed.

'On one condition. Alik must promise the Shaman and he will not use magic without my permission.'

'I promise,' Alik said without hesitation.

A hint of a smile pulled at the side of Delrik's mouth. 'And you must also promise you *will* use your powers when I ask. Whatever I ask of you.'

Gwyn's face blanched and Horace's eyes flickered with interest.

What would Delrik ask Alik to do with his powers? Could it be all that bad?

Then the missing pieces fell into place. Alik recalled their earlier conversation about potentially breaking the alliance with Ivane and Ette. Did the King want him to use his magic against the other nations?

Alik hung his head. Knowing he may be condemning an innocent woman and her child to death, he said, 'I can't make that promise.'

Gwyn was out of her chair, holding her hands out pleadingly to the King. 'You must let the Shaman come. You can't just let Issy and her baby die.'

The King's eyes never left Alik. '*I'm* not letting anyone die.'

'*Please*,' Gwyn begged Alik, and he wished more than anything that he could tell her why he wouldn't agree to the King's demand. That it was bigger than just Issy and her baby. But instead he looked away.

'Sofia will never forgive you,' Gwyn spat at Delrik.

A moment of silence. 'You're right,' Delrik said in a soft voice, as if speaking only to himself. 'Send for—'

'Don't be a fool!' Horace roared. 'You can't invite a Kengian mind-controller into your home.'

Delrik looked from Horace to Gwyn in confusion, before dropping his gaze.

Gwyn jutted out her chin and strode from the King's rooms.

ALIK EXCUSED HIMSELF. He was decided. He wouldn't let Issy and her baby die. He would send for the Shaman, no matter the consequences. He was sure that, given time, the King would back down, especially after speaking to his wife—but Lore's wife didn't have time. Alik had to act now.

He would ask Elos to send a message to the Shaman. Elos would know where to find her, and he was the only person Alik could trust to help him. And while Alik believed he could win back Delrik's favour, he was fully cognisant of the threat Horace posed.

The Chancellor would use the fear of Kengian magic against Alik. Given the right circumstances, the King would turn on him. But there was one way the Kengian Prince could shore up his position within the Lamorian court. There was one way he could help keep Kypria at peace.

All he needed to do was marry a Countess.

## 27

$\mathcal{G}$wyn went straight from the King's rooms to the Queen's apartments and relayed what had happened. A livid Sofia tried to speak to her husband, but the guards wouldn't admit her to Delrik's private chambers. She planted herself in a seat by the main doors and harangued the guards every few minutes, demanding an audience with her husband.

Realising she couldn't do anything to help Sofia, Gwyn went to Issy's room and found two of the King's physicians in attendance. The pair stood in a corner, shaking their heads, their brows scored with worry lines. Gwyn looked immediately to Lore, who refused to meet her eye. He busied himself preparing an elixir from Ivanian ingredients that Gwyn recognised were used to relieve extreme pain in dying patients.

The room reeked of sickness and the heavy knowledge that death was upon them. Gwyn's eyes sought out Issy, who was lying in her bed. Her swollen belly overwhelmed her otherwise slim form. Issy clutched her stomach with the hopeless ferocity of a mother protecting her child from unavoidable danger – a danger that was plain for any to see. Clumps of dark ringlets stuck to her forehead and she thrashed her head from side to side, her eyes scrunched tightly closed. An animalistic cry erupted from Issy's cracked lips and Gwyn raced to her side.

She took Issy's limp hand in hers, wincing at the heat emanating from the woman's skin. 'Issy, it's me, Gwyn. Everything will be alright.' She squeezed Issy's hand, blinking back tears. 'The King is sending for a Kengian Shaman who will save you and your baby.'

Lore dashed to Gwyn's side. 'A Shaman?' The healer's eyes sparked with hope. 'The King has sent for one?'

'The Queen will see to it,' Gwyn said with a certainty she didn't believe, but she couldn't bring herself to convey the extent of the King's heartlessness. More so, she couldn't bring herself to think about Horace's part in all of it. How had she been so wrong about him?

Gwyn's eyes cracked open a sliver. Someone was calling her name.

'Gwyn.' Sofia's voice. A prodding of shoulders as she roused Gwyn from her sleep.

Gwyn's initial reaction to seeing her friend was to smile, but as her eyes adjusted to the ribbons of dawn light spilling into the room, she remembered where she was and why she was there.

'Issy!' She leapt from the chair she must have fallen asleep in, dropping the damp flannel she had used to mop Issy's brow.

Sofia gripped Gwyn's arms. 'The King has just agreed.

He's sending for the Shaman.' Gwyn struggled to comprehend the Queen's bright smile, like she'd forgotten her husband had initially refused to see her and that he had only agreed to do the humane thing after she'd pressured him.

'Let's hope it's not too late,' Gwyn said bitterly, and turned her back on her friend.

She hovered over Issy's still form, searching for signs of life. She held her breath, counting inside her head. *One...* Nothing. *Two...*Still nothing. *Three*— Wait...Was it a movement? Yes – the slightest rise and fall of Issy's chest.

Gwyn exhaled heavily. 'She's alive.' She needed to assure herself as much as anyone else. 'In fact, she looks...better?'

'It's the effects of the medicine,' Lore said in a broken voice from across the bed. He leant over his wife and administered a heavy dose of elixir into her mouth. 'She is beyond help now. All I can do is keep her free from pain.' His words came out choked, as if he'd swallowed a whole storm cloud.

'But the Shaman,' Sofia suggested, to no response. 'I see,' she said after a long pause, and sank into the chair Gwyn had vacated.

Fury ignited to life in Gwyn's stomach, shooting through her veins, threatening to explode from her in a cataclysmic upheaval of words. How could Issy be taken from them? How could the King and Horace be so cruel? Why had they ever come to this place? But that would be giving into her own selfish pain. Right now, she had to honour Lore and his wife and their suffering.

She fetched a bowl of water and a fresh flannel and did all she could think to do: mop Issy's forehead, praying the pain would end soon.

A commotion sounded in the corridor outside and the door was flung open. Elos rushed into the room. A woman with long wavy hair and skin that had a shimmery, ethereal quality to it followed in his wake.

'The Shaman,' Elos announced, and Gwyn stepped away from the bed to make room for the Kengian, who had somehow made it to the castle mere minutes after the King had summoned her.

OVER THE NEXT twenty-four hours the Shaman put Lore to work preparing medicines using Kengian herbs, powders and vials of colourful liquids she had brought with her. Each time she administered any treatment, she did so with a series of complicated hand movements and strings of Kengian words – spells, perhaps.

Gwyn and Sofia were also put to work, tasked with making sure Issy's entire body was smothered in cool, wet cloths, which they changed regularly. They took turns catching snatches of sleep.

In the wee hours of the next morning, the Shaman broke the news that the only way Issy could be saved was if the baby was cut from her belly. Lore gave his permission, but sat with his head in his hands as Gwyn and Sofia assisted in the surgery.

No one said anything when the nearly full-term baby boy was lifted from Issy's womb without a whimper. His perfect tiny rosebud lips destined never to open.

The Shaman placed the child into Lore's arms and the Ivanian cried enough tears to drown a thousand souls.

A miracle did come, though. Mid-morning there was a woman's cry, followed by a scratchy voice. 'My baby.'

Issy had survived, only to bear witness to all she had lost.

GWYN STORMED THROUGH THE CASTLE, enraged that the King had delayed the care Issy needed. The only reason Delrik may be able to claim his conscience was clear was because someone must have sent for the Shaman earlier. It was the only way she could have arrived so quickly. It was this reason, and this reason alone, that Issy lived. Gwyn couldn't forgive Delrik. Yet she reserved her real fury for someone else. Someone whose cruelty knew no bounds.

She strode straight past Horace's guards into his private study.

The Chancellor stood up from his desk with a tentative smile on his face. 'Gwyn, what a pleasant surprise.' He walked over to where his chessboard was set up on a small table. 'A bit early for a game, but—'

Gwyn met him at the table and swept her arms across the chessboard, sending pieces flying across the room and clattering to the ground. Every piece was toppled or gone completely from the board, except for one rook that remained standing in defiance.

'What was that for?' Horace shouted.

Gwyn crossed her arms. 'You'll be pleased to know that the baby is dead.'

Horace squared his shoulders. 'Yes, I had heard that, but I am not pleased to know it. I'm sorry for your friend.' The Chancellor sounded genuinely sorry.

Gwyn unfolded her arms, but she wouldn't let him off the hook that easily. '*Are* you sorry? You did convince the King not to send for a Shaman.'

Horace's brows bunched in confusion. 'But the Shaman did come and still wasn't able to save the baby. I'm not sure how that is my fault.'

Gwyn's anger returned tenfold. 'What *is* your fault is that you were willing to sentence Issy and her child to death in the first place. Issy would have died if it weren't for the Shaman.'

'But Issy didn't die.' Horace walked back to his desk and took a seat. 'And to be perfectly honest, I have more important things to worry about right now.'

Gwyn followed him and planted her palms on his desk so she was facing him. 'What could be more important than someone's life?'

'You ask questions that insult your intelligence,' he said through clenched teeth. 'What is clearly more important than *one* person's life is the lives of many. And I am tasked with ensuring the best interests of the many – of all Lamorians.'

'The many are not your responsibility. You're not the King. You don't even have the King's ear.'

Horace jumped to his feet and mirrored Gwyn's pose. They glared at each other across the desk.

'What the last day or so has proven is that the King does still listen to me. I planted fear of Kengian magic in his mind and he refused to send for the Shaman. And it would have gone to plan if it weren't for the Queen's interference and Alik defying the King's orders.'

Gwyn stepped back from the desk. 'Alik?'

Horace's mouth curled in disgust, and he too stepped back. 'The Kengian Prince sent for the Shaman as soon as he left the King's rooms. I would have thought Delrik would be furious, but he has forgiven the Prince. He hopes to convince his wife that he had sent for the Shaman much earlier in the night and hadn't wanted to say anything in case she didn't come.'

'But Sofia won't believe...' Gwyn shook her head. Of course Sofia would believe him. 'In any case, Alik and Sofia still stand between you and the power you seem to love above everything and everyone.'

Horace flinched at the last part. 'I'm doing this for you too. For us.'

'Doing what, exactly?' Gwyn scoffed.

'I will undermine Alik. It may take time, but I will succeed, now I know that his magic is his weakness. I will feed on the King's fears and won't stop until the Kengian is destroyed.'

Horace's cold black eyes bored into Gwyn, sending a shiver through her body.

'And what of Sofia?' she asked, almost afraid of the answer.

'Simple. I will convince the King to invade Ivane and take back what is rightfully ours.'

Gwyn stepped away, shaking her head. 'The King will never agree to it.'

Horace clasped his hands together in front of him. 'But he will. The Ivanian King still hasn't paid the dowry and never will. Soon we will run out of money, and Delrik will have no choice. Yes, it may take time, but I will succeed.'

Gwyn stuck out her chin. 'Not if I have anything to do with it.'

Horace chuckled. 'I've always admired your spirit, Gwyn. But you're also pragmatic and will see that my way is the only way – *our* way.'

Gwyn's hands balled into fists. 'There is no *our* or *us*, and there never will be.'

The words seemed to strike Horace like a stake to his heart. Judging from his silence and the sudden change in his pallor, he was shocked by Gwyn's announcement that they would never be together.

Gwyn was so angry she wanted to drive the stake in further by adding that they weren't friends either, but instead she strode away, shaking with rage.

GWYN COULDN'T BELIEVE she had once thought there could be something between her and the Chancellor. She'd been right all along: Lamorians couldn't be trusted. They could never be anything other than her enemy, but she was stuck here now. And if she was stuck here, she would do something about it. She would protect Sofia and both their homelands. Somehow. She had to do something!

She was so consumed by her anger and newly formed determination to undermine Horace's plans that she didn't notice the Kengian Prince until she rounded a corner and crashed into him.

Alik grasped her shoulders, steadying her. His silver eyes, clouded with concern, raked her face. 'Are you alright?'

All Gwyn could manage was something between a strangled cry and a laugh.

Realisation washed over Alik's face. 'Of course you're not alright.' He lowered his hands and his head. 'I'm so sorry about Issy's baby. I wish I could have done something.'

Gwyn gave a fragment of a smile. 'But you did do something. You sent for the Shaman, against the King's wishes. Thanks to you, Issy lives.'

Alik held his hands out, almost in apology. 'It was the right thing to do. But you mustn't speak of it. The King would prefer others to think she arrived at his bidding. And I can't risk the King's wrath.'

Gwyn frowned. 'You can't risk *anyone's* disfavour.'

Alik nodded. 'You speak of the Chancellor, but I have a plan to stay in the King's good graces.'

'You do?'

'I'm to marry Countess Datanya. I have just spoken to the King now and it is agreed.'

'Oh,' Gwyn said, unable to conceal her disapproval.

Alik raised a brow. 'Oh?'

'My apologies. If you're in love, then I wish you all the best.' It was a lie. Up until now she had always thought Datanya and Alik were perfect for each other, but after what he had done for Issy, the personal risk he had taken, she was beginning to think she had misjudged him too.

Alik shrugged. 'She loves me, and it's the right thing to do for our kingdoms. It will unite Kengia and Lamore.'

'But it will put you dangerously close to the crown. You can't underestimate Horace. I don't think any of us know what he's truly capable of.' She fixed Alik with a serious gaze. 'I think you should leave. Go back to Kengia, where you will be safe.'

Alik chuckled.

'I mean it.'

'I know. I only laugh because I've always thought you despised me and pretty much all Kengians, and that is why you want me to leave.'

Gwyn's cheeks flushed hot. 'I don't despise you. I don't know you. And I don't despise Kengians.' She thought of the Kengian healer, Nima, who had saved her life all those years ago. 'But I do dislike how your country wouldn't come to Ette and Ivane's aid all these years.'

Alik shifted the weight between his feet. 'I agree. It is why I insisted on coming here to help Lamore and Ivane make peace. I want to make amends and help unite Kypria. This is where my destiny lies.'

'But your destiny might mean dying here!' She couldn't understand why he just wouldn't go home.

Alik's jaw tightened. 'I'm the Earth King's heir, and it's my responsibility to secure my country's future, regardless of the danger. Can you understand that?'

The cloudiness in the silver lakes of his eyes immediately cleared, and she couldn't help but be moved by his earnestness. In that moment he was far from the frivolous man with his head in the clouds she had thought him to be. He was someone who thought he was destined to help unite Kypria, like her. He was an Earth King's heir, like her. Of course she understood what he meant.

An icy draught gusted down the stone-floored corridor, and Gwyn held her cloak tighter to her. 'I just fear that we are heading toward something. Maybe the end of everything, if Horace has his way. And you will be the first casualty, if you give Horace or the King reason to fear you.'

'What reason would I give them?'

It was Gwyn's turn to be earnest. 'Using your magic.'

Alik looked down at his hands and flexed his fingers. 'You're right. It's too big of a risk.'

'Promise you won't use your powers again.'

'I won't,' he mumbled.

'Can I believe you?'

Alik looked up again. 'You can trust my word. Where I come from, honour and courage are everything.'

A bittersweet memory came to Gwyn of her father's tales of the Ettean Princesses – the Guardians of Honour, Justice and War. Maybe she and Alik weren't so different from each other. They were both bound by duty and fate to stay in Lamore and fight for Kypria's future.

'Gwyn!'

Horace's voice, uncharacteristically etched with something that sounded like fear or desperation, echoed down the hallway. She didn't look back to face him. Instead she met Alik's eyes with unwavering steeliness.

'Remember what I told you.'

She picked up her skirts and hurried around the corner,

away from the two men who had traded places in her estimation, and toward an uncertain future. A future that would require every ounce of her resolve and the heart of a warrior.

## 28

*A*lik had spent his whole life wanting to leave Kengia, and while he had no regrets about coming to Lamore, some days he pined for the familiarity of his homeland. Most of these days happened to be in summer, which had always been his favourite time of year. Alik had fond memories of swimming with his siblings in Lochlen Lake and spending lazy afternoons fishing under the shade of the sacred yew tree. Some nights Alik and Amund would set up hammocks under the stars, with the younger brother pointing out the constellations by name and the elder marvelling at his sibling's seemingly infinite knowledge. They would drift off to sleep with the sound of chirping crickets and croaking frogs singing in their ears, and Alik would dream of adventures and a paradise beyond the Nymoi Alps.

In his dreams, he never pictured the reality that was the hottest summer on record at Lamore Castle. The castle was built to withstand the country's bitter cold winters. The warmth from the heavy rugs and tapestries that adorned every room's floors and walls was enthusiastically welcomed during the colder months, but equally cursed on days like today.

The window shutters in Alik's rooms lay open, ready to capture the tiniest sea breeze, but this morning there was none. The oppressively still air shrouded the castle like layers of thick fur cloaks that couldn't be shaken off, leaving a lethargic mark on all its inhabitants.

Tired and already homesick, Alik wiped the sweat from his brow and read the latest starling message from Amund. Like all recent messages, this one urged Alik to come home, saying Kairi's vision of him being in imminent danger persisted.

*It can't be all that imminent,* Alik thought. His sister had first given the vague warning months ago, and nothing *terrible* had happened. Yes, Delrik had become increasingly erratic, one day declaring his unwavering support for Alik and the Kengian farmers, the next spouting doubts over Alik and Kengia's motivations. He'd mutter about 'magic being a threat to Lamore and all of Kypria', sounding eerily like Horace, who was as hostile as ever to Alik.

The Prince had heeded Gwyn's warning about the Chancellor and hadn't used his powers since the day he'd saved Datanya. He'd also sent missives to his countrypeople in Lamore, advising them to exercise caution when employing any Kengian practices that could be interpreted as 'magic'. Even so, Alik knew none of them were safe.

Only yesterday Delrik had requested that Alik 'perform a magic trick' in the King's presence chamber, in front of all the nobles and petitioners. In some kind of twisted logic and test of loyalty, Delrik demanded Alik do the trick to 'prove Kengian magic poses no risk'. When Alik politely refused, Delrik changed tack, claiming the demonstration was necessary to prove he would only use magic at the King's command, 'and no other's'. Again Alik had refused.

Delrik's face had contorted – and Horace had seen his opportunity. At that exact moment he had brought forward a trio of landowning lords from Lamore's Lowlands, who had each bowed before the King, hats in hand, and cried poor that they had lost their lands to the 'Kengian thieves'.

Again the Chancellor had raised his objections over the Kengian farmers being given access and titles to common land that had been the 'ancestral rights of the landowning nobles to use for their sheep and wool trade'. And again Alik had countered that the farmers had transformed the marshlands, previously unsuitable for farming, so they now supported all sorts of crops that would feed and sustain Lamore.

The King had thrown his hands into the air. 'I'm sick and tired of these petty arguments and promises that never come to fruition.'

'But they are coming to fruition, Your Majesty,' Alik had said gently. 'Why don't we go see for ourselves?'

After a drawn-out pause, Delrik grunted his agreement and dismissed everyone but Horace, who smirked at Alik like he'd fallen into the trap that had been set for him.

The latest encounter had confirmed that Alik was on shaky ground, but he couldn't allow himself to believe he was in any immediate danger. Because he wouldn't leave. He couldn't. He was intrinsically bound to Lamore. He knew in his heart, more than ever, that his future was tied to this place. *If only it wasn't so blasted hot!*

Alik abandoned his brother's message and escaped the oven that was his room.

The Kengian Prince found himself in the Queen's Gardens, a geometric series of defined gravel paths, lush plantings and water features commissioned by King Delrik for Sofia. Delrik had been determined to honour his new wife with gardens reminiscent of her homeland. He had sent for mature figs and rose bushes in every colour of the rainbow from Ivane. He'd engaged the finest artisans to create fountains and ponds like those he'd seen in Nadis. And while it was nothing like the gardens of Alik's homeland, it was a welcome haven, particularly in recent days.

Alik gave in to the heady scent of roses and followed the sound of running water to his usual spot. The sound alone was enough to have a cooling effect on his body. With each step beneath the canopy of fig trees, he felt revived.

He turned the last corner that would bring him to the centre of the garden and the Fountain of Courage: a two-tiered fountain ringed by twelve standing lions, all carved of white marble. In an impressive display, water spurted skyward from a central pillar, splashing down into the first-tier basin that fed into the second tier. In turn, the second basin diverted water to the lions, which spouted streams from their mouths.

The spectacle never failed to capture Alik's attention, but today something else drew his gaze. The Queen, Gwyn and Issy were approaching the fountain from another path. Issy nodded him a brisk acknowledgement, seeming intent on getting Sofia to take a drink of water from a flask. The latter gave Alik a weary smile before accepting the offer. Gwyn offered her own smile – something he'd become accustomed to ever since that day she had thanked him for helping Issy. But today something was different. The smile was genuine, but didn't reach all the way to her eyes.

'Is everything alright?' he addressed the three women.

'Perfectly fine, thank you, Alik,' Sofia assured him. 'But these Lamorian fashions...' She indicated her heavy skirts. 'They just aren't made for such heat. I think I must retire to my rooms.'

Alik offered his arm, but Sofia waved her hand.

'Please, stay and enjoy the gardens.'

Issy took the Queen's arm and led her away. Gwyn, though, stayed behind.

'Is everything alright?' Alik repeated.

Gwyn gave a heavy sigh. 'Yes and no.'

Alik cocked his head. 'Sorry?'

'The Queen is with child.'

'That's fantastic news!' Alik exclaimed. 'The King will be so pleased.' He didn't add that it may help stabilise the King's mood and make him look more favourably on the Kengian farmers.

Gwyn bit her lip in response.

'And Sofia? She is pleased?'

Gwyn nodded. 'She is very pleased. It is what she and the King have wanted. She's hopeful Delrik will now return to the man she first fell in love with. And perhaps he will.'

'But...?'

'But I fear what will happen when Sofia goes into confinement, and me with her.'

'Confinement?'

'It's some archaic Lamorian custom where noblewomen must be confined to their rooms for many weeks leading up to and after the birth of their child.' Gwyn's eyes flashed with anger. 'The only people allowed to see them are their lady companions and physicians.'

'But that's ridiculous!'

'Worse than ridiculous.' Her pupils dilated. 'It means

Horace will have free rein over Delrik and the kingdom while we're locked up.'

'Surely Delrik can be reasoned with about this custom?'

Gwyn shook her head again. 'Sofia only told the King yesterday, but Horace caught wind of it almost immediately and brought in Delrik's personal physicians to make sure the custom is adhered to. He had them claim the baby and Sofia's health would be at risk otherwise. The only thing she could negotiate was having Lore with her in confinement, rather than the King's men.' She looked away then, in the direction of the castle and Obira City. 'So the Queen will be looked after, but what will we emerge to? What will happen while we're gone? Everything we've worked so hard for… Everything we were destined for…'

Alik's head reeled. Gwyn was right. With Sofia in confinement, who would temper Delrik and counteract Horace's scheming? Of course, he knew the answer.

He reached for Gwyn's arm. 'Don't worry. I'll take care of everything. I'll make sure Horace is kept in check. And I'll be here waiting when you get out to make sure all our destinies are fulfilled.'

Her gaze went first to where his hand touched her arm, and then to his face. Her eyes, the colour of rich honey, brimmed with tears.

'I promise,' he emphasised.

'You shouldn't make promises you can't keep.'

'I don't. Because I always keep my promises.'

Gwyn gave a bitter laugh. 'Like the promise you made to Datanya?'

Alik held his hands up in protest. 'I've told her we won't be married, but she won't accept it.' He hadn't been able to go through with marrying the Countess, even if it would have helped shore up his position with the King. There was no honour in marrying someone you didn't or couldn't grow to love.

'Well, I'm sure you'll have plenty of opportunities to convince her on your trip to the Lowlands. I understand you'll be staying at Datanya's main estate when you go to visit the Kengian farms.'

Alik gave a small nod.

Gwyn's tears suddenly evaporated. She jutted out her chin and grinned. 'Maybe you'll get there and decide she is worth the effort after all.'

Alik grinned back at her. 'I very much doubt it.'

# 29

$\mathcal{W}$hen Alik first arrived in Lamore, his journey had taken him east to Talbot then south via Lakelands Road to Dunhin Village, where they had transferred to the King's Road to Obira. This route traversed the picturesque Lakeford counties and a small amount of marshland just before reaching the city.

The Lowlands in Lamore's west were nothing like Lakeford, and took marshlands to an extreme level. Calliope, the estate Datanya had inherited when her parents died, sat among woody reeds and swamps reeking of stagnant mud, which had inexplicably persisted in the stifling summer heat. Alik had travelled to Calliope in Datanya's carriage at the King's insistence. It had been a cumbersome trip, with the carriage becoming bogged several times – and there was also the fact that he had taken the opportunity to ensure Datanya understood they would never marry.

He had let her down as gently as possible, explaining that she deserved a husband who loved her more than anything. Someone who appreciated her many virtues. He had explained that he couldn't commit himself to anyone while he was focused on strengthening the relationship between Kengia and Lamore. Some of it was true. Some of it was not, but he didn't want to hurt her unnecessarily.

By the time the carriage came to a sluggish stop outside Calliope Manor, Datanya, between sobs, had accepted the rejection. She held a lace handkerchief to her nose and rushed inside the grand stone residence. Alik wasn't sure if she was shielding herself from the stench of swamp mud or trying to mask her upset. Perhaps both.

'Should we visit one of these *miraculous* Kengian farms?' Delrik appeared beside Alik. His glowering shadow, Horace, stood behind him.

'Let's do that,' Alik said, glad for the distraction.


THE FARMER REEVE of Datanya's estate, Sergei, escorted them a dozen miles or so away to what was formerly common lands, but was now owned by several Kengian farmers.

The change in landscape was as marked as it was magnificent. Endless rows of green replaced brown mud. Farmers hunched over crops of potatoes, cabbages, squashes and greens, tending to them, harvesting them. Bullocks pulled heavy ploughs through freshly tilled earth, creating furrows for new seeds. Alik had always had faith in the Kengian farmers, but being able to drain the land so expertly and bring it to fruition on such a scale was something he'd never anticipated.

Sergei shook his head to himself. 'It's hard to believe until you see it with your own eyes. I have half a mind to sell off all of the Countess's sheep and ask some of these Kengians to help me do the same at Calliope. Wool may keep the lady in riches, but this' – he indicated the green fields – 'is the future of Lamore.'

'Indeed,' Delrik said, his eyes sweeping the vast enterprise before them.

Alik looked to Horace, keen to gauge his reaction, and admittedly wanting to savour his victory. But the Chancellor's face was expressionless.

Delrik slapped Alik on the back. 'I knew you'd do it. I knew it.'

Alik didn't point out that he'd done nothing – it was the Kengian farmers who'd done everything. He merely nodded.

The King shifted his attention to the Chancellor, casting Horace an accusatory gaze. 'And what say you, Horace?'

Horace didn't get a chance to respond. An ear-piercing scream split the air. A child's scream.

Alik's eyes went to the source of the cry. In the distance, he could just make out a boy pinned under a plough. Farmers ran from every direction to help the screaming boy. Alik raced to follow them.

BYSTANDERS SPOKE in rushed Kengian between the boy's cries.

'Something spooked the bullock…Knocked the boy over…Dragged under the plough…Right before it broke free of its harness.'

A group of Kengians had banded together to try to lift the equipment from the boy, but they struggled to raise it more than an inch before he howled even louder in pain.

'He's half caught up in it.' One of the farmers indicated the plough's cutting blade with a shaking hand. The coulter was pressing into the boy's abdomen. 'Don't know how we'll move it without kil—'

'But we have to do something, quickly,' another said, 'or he'll die anyway.'

Then it was silent. The boy no longer screamed or cried. Alik looked at him directly for the first time, praying he was still alive. And that was when he realised it was the Lamorian huntsman's son – the boy he had helped in the woods the day of the fox hunt. He was alive, albeit barely, judging by the shallow rise and fall of his chest.

'But I told him to go to Lakeford,' he lamented to himself in Kengian.

'He was in Lakeford,' a farmer beside Alik said, her voice quavering. 'But he came here with my family when we were offered our own land.'

'Why aren't they doing something?' The King had joined the group and was waving his hands frantically. 'They could just use their magic.'

'Most Kengians don't possess those sorts of skills.' Alik stopped short of adding, *As I have told you a dozen times.*

'But *you* do.' It was Horace speaking beside him.

Alik spun to face the Chancellor. His face was blank, but his eyes danced, taunting the Kengian Prince.

By now the farmers had registered Alik's presence and all looked at him expectantly. Yes, Alik had made a promise not to use his magic. A promise made for good reasons, but there was no question: he had to help the boy in spite of any consequences.

He asked everyone to clear the space around the plough. He closed his eyes and thought of those he'd made promises to. 'Forgive me.'

Alik opened his eyes and lifted his hands. The familiar energy surfaced inside him, buzzing through his veins until it reached his palms. His hands bloomed with heat and a silver glow. He aimed one palm directly at the blade touching the boy and focused the other on the top of the coulter where it was fixed to the plough. Ribbons of wind sprang forth, and Alik's hands worked independently of each other to control them. The fingers of one probed and pulled at the air, freeing the coulter from its fixings. The wind from the other hand held the blade in place so it wouldn't stab the boy.

Alik's arms burned, every muscle on fire from lack of use, but he pushed on until the coulter was completely free. With one controlled *swoosh*, he lifted the blade high into the air and flung it across the field, where it landed, plunging deep into the rich earth.

The Kengian farmers sprang into action and extricated the boy from the plough. Alik's arms dropped limply to his side. He heaved big lungfuls of air as he tried to recover from the strain on his body – but his breath caught in his throat at the King's venomous stare, and at Horace smirking beside him.

Horace addressed Delrik. 'You have asked him, time and time again, to demonstrate his magic for you, Lamore's anointed King, and he refused. But he will use it to save a boy.' Horace turned his nose up in disgust. 'A *nobody* of a boy. He is not your friend.'

'Delrik.' Alik held his hands out placatingly. 'I *am* your friend.'

Horace scoffed. 'A friend wouldn't humiliate you as he has done, sire.' He dropped his voice to a sinister growl. 'Make no mistake. The Kengian Prince is your enemy, and with the powers he wields, he thinks he is more powerful than you. You must prove otherwise.'

Slowly, the King nodded.

'Delrik!' Alik cried.

'You shall address me as Your Majesty,' Delrik hissed.

'And until you can prove that you can be trusted, you will stay here with your *Kengian* farmers and make sure they deliver.'

'A wise decision, Your Majesty,' Horace said earnestly. 'And I will leave my personal guards here to ensure your wishes are *executed*.' He said the last word with his signature smirk.

'Your Majesty!' Alik tried to appeal to the King again, but Delrik had already turned his back on him and was walking away.

Horace turned to the captain of his guards. 'The Kengian Prince has been banished from court. If he tries to leave, kill the first farmer you see, and anyone else who stands in your way.'

Alik's heart hammered in panic. He had to get back to court. He had promised Gwyn he would keep Horace in check, that she had nothing to worry about.

But it was a day for broken promises.

## 30

When Gwyn learnt that Alik had been exiled to the Lowlands, she saw the future crumble before her. Soon Sofia would have to go into confinement and Horace would face no opposition. Alik needed to be at court.

Gwyn was absolutely terrified. She didn't need to explain her fears to Sofia – her best friend knew exactly what was at stake and wasted no time confronting her husband.

'What's the meaning of exiling the Prince?' Sofia shot at Delrik in his rooms, in front of Horace and several retainers who were serving up a late supper and goblets of wine.

Delrik initially had the decency to look like a naughty boy being scolded, but it was Horace who replied.

'How dare you question your King!'

Sofia crossed the room to stand just inches from the Chancellor's face. 'And how dare you speak like that to me, your Queen?' she said through gritted teeth.

Delrik took a large gulp of wine.

'His Majesty has only done what is right for the kingdom,' Horace persisted. 'He has taken steps to ensure Lamore's crops are secured, while also keeping a *dangerous* threat from court.'

'Dangerous!' Gwyn scoffed. 'The Kengian Prince has done nothing but help people since he's been here, which is more than you can say.'

Horace scowled back at her. 'Yes, *dangerous*. He performed magic without the King's permission.'

Gwyn had heard what Alik had done to save a young boy, and while she wished he had never used his powers, she understood why he'd done it.

'Enough!' The King was finally speaking. 'Alik will stay in the Lowlands until he can prove he can be trusted and is loyal to the crown.'

'But he is needed here,' the Queen argued.

'Pray,' Horace drawled, giving a dramatic wave of his hand, 'enlighten us as to why a dangerous Kengian is required at court.'

The Queen stuck out her chin. 'Because while I am locked away in your archaic Lamorian custom, you can't be trusted to be the lone adviser to the King.'

Gwyn bit her lip at Sofia's words. In calling out Horace, she had inferred that the King was incapable of making the right decisions without her or Alik.

Catching her meaning, Delrik grabbed his wife's arm and spun her to face him. 'I do not appreciate what you're imply-ing, *wife.*' His nostrils flared. 'The Chancellor is right. Do. Not. Question. Me.'

Gwyn touched Sofia's other arm, urging her without words to back down. Now the King's temper had been trig-gered, it was reckless to further antagonise him. But Gwyn also knew her best friend better than anyone. Sofia was a born warrior, like her. She'd never back down.

Sofia yanked her arm from Delrik's grip and issued a

threat that surprised even Gwyn. 'You allow Alik to return, and put an end once and for all to Horace's calls to invade Ette and Ivane, or we are done.'

Delrik stumbled back and blinked rapidly. 'Done? What…what does that mean?' he stammered.

'It's an empty threat,' Horace scoffed. 'She is with child, your child. She can't leave the castle.'

Sofia didn't deign to look at Horace. She maintained a steady gaze on her husband. 'I know you won't let me leave the castle, but I will go as far away as possible. I'll move out of my apartments next to yours, to the south-east tower.'

Gwyn was rendered silent, along with the King and Horace. The disused south-east tower was on the opposite side of the castle and hadn't been inhabited for a century or more. From the little Gwyn had seen, it had fallen into a state of disrepair. Delrik would never let his heir be born there. He would capitulate.

But Gwyn, and Sofia, it seemed, had sorely misjudged what the King was capable of when threatened. He took a slow and deliberate sip of his wine and said, 'We'll see who backs down first.'

With that, Sofia spun on her heels and marched out of the room. Gwyn made to follow, but was stopped by Horace's hand on her arm.

'The King will not yield,' he said tonelessly.

'And neither will the Queen.'

Horace released her arm and shrugged. 'To her detriment. But I hate to think of you having to endure the conditions of the south-east tower.'

'Since when do you care about my welfare?' she spat.

'You know how much I care,' he said in a whisper. 'Just say the word and I will support your cause.'

Gwyn's heart stilled. Horace was offering his support…if she agreed to be with him.

She had cared for him before; perhaps she could do it again. But it had only ever been as a friend, and she wasn't sure she could even offer friendship after she'd seen the extent of his true nature. It would be a lie. Perhaps a lie she would have been willing to live with…before. Not now. Everything had changed.

'I'm sorry, Horace, but I can't be with you,' she said, as kindly as possible.

Horace clenched his jaw. 'In that case, I'm not sorry. I'm not sorry for the fate I will make sure befalls you and your friends.'

## 31

---

*A*s ordered, Alik stayed in the Lowlands, lodging with the Kengian family and the huntsman's son, who'd made a full recovery after the plough accident. The Kengian Prince had taken the boy – Kit – under his wing, teaching him about *kira* and the importance of balance in nature. Kit may never possess a Kengian's affinity with nature, but he was a keen student and applied his learnings to his own small plot of land, which flourished with burgeoning cabbage heads and verdant green carrot tops.

When Alik wasn't watching over Kit he was hard at work in the fields, determined to do his part and prove to the King that he was his ally. He joined his fellow Kengians from dawn to dusk, digging, picking and tending to the crops. He soothed his blistered and calloused hands in warm salted water at night, grateful for the pain – a reminder of his unfulfilled promises, and his anger.

When Alik allowed himself to think about his exile – which he tried not to do too often – the fury he had buried deep inside him would resurface with a vengeance. Fury not so much at Horace, whom he had never expected to act any differently, but at Delrik. Alik had honestly thought he and the King were friends. He had been convinced that together they would transform all of Kypria for the better. He'd even been able to disregard Delrik's changeable nature and occasional lapses in judgement, sure that he could always bring the King back to the right path, but his banishment had unravelled everything. He came to the conclusion that he had never really known Delrik, and that perhaps the King didn't really know himself.

When Alik's anger eventually subsided, he would turn to working through the problem. Part of him argued that the King could still be reasoned with. Alik just needed a chance to speak to him. So he focused on what he could do to be allowed back at court. He had to get back to court. He had to.

He'd written to Delrik regularly asking for permission to return, but the King had replied only once, saying he was counting on Alik to ensure the Kengians delivered plentiful winter crops, that it was 'critical to Lamore's future, as the treasury is near empty and the treacherous King Arlo still hasn't paid the dowry'.

But Alik couldn't wait until winter. By then Sofia would be in confinement, and Gwyn along with her. He needed to be there to counter Horace's influence.

Gwyn had confirmed in letters to him that the Chancellor had tightened his grip over the King. Immediately after Sofia had moved to Lamore Castle's south-east tower, Horace had taken up residence in the vacant Queen's apartments adjoining Delrik's rooms, giving him unfettered access to the King.

Most recently, Horace had been campaigning to have the Kengian farmers stripped of their land titles. Gwyn had said the Queen was heavily opposing it, and so far, the King was heeding her advice, but he would make no promises while she insisted on staying in the south-east tower. In turn Sofia maintained she wouldn't return until he *did* make such promises, and until he allowed Alik to return, leaving the King and Queen at a stalemate.

Gwyn said the situation at court had been exacerbated by the continued dwindling of the treasury funds, which she suspected would never be alleviated with a dowry payment. *Sofia and I,* she wrote, *suspect King Arlo lacks the funds himself, as he is still rebuilding Ivane and repaying all of the supporters who helped him win the war.*

Alik thought about heading back to the castle anyway, but the Chancellor's guards were always near, and he hadn't forgotten Horace's orders to kill farmers if he attempted to leave. He just hoped the King would relent soon, so he wouldn't fail in his duty and break his promises to those he cared about.

'Alik! Alik!' Kit's excited voice. The boy ran toward the cottage threshold, where Alik was taking off his muddy boots. 'A letter! A letter!' he exclaimed.

A smile crept across Alik's face at Kit's joy. 'It's just a letter,' he said good-naturedly as he stood up to receive the sealed message. He recognised Gwyn's seal straight away and was filled equally with anticipation and anxiety. Would it be good news?

'It's not just a letter,' the boy panted. 'Look who brought it.'

Only then did Alik notice the approaching figure. A travel-worn man, not a nobleman but someone who seemed familiar. He dropped to one knee in front of Alik and bowed his head. 'Your Highness.'

'It's Father!' Kit cried.

The huntsman from Lamore Castle. Alik urged the man – Blake – to get to his feet. The huntsman did as he bid, then took off his hat and held it to his chest.

'Thank you. Thank you a thousand times for saving my son. I'm indebted to you.'

'There's no need to thank me. I only did the decent thing, but I don't understand why you are here…I mean, here *now*. How did you convince the King to release you?'

Blake squared his shoulders. 'I didn't. I ain't going to take orders from the likes of him anymore.' He spat on the ground. 'His mood changes more than the weather. Only a matter of time before he turns on all of us. I've come to help you.'

'Help in the fields?' Alik asked, confused.

The huntsman nodded at the letter.

Alik broke the seal and began reading. There were no pleasantries.

*Dear Alik,*

*The situation at court has not improved. In fact, it has deteriorated.*

*Horace seems intent on undermining all of the good work and attempts to unite Kypria. He has intensified calls to invade Ivane and Ette, saying Lamore is left with no choice because the kingdom is running out of money. He has also halted the hospital plans and increased the taxes on the poor, so they are higher than they've ever been.*

*Horace has perfectly apportioned the blame for what he describes as 'Lamore's untenable situation' to the Kengians, the poor and the Ivanian King, and Delrik, whose vanity won't allow him to accept any responsibility, appears eager to accept these parties as villains.*

*Sofia appears to have given up, resigning herself to the impending imprisonment of being confined to her rooms, but I don't judge her. She has been worn down, not by her pregnancy but by heartbreak and the malignant presence of the Chancellor. I cannot believe he and I were once friends.*

ALIK SCREWED UP HIS MOUTH. He couldn't believe the pair had been friendly either. He read on.

*You must find a way to get back to court...soon. You are the only other person Delrik may listen to.*
*The King needs you. We need you.*
*I dare not imagine what will happen if you don't return. All hope would be gone...but I will not have it.*
*I have endured a lifetime of disappointment and loss, and through that, I have come to learn that if I want change, it is up to me to make it. I must take action. So that is what I am doing.*
*I have sent you a gift.*
*Yours,*
*Gwyn*

ALIK LOOKED up and caught both father and son's eager gazes. He scratched his head.

'So *you* are the gift?' he asked Blake.

A great belly laugh was the response, followed by another voice: 'No. I am.'

Another rider had arrived. Alik knew their identity instantly.

'Elos!' He raced to shake the towering knight's hand vigorously. 'It's so good to see you.'

The humour had disappeared from Elos's face, replaced by a serious expression. 'I venture it is better to see me than you think.'

ELOS EXPLAINED HIS MISSION: Gwyn had sent him to liberate Alik from the Lowlands.

'I appreciate the thought, but Horace's guards don't let me out of their sight for a second,' Alik lamented. 'The moment we subdue one of them, the others will attack the farmers, and I can't risk their lives like that.'

Elos nodded sagely. 'You're right. We can't subdue one of them.' Then a mischievous grin spread across his face. 'So we will subdue all of them…at once.'

Alik inclined his head. 'But how? I won't put anyone here in danger like that.'

'And I don't expect you to.' Elos nodded at the huntsman. 'We have a plan.'

The pair then detailed how, before dawn, Blake would go to the guards and say that he had seen Alik escape. He would claim he had seen the Prince heading toward Calliope, and there he would lead the guards in the dark – straight into the marshland.

'I grew up in these parts and know the peat bogs like the back of my hand, unlike those guards who 'ave never set foot outside Obira,' he explained. 'Before they know it, they'll be up to their necks and sinkin' in a bog.'

Alik grimaced. 'But what makes you think they'll follow you?'

The huntsman grunted his conviction. 'They'll trust me. I'm a Lamorian, and as far as they know I'm still in the service of the King.'

'And while they are stuck in the swamp,' Elos said, 'I'll be helping you make your actual escape.'

Alik mulled it over. It could work…maybe.

'But we can't let the guards die,' he reasoned. 'The King would never forgive such an affront.'

'We won't,' Elos said. 'We will get the farmers to go to Calliope to offer to save them. They will pull the men from the bogs, on one condition: the guards don't harm a single person and they leave immediately. They'll desert, of course, because Horace would hang them if they returned to the castle – leaving us all in the clear. As long as no one talks.'

'You can trust everyone here,' Alik asserted. 'But…'

Elos held up his hand. 'I know what you're about to say – that you can't put the farmers at risk. But let it be their choice.'

There was no argument from the Kengian farmers. They'd committed themselves long ago to supporting their future King, and like him, they lived with honour and courage.


ON THE RIDE back to Lamore Castle, Elos filled Alik in on the latest from court. It was worse than even Gwyn had described. The King, under pressure to bring the nation back to prosperity, had been looking for anyone and everyone to blame. He'd grown incredibly superstitious, reading up on the Water Catcher prophecy, convinced his regime was about to fall all because he had invited Kengians into his country and home.

'He thought he knew how to run the kingdom better than

his father,' Elos said. 'But under his father, Lamore thrived, even if it was at the expense of Ivane and Ette.' He shook his head to himself. 'And Horace continues to plant seeds of doubt, suggesting Delrik's father was right not to trust Kengians and to favour securing Lamore's future through oppression, not peace.'

Alik's grip tightened on his reins as his anger resurged. 'I'll tell him in no uncertain terms why that way is wrong.' His voice rose with every word. 'I will *make* him listen.'

Elos huffed a heavy sigh. 'I understand your anger. We're all angry, but that is not the way to handle the King. He is unpredictable, but one thing remains constant.'

'One thing?'

'His pride.'

*Of course.* Alik had seen it himself from his first encounter with the King. He'd watched Delrik practising swordplay, the way he acted with a sense of theatre, desperate to be admired, as well as desperate to win. Confronting the King or showing him up in front of his subjects would get him nowhere.

'So the secret to managing the King is managing his pride,' Alik concluded. Even if it meant sacrificing his own. But with the stakes so high – not just for himself, but for Kypria at large – it was a price he was willing to pay.


ALIK WENT STRAIGHT to the King upon arriving at the castle. Delrik was in his presence chamber, receiving petitioners. He was currently listening to a grievance between two neighbouring landowners. All the court appeared to be there. It was the perfect audience for Alik. He knew exactly what he needed to do.

But to keep one promise, he would need to break another.

Horace, Sofia and Gwyn all looked up at his harried arrival. Shock turned to undisguised hatred on the face of the former, while relief washed over the latter. The Chancellor leant over and dropped something in the King's ear, and Delrik shot his attention toward Alik, his gaze narrowing to slits.

Horace dismissed the petitioners with a flick of his wrist. A curtain of silence fell over the room and the crowd parted for Alik to approach.

He walked slowly, with what he hoped was a contrite expression on his face. Anger coiled inside him. Every nerve in his body stood to attention. But he had to maintain the act. So much relied on him.

He stopped a few feet short of the King and fell to his knees. Looking down at the stone floor, he said in a loud and clear voice, 'I am here to declare my fealty and undying fidelity to you, Your Majesty. I have wronged you by not doing your bidding at all times.' Alik paused to swallow the bitter taste of his words. 'But I have seen the error of my ways and throw myself at your mercy.' He lifted his head then, and locked eyes with the King. 'I am your most faithful servant. And you are the most magnificent and benevolent of all Kings.'

A muscle in Delrik's cheek twitched, but he said nothing.

Alik stood up, turned and addressed the courtiers. He could feel every eye drilling into him. 'The King tasked me with ensuring the security of Lamore's food crops. And now that I have delivered, I seek the privilege and honour of being back at this court. Here I can further prove my loyalty to your King and country, and do his bidding.' Alik took a deep breath. 'His Majesty, in this very room, once bid me to demonstrate my magic and show that it was his to command, but I made the grave mistake of not complying.'

Gwyn caught Alik's eye and shook her head, but there was no going back. He broke her gaze and turned back to face the King.

'Today, with your permission, Your Majesty, I will rectify that.'

Delrik tapped his fingers on the arm of his throne for several beats, then stopped. He gave the slightest nod and Alik closed his eyes.

The Kengian Prince had thought hard about the next part. He was taking a significant risk, but if it panned out, he would have the King's ear again.

He opened his eyes and raised one hand. He swept his arm to the right so his palm was facing Horace's feet. His hand was wrapped in silver light. Alik gave an apologetic shrug as he lifted his arm, raising Horace's robes with it.

A collective gasp echoed through the chamber. Horace's eyes darted in confusion. He tried to bat down his robes, but they kept rising. The black material was now floating at Horace's knees, revealing the pasty white pins of his legs.

'Stop! Stop it now!' Horace screeched.

The King remained silent. No one else dared to make a sound. Then another twitch in Delrik's cheek. The hint of a smile. A chuckle that quickly crescendoed into a chortle.

And with that cue from the King, the room erupted in laughter.

Alik released his power over Horace's robes and Delrik rose from his throne.

'Welcome back, my friend!' the King cried, and the courtiers clapped enthusiastically.

As Horace stomped from the room, Delrik wrapped Alik in a bear hug.

'Don't you ever defy me again,' he hissed in Alik's ear. An *or else* was implied by the fingers digging into Alik's ribs. But the Prince was able to push aside the pain – for his plan had worked.

LATER, Alik found Gwyn in the Queen's Gardens. He didn't know what reception he would get, but judging by her furious pacing in front of the Fountain of Courage, he guessed it would not be a good one. On noticing his arrival, she strode toward him, her brown eyes flashing – and slapped him in the face.

'Hey!' he protested, holding a hand to his cheek.

'You said you wouldn't use your magic, but you have…twice!'

He held his hands out in appeal. 'You know I had to save the boy in the Lowlands.'

She crossed her arms. 'And it got you banished. What's your excuse for today's little performance?'

'I had to do it. The only way to keep my promise to keep Horace at bay was to break my other promise to you. Delrik needed to see I would do his bidding.'

Gwyn made a *harrumph* sound. 'So you thought you'd also humiliate Horace in the process?'

'It was important to publicly position myself above him,' he argued. 'And it worked. I know I'll have the King's ear now.'

She threw her arms up in the air. 'If Horace doesn't kill you first. And that can't happen…We need you alive. We're counting on you.' She said the last part in a choked whisper.

A chilly breeze gusted through the garden and Gwyn pulled her heavy fur cloak tighter around her.

'I'm sorry I let you down,' Alik murmured. 'But I'm here now. Everything will be alright. I pro—'

Gwyn pivoted to face him, her eyes awash with tears. 'Don't make promises you can't keep.'

Instinctively, Alik wanted to embrace her, but he wasn't sure she would welcome it. He looked instead at the ground, where he noticed a single dandelion that had sprung from the gravel path and lived long enough to go to seed. A lone survivor in the otherwise meticulously weeded gardens.

He bent down and plucked it from the ground. He held it out to Gwyn. 'If promises aren't enough, then make a wish.'

A faraway smile slowly bloomed on Gwyn's face, as if she were harbouring some great secret. She blew on the flower head and grinned as the breeze caught the feathery seeds and lifted them up into the air.

As they watched the seeds arc their way through the grey sky and embark on their new life, Alik was filled with certainty. A certainty as constant as the sun and the moon that there was hope, and that their destinies would be fulfilled.

## 32

*T*he King's message arrived after supper, setting Alik immediately on edge. The unexpected summons was yet another sign that nothing was right in the Lamorian court.

Sofia was still in confinement after giving birth to a Prince two weeks earlier. She remained in her chambers in the south-east tower, along with Gwyn, Lore and his wife, Issy. With Alik back, Delrik had pressured the Queen to return to her original apartments, but Sofia maintained she wouldn't until he swore not to invade any territories. So by the time she went into confinement, the King was already on edge. And as expected, Horace had taken advantage of the Queen's absence, regaining Delrik's confidence.

Alik, in turn, had focused on assuring the mercurial King that he and the Kengians would never turn on Lamore, and that the farmers were committed to the kingdom. Depending on the way the wind was blowing, the King did or didn't listen to him. One day Delrik would fawn over Alik and express his gratitude for their friendship and everything the Kengians had done. The very next, he'd implement some new restrictions. First he banned all Kengian harvest festivals. Then he banned any form of Kengian culture being practised, including the wearing of traditional costume.

Alik had tried everything to get Delrik to see sense, but without the Queen by his side he was incorrigible. He stalked the castle like an injured bear, bellowing at anyone who came within striking distance. And with each day that passed with no sign of the promised dowry, his mood only worsened. Just today, Delrik had dismissed the last of Alik's retainers at court, his personal guards, replacing them with men from Horace's household.

Alik could have left court. He could have heeded his father and brother's pleas for him to return home. But there was no abandoning Lamore now. He was committed to the place and the people in it.

He was doing everything he could to keep his word, including a renewed promise to Gwyn not to use his powers. They only needed to hold on a little longer. They needed just a little more time.

Time they may not have.

DELRIK WAS BARELY visible in the amber glow coming from the fireplace in his unlit privy chambers. His shadowy figure paced the floor, leaving a trail of mumbled words and an overwhelming fetor of stale wine in his wake.

A guard announced Alik's arrival, but Delrik didn't so much as look in his direction. The King doubled back to a side table, where he refilled the large mug in his hands with wine. Noticeably, he didn't offer Alik a cup.

Delrik went back to pacing and muttering, and Alik

strained his ears to try to discern his meaning. He caught the word 'bewitched'.

'*Bewitched?*' he asked.

Delrik looked at him then, startled. He rushed across the room, stopping just short of Alik's face.

'Yes. Bewitched,' he snarled. 'Horace says you have bewitched me...Used suggestive powers.'

Alik tried not to turn up his nose at the King's alcohol-tainted breath. He took a step back. 'Your Majesty. As I've told you, I'm not versed in Kengian suggestive powers, and even if I were, to what end would I use them against you?' He made a conciliatory hand gesture. 'You are my friend.'

Delrik peered closer at Alik, his bloodshot eyes clearly visible despite the dim light. '*Are* you my friend?' He tilted his head from side to side. 'Are Kengians my friends? Horace says you want to take all of our land...Take it as your own,' he slurred, jabbing his finger.

Alik felt somewhat relieved that Delrik was affected by alcohol. Once sober, he would see the ridiculousness of his accusations. In the meantime, Alik would offer his best assurances and placate him as if he were a child.

He rested his hands on Delrik's shoulders. 'Of course Kengia and I are your friends. We have done nothing but try to help you, and you have just begun to see the fruits of everyone's labour.'

The King's eyebrows danced furiously as if he were trying to process what Alik was saying.

'The winter crops may not be as fruitful as the other seasons', but they will make a big difference to Lamore's position, and will help bring you all of the prosperity you've been waiting for,' Alik pressed.

Delrik looked as if he were about to rub his chin in thought, but forgot he had a mug in his hand and whacked himself in the face with it. He shook his head and stepped back, several paces away from Alik.

'It won't be enough,' he said, still shaking his head. 'We have no money, and King Arlo will never pay the rest of the dowry...even with the birth of an heir.' Delrik spat the last words and slammed his mug down on a table. Then he went suddenly still. 'We have no choice.' There was unexpected resolve in the King's voice that belied his drunken state.

'No choice?'

Claws of glowing light from the fireplace crept their way across the floor, stopping at Delrik's feet.

*You were warned,* the fire crackled.

'We must invade Ette.' Delrik's jaw hardened. 'And Ivane.'

'No, no, no.' Alik closed the distance between himself and the King in a few swift steps. 'Kypria must be at peace. It is your dream!'

'An impossible dream,' Delrik said with conviction. 'I don't have any appetite for war, but it would be for the good of my country.'

'But what about Sofia?' Alik countered.

Delrik winced only slightly. 'She will understand that I'm only doing what I have to do.'

Alik cursed himself for not realising the full extent of Horace's influence in Sofia's absence. 'Please don't do this,' he begged. 'You can still deliver on your duty to your people without going to war. Let me help you.'

Delrik's lips jerked into the semblance of a smile. 'You would help me?'

'Of course. We are friends.'

'I am glad to hear it. But I will need you to use your powers.'

Alik's throat constricted, remembering the last time

Delrik had asked him to promise to use his powers. 'I thought you banned Kengian magic in Lamore.'

Delrik gave a dismissive wave. 'I will make an exception. For the good of my country.'

'I don't understand.' At least, Alik hoped his understanding was wrong.

'It is simple. I want you to join my army to help them defeat Ivane and Ette.'

Alik shook his head vehemently. 'You're not making sense.' He made to walk away. 'Let's discuss this in the morning.'

'I know exactly what I'm saying, and you must hear it. Because if you don't join me, you are my enemy. As is your homeland.'

Alik spun back, rounding on Delrik. 'Are you threatening to invade Kengia as well?'

'My enemies will come to learn exactly why Lamore dominated the Kyprian Empire for so long, and what I am capable of.'

'Are they your words as King,' Alik sneered, 'or the words of Lamore's true ruler, Horace?'

Veins threatened to pop from Delrik's forehead, but before he could respond, the Chancellor himself barrelled into the room.

'Have you seen it?' he demanded, only giving Alik a cursory glance. He ran toward the window and flung open the shutters to reveal the true source of the claws of orange light that now flooded the room.

'A blood moon,' Delrik said in a hushed tone.

Alik stared at the sky, where the full moon had transformed into an orange-red orb, bleeding into the night.

Horace turned back to face Alik and gave a triumphant smirk. 'It is the first sign in the prophecy.'

'*Darkness and defeat,*' Delrik began to recite.

'*Heed the three signs by looking to the skies,*' Horace followed.

'*The first will be seen in a blood moon's rise,*' Delrik added.

Delrik's eyes widened, mirroring the full moon. 'The Water Catcher is coming, then. To destroy Lamore.'

'But you don't believe in the prophecy,' Alik argued. 'We know it's not true.'

Horace took up a position next to the King. 'He would say that, wouldn't he? The Water Catcher, after all, is from the firstborn line – like him.' The Chancellor leant in closer to the King. 'This has all been part of their plan to gain your trust and infiltrate your court, before releasing their Water Catcher on us and seizing power.'

'This is ridiculous!' Alik shouted. 'There is no Water Catcher!'

'Arrest him. Arrest him now,' Horace hissed. 'Proclaim that all Kengians are enemies of the state.'

Alik didn't wait to see how Delrik would respond. He rushed from the King's apartments back to his own room.

His first instinct was to pack his belongings and run. Horace's guards were outside his chambers, though he reasoned he could overpower them – but that wasn't what stopped him. He was bound to Lamore. He'd made promises, and there was much more than honour at stake. His destiny was here. It was his heart's truth.

Tomorrow, he told himself, Delrik would see sense.

But the appearance of Elos at his door soon after, hand on the hilt of his sword, told Alik otherwise.

'I'm here to arrest you,' Elos said formally. His expression and manner lacked any sign of the friendship between the pair.

'On what charges?' Alik challenged.

'Your charges will be read when you get to the castle dungeons,' Elos said, grabbing Alik roughly by the arm.

Alik shuddered. He had heard tales of the inhumane dumping grounds for Lamore's criminals, where no one left alive, unless they were on their way to the gallows.

'I demand to speak to the King,' he said as Elos shoved him past Horace's guards.

'You have forfeited any rights to make demands,' Elos said gruffly, shoving him even harder, to the snickers of the guards.

As Elos led him through the castle at swordpoint, Alik considered his options. He was no use to anyone if he was in the dungeons, so he would need to escape. But with no weapon, he stood little chance against Elos – unless he used his powers. Yes, he had made a promise, but this was the only way…

As they reached the base of a set of stairs near the entrance to the main courtyard, Alik stared down at his hands, focusing on the pulsing energy in his veins. Silver light washed from his fingertips to his palms and he snapped his hands into fists. But before he could do anything, Elos's blade was at his wrists.

'You don't want to do that,' he whispered, and swept his gaze around them as if checking if anyone was nearby – there was no one. No doubt every eye on the castle was on the blood moon as the nobles watched from the safety of the castle interior. Elos then nodded toward the courtyard entrance, which Alik was certain didn't lead to the dungeons. He didn't have a chance to question Elos, who pinned himself against the outside wall and started edging along it through the shadows, indicating for Alik to follow suit.

Soon they found themselves at the stables, where Elos

showed Alik to his horse, Meteor, who was already saddled. The mare whinnied a soft hello and nuzzled Alik's hand.

'Head for the woodland and north-east gate,' Elos said, looking around again as he spoke. 'There are only two guards there that you will need to take care of. From there you have a clear run down the hill to the city.'

But Alik didn't move. 'I don't understand.'

'What is there to understand?' Elos said. 'I'm helping you escape.'

'But what about back there? All the shoving.'

The knight grinned. 'I had to put on a good show, now, didn't I?'

'But *why* are you helping me?'

Elos's smile slipped away. 'I made a pledge to my King and to Lamore. My oath was to stand up for fairness and justice, and to protect those who needed protecting. But now the King is asking me to lead an invasion of Ivane and then Kengia.' He screwed up his nose. 'There is nothing true and fair about that.'

'I agree, but how do I come into that?'

'Well, I had more than an order to arrest you. Horace told me to kill you.'

Alik wasn't surprised by the news, and neither was Elos, it appeared.

He play-punched Alik in the arm. 'And as I said, I pledged to protect those who need protecting.'

'Hey!' Alik protested. 'I can look after myself.'

Elos raised a brow. 'Didn't look like it back there.'

'Thank you.' Alik made to embrace the giant of a man, but Elos stepped out of his reach and rubbed the back of his neck, eyes darting around once more.

Alik would make his escape, for now. His business at

Lamore Castle was far from over, but he would have to wait until it was safe to return.

'Here.' Elos handed over his sword and a cloak he took from a hook on the stable wall. 'Be careful in the city. Horace has issued an edict that all Kengians are our enemy.'

Alik nodded gravely. 'You take care as well. Horace won't believe I overpowered you to escape.'

Elos winked. 'I'll say you used your magic.'


ALIK MADE his escape in the red-tinged moonlight. The two guards at the north-east gate were so busy gaping at the blood moon they didn't notice Alik's presence until it was too late. In quick succession he rendered each of them unconscious with the hilt of his sword. He then bound their wrists and tied them to a post in the guardhouse.

As sure-footed as always, Meteor navigated the gravelly hillside littered with granite boulders and led them to Obira City. Unlike the castle, where everyone remained in their rooms, it appeared that every resident of the city was out on the streets, marvelling at the blood moon, conjecturing about its meaning and whether it was a bad omen.

As Alik rode by he caught snippets of conversations with several references to the prophecy, but as he continued further into Obira, the mood thickened. He lost count of the number of times he heard 'Kengians' uttered in disgust, followed by the phrase 'enemy of the state'. Alik pulled the hood of his cloak down to shield his face from view.

He arrived in the marketplace to a disturbing scene. A man Alik recognised as one of the farmers who had come with him to Lamore was being strung up to a shop sign, to the screams of his wife. A burly Lamorian held the woman back while cheering on the men who were hanging her husband.

Alik lifted his hand, about to use his magic to help the man – but then he realised he would only make it worse.

He could save one Kengian, but how many more would die if Lamorians had more reason to fear their magic?

He looked down at the sword by his side. He was severely outnumbered. But he couldn't abandon his people, or Lamore, for that matter. Maybe he could still make Delrik see sense. Maybe he could still deliver on all of his promises.

So he turned his back on the Kengian couple in the hope he could save many more like them.

# EPILOGUE

*T*he horse reared, spooked. There was the sensation of falling to the ground. A crack of skull on cobblestone.

Darkness. Nothing. Then Alik was standing up, dazed. Holding his hand to a gash on his head.

A Lamorian man jabbed an accusatory finger at his face. Garbled words that Alik couldn't quite make out...*Silver...Eyes. Silver-eyes.* The man was talking about him.

But nothing made sense.

He couldn't remember how he got here, just a series of staggered images shuddering through his mind.

*Riding back toward the castle. Elos finding him, insisting he make his escape. Elos telling him something to convince him to leave. Something...*

One wobbly foot in front of another. Dozens of Lamorians circled him. One man pounced. Another. On the ground again. Boots connecting with ribs. Fresh pain tearing through his body. A punch to his face. Another. Another. More boots driven into flesh and bone. Excruciating pain. Eyes swollen almost completely shut.

What had Elos said to him? What had spurred him on to the castle? He remembered being there. A confrontation. Arguing with Horace. A frantic determination to do something. What?

He grimaced from the effort of trying to remember, and from the pain that riddled his entire body.

Then he saw himself again, riding back to Obira City. Not on Meteor. Another horse. An angry mob in the marketplace. He couldn't go forward. Couldn't escape.

The horse had spooked. He'd fallen.

It was now again. Alik's limbs and body were unresponsive. There was a sense of knowing he needed to use his powers, but he couldn't.

Being a Kengian with silver eyes and magic in his veins had been his death sentence as much as it could have been his saviour, but he had made a promise. He was bound by honour.

No one could have guessed it would ever come to this.

More images.

*Blood.* The metallic taste of it filling his mouth. *Fire.* Snatches of a sky haemorrhaging crimson between laboured blinks. *A girl – a woman and her warning.* His last thought.

Destiny seized in a final breath.

# CAN I ASK A FAVOUR?

Thank you for reading *The Earth King's Heir*. I hope you enjoyed it and would appreciate if you could take a moment to leave a review. Reviews are the lifeblood of independent authors and key to others learning about our books.

You can **share your review** via your favourite online bookstore or Goodreads.

## About *The Firemaster's Legacy:* The Kyprian Prophecy Book 1

A young adult, fantasy novel perfect for fans of *Throne of Glass*, *Red Queen*, and *Shadow and Bone* series.

*Firesky is the ultimate weapon. It will either obliterate or liberate all of the Kyprian nations. One silver-eyed girl has the power to determine their fate — if she dares to question everything she believes in.*

**Read on for an excerpt from the *The Firemaster's Legacy* now!**

# THE FIREMASTER'S LEGACY

## THE KYPRIAN PROPHECY BOOK 1 (AN EXCERPT)

*Darkness and defeat, a King is to blame;*
*A regime must fall for everything to change.*

*Heed the three signs by looking to the skies:*
*The first will be seen in a blood moon's rise.*

*On the brink of war, the next is firesky:*
*Promises of destruction, many sure to die.*

*An empire's fate uncertain, until comes the third:*
*A catcher of water. Kengia's firstborn returned.*

*Hopes will be tested; some will be betrayed.*
*Fire or water — the choice must be made.*

**— Old Kyprian prophecy**

# PROLOGUE

*Hope is for fools and the damned.*

*Arisa was eleven-and-three-quarters when she vowed she would be neither.*

*It was the first time they came for her. It was the day she learnt that being Kengian and one of the silver-eyes was the surest path to death. And it was the day she knew for sure that the Water Catcher would never come.*

✧

The silver sun was high in the sky casting welcome beams of shimmering light into the shadows made by the school's high stone walls. The cherry blossom tree sighed as it surrendered its last flower. Arisa watched with a dreamy smile as the white petals floated through the crisp wintry air and landed at her feet.

'Arisa.' Rea cast an accusatory glance at her. 'Are you watching?'

She turned to her friend, who was standing perfectly poised on one leg in the hopscotch square. 'I'm watching.'

Rea nodded and tossed her chestnut braids back over her shoulders. She screwed up her mouth in concentration and threw the stone along the line of squares marked out in the playground dirt. It fell just outside a space three places ahead of where Rea stood. She pouted for a moment, before scrunching her eyes shut and reaching out with her left hand. Her fingers glowed, and with the tiniest flick of her wrist, she sent the stone catapulting until it came to rest neatly in the middle of the square.

'Ha!' Rea clapped her hands in delight and looked back at Arisa with a grin. 'Did you see that?'

Arisa should have smiled and said yes, but she couldn't share Rea's enthusiasm. It wasn't just the fact that she was nearly three years older, so had outgrown many of the games Rea liked to play. It was because a jolt of fear had coursed through her when Rea had used forbidden magic. She was scared for her friend – her only friend.

Their friendship had been instantaneous when Rea had arrived at the King's School. Arisa had been drawn to the girl with the glittering silver eyes. They were kindred spirits – each of them an outsider. Arisa was the lowborn orphan and ward of an eccentric healer, at a school reserved mainly for the nobility. Rea was a Kengian. Part of a people displaced from their homeland, only tolerated for their uncanny ability to nurture crops in the barren land of Lamore. Being a Kengian made Rea a pariah in Obira City, and a source of admiration for Arisa – especially given Arisa's guardian made her hide her identity.

Rea had left her farming family outside the city's gates

and was boarding at the school, but she still embraced her Kengian heritage and beliefs. Arisa had never been beyond Obira City's walls. Her guardian, Erun, wanted to keep her close to him. He said it was the only way to keep her safe. So she had never met anyone who lived openly as a Kengian – until she'd met Rea.

The way Rea lived was admirable and terrifying at the same time. Arisa asked her hundreds of questions about her powers. Rea shared her language, her traditions, her Kengian affinity with nature. Arisa was spellbound by tales of the nation cut off from Lamore, and of its people. Rea was her teacher, and Arisa was Rea's protector. But every time Rea used her powers in the schoolyard, Arisa's job got exponentially harder.

Rea tilted her head, as if trying to read her mind. 'Let's play something else. You can pick.'

'It's alright. You choose.'

Rea's dazzling smile returned. 'Let's chase each other. I'll be the Water Catcher and you can be the evil king and try and get me.'

A cold gust of wind manifested from nowhere, sending shivers up Arisa's spine. She could have sworn she heard the word *'shhh'* whispered on the breeze.

Kengians who defied the King's rule were routinely sent to the dungeons under Lamore Castle, never to be seen again, or else ended up hanging from the gallows. But something even more disturbing had been occurring in recent days. There had been stories of silver-eyes being taken from their homes in the night – permanently vanishing. It wasn't just silver-eyes, either. Kengians who hadn't defied the King's rule but openly practised traditional customs had also been targeted. And it was rumoured that anyone who openly sympathised with the Kengians would be next.

Erun had implored Arisa to temper her outspoken tendencies and not to publicly support the Kengian cause. He knew she would never distance herself from Rea, so he begged her to try to stop Rea from doing anything that would draw any extra attention to either of them.

Now, she hurried to Rea's side. 'You can't mention the Water Catcher, or anything to do with the prophecy.'

Rea crossed her arms and glared at Arisa. 'What's the matter? Don't you believe the Water Catcher will come?'

Arisa glanced around to ensure they couldn't be overheard. All the other students were well out of hearing range, but it didn't mean they would escape notice. She dropped her voice to a whisper. 'Erun says the prophecy will come to pass, but he also says we should be careful speaking about it. Especially now.'

Rea rolled her eyes. 'Everyone I know believes the Water Catcher will come.' Her tiny voice rose. 'And they aren't scared to say so.'

Arisa grasped her friend's wrists. 'But you *should* be scared. Speaking about the prophecy is the same as speaking out against the King, and he has spies everywhere. It is said Kengians are being kidnapped on his orders.'

'The King should be the one who is scared. The Water Catcher is coming to get him.'

'I don't know what it's like in the rest of Lamore, but here we can't talk about the prophecy and threaten the King. And you can't keep using your magic.'

Rea put her hands on her hips. 'Why not? What will they do to me?'

*They will come for you. They will come for me,* she thought, wondering desperately how to get Rea to see sense – but she was distracted by the sudden clattering of wheels and horses' hooves on the school's cobblestone driveway.

A lump caught in her throat as she took in the wagon with its barred windows. An impeccably dressed nobleman and a boy, each on horseback, preceded the wagon, and stopped to speak to the school's groundsman. Arisa couldn't make out the words, but could guess their meaning when the visitors looked in their direction.

She bent down to Rea's eye level. 'We have to go. Now.'

Rea stood frozen. All of her earlier brazenness and courage had slipped away.

'Rea!'

Arisa tried to shake her friend to life, but it was too late; the man on horseback had already ridden over and dismounted. He was now standing before them, examining each of the girls with cold eyes. She held Rea's hand tightly in hers as a groomsman wearing the King's livery leapt from the top of the wagon and ran to help the boy from his pony. Arisa noted that the boy wore an ermine-trimmed purple cloak – the colour reserved for royalty.

The boy scowled at them, his black eyes narrowed, as he joined the nobleman. He was a heavyset lad, a good half-head taller than Arisa, but slightly younger, judging by the boyish roundness of his face.

'That one.' The nobleman pointed at Rea.

The boy peered suspiciously at her. 'How do you know?'

The nobleman yanked Rea's arm, wrenching her away from Arisa. He grabbed her jaw and turned her to face the boy. 'Take a look yourself.'

The boy stepped forward hesitantly until he was close enough to properly examine Rea's face. He gasped. 'Silver eyes.'

Rea hissed in the boy's face, and he stumbled backwards. Arisa was torn between unspeakable fear and an urge to smile.

The boy recovered himself and shot an angry glance at Rea. 'I've never seen one before. Not one of the silver-eyes.'

'It's an anomaly. Silver eyes only appear in the most dangerous Kengians.' The nobleman then addressed Rea. 'We hear you've been telling tales about the prophecy.'

Rea lifted her chin and met the man's gaze defiantly. '*Mikret Tawreh elli tacusa.*'

'What did she say?' the boy demanded.

Arisa's lips thinned. She wasn't about to tell him what Rea had said in Kengian: *The Water Catcher will come.*

'Who cares?' The nobleman waved his hands. 'It's enough that she's Kengian, and one of the silver-eyes. The King wants them all out of the city. He feels safer if they're far away in the fields where they belong.' He paused to smile to himself. 'Or even further away.'

Arisa noticed a small crowd of their fellow students gathering around them. 'Get help,' she appealed to them, but they were silent and unmoving. Some smiled slyly, as if they had known this day would come.

'*Rhe sri.*' Rea projected her voice so everyone could hear. She focused her gaze on the boy; her eyes were burning silver-hot. '*Noy hno uebu tof rom, eo Mikret Tawreh.*' *The King's right. He's not safe from me, or the Water Catcher.*

The boy clamped his chubby hand around Rea's arms. She struggled hard against him, as Arisa pulled at the boy's wrists. 'You can't take her.'

The boy spun toward her, his face flushed red. 'What did you say?'

She stood a little taller, determined not to show the fear gurgling inside her stomach. 'I said, you can't take her.'

'What about this one?' The boy indicated Arisa as he called back to his companion.

The nobleman approached her and closed his hand

around her chin. 'She was mentioned in the report. Doesn't have silver eyes, but doesn't mean she isn't Kengian. She could be one of the ones in hiding.' He released his grip and glanced down at her worn gown and battered boots. 'More likely she's just lowborn.'

The boy stepped menacingly toward Arisa and made a show of sniffing the air near her. 'Smells like a Kengian to me.'

She could hear in her mind Erun's warning to keep her head down, but she couldn't stop herself. Someone had to stand up to this bully. Someone had to stand up to *them*.

'*Noy farik noy, aodru-tec.*' She spat the words in the boy's smug face. *You're smelling yourself, turd-face.*

The boy flung his hands over his ears. 'Now she's speaking Kengian, too. She's trying to bewitch me, Sir Marcus!'

*Sir Marcus?* Arisa shivered. The nobleman was Lamore's High Sheriff, which didn't bode well for them.

Sir Marcus exhaled heavily. 'Kengian magic doesn't work like that. She's just baiting you.' He picked up Rea and headed toward the wagon.

'You can't take her!' Arisa cried. 'She's done nothing wrong.'

The boy poked her hard just below her shoulder blade. 'You can't tell me what to do. Do you know who I am?' he snarled, not waiting for a response. 'I'm Lord Guthrie, the Earl of Chisolm, and kin to King Delrik.'

She had heard of the belligerent boy, Guthrie, who was also the son of the King's closest adviser, Chancellor Horace, but his titles didn't scare her. They only made her angrier.

'So?'

'*So!*' Guthrie's face distorted and turned beet-red.

'So, you're no one to me.'

A smirk tugged at the corner of Guthrie's lips. 'But I *will* be someone to you. You were reported too. You're coming with us.'

Arisa's throat closed up and her palms dripped with sweat as Guthrie's arms went around her. He half yanked, half shoved her toward the wagon, where a burly-looking guard lifted her up and threw her roughly inside. She landed heavily against Rea. Her friend's normally carefree face was drawn with terror.

Arisa scrambled back toward the wagon's open door to see the Schoolmaster running toward them.

'Sir Marcus,' he panted, trying to catch his breath. He bowed hurriedly. 'These girls have done nothing to afford you taking them. They are innocents.'

Sir Marcus shook his head. 'You know the King's orders. No silver-eyes in the city. He will not abide anyone defying his laws, or threatening to disrupt his rule.'

The Schoolmaster pointed at Rea. 'But Rea has permission to be here. She's sponsored by the Duke of Lakeford and is the daughter of one of his most trusted tenants.'

Sir Marcus's brow furrowed. 'You can take it up with the Duke, but I'm afraid by the time you speak to him, it will be too late.'

'Too late?' the Schoolmaster and Arisa said in unison.

'We're taking them to Ette.' It was worse than Arisa had feared. There was little chance they could be saved if they were all the way across the Kyprian Sea. 'You're looking at Ette's new Governor.'

Guthrie puffed out his chest. 'And I'm to be his Lieu-tenant-Governor.'

Arisa thought she saw Sir Marcus wince slightly.

'Yes. Lord Guthrie will be under my tutelage. And these girls will serve in my household. We set sail at first light.'

*More likely we'll be treated as slaves,* she thought.

'The King has agreed to this?' The Schoolmaster's voice was impossibly high.

Sir Marcus nodded. 'We have need of a household befitting my and Lord Guthrie's positions, and the local servants are notoriously unreliable.'

'It was my idea to take the Kengians.' Guthrie thumped his chest. 'The silver-eyes' magic won't work in Ette.'

The Schoolmaster seemed to collect himself. 'Congratulations on your new post, Sir Marcus, and yours, Lord Guthrie. But only one of the girls you have apprehended is Kengian. Arisa' – the Schoolmaster pointed at her – 'is as Lamorian as you or I. I have known her since she was a babe.'

A bolt of relief shot through her, but it was just as quickly overcome with guilt. Being saved meant she would have to abandon Rea.

'She's a known sympathiser,' Sir Marcus said.

'And she tried to curse me with her filthy Kengian words,' Guthrie said.

The Schoolmaster shot a desperate look at Arisa that said, *Really?* She bit her lip, unable to deny it.

'I'm sure it was a misunderstanding, Lord Guthrie.'

Sir Marcus sighed. 'Both girls are coming with us.'

He mounted his horse as Guthrie was helped on top of his pony. Guthrie shot a triumphant smile at Arisa as the guard slammed the wagon door in her face.

The wagon lurched into action, leaving her to contemplate her fate. She hadn't heeded her guardian's many warnings. She hadn't protected Rea. And look what had happened. She couldn't put Guthrie's cruel smirk or his lifeless black eyes – the colour of death – from her mind.

Rea sat beside her. 'It's alright, Arisa. The Water Catcher will come.'

'Stop saying that,' she snapped. 'That's how you got us into this mess.'

Rea's face fell. 'I'm sorry.'

She immediately regretted her comment. Rea had done nothing but be proud of her heritage and who she was. 'It's not your fault,' Arisa said in a softened voice. 'You didn't do anything wrong.'

'I did. You told me to stop talking about the prophecy and not to practise my magic. But it's not proper magic; I can only do a few little tricks. I can't actually hurt anyone. I didn't think anyone would care.'

Arisa's gut churned with anger. Rea was in the right, but it didn't matter. Being right and just held no power in Lamore. 'Don't blame yourself. You can't help who you are. It's not fair that we can't say what we want.'

Rea nodded her head miserably. 'We'll be alright. They might not really take us away.'

Arisa took the girl's shaking hands in hers. 'Sure, they might not,' she lied.

THE WAGON JOSTLED its way through Obira's winding alleyways until it came to a stop at the port, where Arisa and Rea found themselves being pulled across the gangplank of a cargo ship. The King's peregrine falcon flag flew high on the mast.

They were shoved down three floors until they reached the ship's hold. Arisa shuffled forward in the dark, the guard pushing her further toward the sound of Kengian voices. He threw her to the floor. Her back thumped hard against a post. She could feel a sea of limbs moving around her, and hear the clinking of chains as the prisoners made room for the newcomers.

'Sorry.'

Her apology went unanswered in the fetid hold. Straw scratched at her legs. The space reeked of human waste. Arisa shuddered at the coldness of the metal as manacles snapped closed around her wrists. She heard the click of a second pair next to her. She reached out for Rea's hand.

The guards left them, and her eyes adjusted to the darkness. Dozens of eyes peered back at her. Many of them were silver, but a few weren't. Some of the captives looked like they hadn't seen light or a good meal for years. She wondered if they had been freed from the dungeons, only to now be bound to a life of servitude.

A frail-looking man fixed a blank silver stare on her. His eyes were empty, as if he had long ago given up trying to make sense of what was happening.

'Arisa?' Rea squeaked.

'It's alright.' She squeezed Rea's hand. 'It will be alright,' she lied again.

'I'm never going to see Mother and Father again,' Rea cried.

'It will be hard. Trust me, I know. But at least we're together. We can survive, as long as we're together.'

'You promise you won't leave me?'

'I promise.' Arisa could feel Rea's warm tears as they dropped onto her hand. 'Don't cry.'

*Never let them see you cry*. Erun's words were etched in her mind. Words she'd never hear again.

'Don't cry,' she repeated, biting back her own tears.

⌁

ARISA WASN'T sure how long they had been in the hold. She couldn't tell if it was day or night. She had managed to fall asleep at some point, despite the voices all around. A Kengian chorus repeated the same mantra over and over: *Mikret Tawreh elli tacusa* – the Water Catcher will come. Others just rocked themselves back and forth, moaning.

Arisa propped herself up against a barrel, being careful not to disturb the sleeping Rea snuggled up against her. On the deck above, she could hear the crew as they prepared to set sail. Supplies had been delivered periodically into the hull where they were being kept.

Rea's eyes opened with a start as the noises above them intensified. A guard appeared at the bottom of the ladder.

'This way.'

The guard led a man toward them. He was carrying a wooden case, and wore a uniform Arisa recognised from Smith & Son – the establishment of a merchant friend of Erun's. There was something familiar about the man's gait; the way his lanky limbs knocked together.

He lowered the case to the ground next to her. The bottles inside it chinked together, and the guard licked his lips greedily. 'The finest rum,' the man said.

Arisa bit her tongue as she recognised her guardian's voice.

'I don't suppose you'd like some?' Erun reached into his coat. 'I've got a little extra here.'

'Could I?'

'Of course – but you will *want* to do something for me in return.'

'Yes, I suppose so.' The guard's voice had turned flat and mechanical.

'You want to let one of these girls go.'

'No...' The guard shook his head slowly. 'No, I don't.'

*Take it easy, Erun,* Arisa thought. *He has to believe your words.*

'No one will notice one little girl gone. No one.'

The guard's face distorted in the dim light.

'And a little Lamorian girl at that. A Lamorian, just like you.'

After what seemed like an age, the guard nodded. 'A Lamorian girl.' He took the rum and shoved it in his coat, before unlocking Arisa's manacles.

She didn't budge.

'Come on,' Erun hissed in her ear.

'Not without Rea,' she whispered back, relief and guilt warring within.

Erun approached the guard again and pointed at Rea. 'That one too.'

The man shook his head, trance-like. 'Not that one. She's Kengian.' He was still under Erun's suggestive powers, but only just.

'She's a wee little thing.' Erun's voice was carefully measured. 'No one would notice if she was gone.'

The guard shook his head violently, as if he had a tic.

'It's no good,' Erun whispered. 'He will never agree to releasing Rea.'

'No!' Arisa cried, but Erun clasped his hand over her mouth and pried her away from her friend.

'The Schoolmaster is speaking to the Duke about Rea, but right now you have to come with me. Put this on.'

He handed her a uniform. She shook her head, refusing to leave – but Rea nodded her encouragement, as did some of the other prisoners present enough to realise what was happening.

'Rea, I – I'm going to get help.' She choked on her words. 'I promise.'

Rea smiled a little too brightly. 'I know.'

Arisa put on the uniform. It was large on her, but she could probably pass for a delivery boy. After a long hug with Rea, and more promises to be back soon, Erun led her up out of the hull, onto the upper deck, and across the gangway to the wharf.

Everyone on the ship was too busy with their own duties to notice the deliveryman and boy. But all the while, Arisa didn't dare to breathe. Erun led her wordlessly along the wharf and up the steep path leading back into the city. He didn't slow his pace until they made it back into the anonymity of Obira's bustling streets. They stopped in the shadows of a quiet laneway.

'Where's the Schoolmaster? We have to make sure…'

Erun's downcast eyes stopped Arisa in her tracks.

'We have to get help for Rea,' she finished.

'We can't.' Erun's voice broke. 'We can't help her.'

'What do you mean? You said—'

'The Schoolmaster went to the castle and tried to get an audience with the Duke, but he is away at Talbot. The Chancellor was hearing petitions on the King's behalf and laughed him from the room.'

The realisation washed over Arisa like a series of needles stabbing into her one by one. She tried to ignore the heartbreak she saw in Erun's eyes.

'We have to go back.' She clutched her guardian's arms. 'You have to use your powers.'

'You saw what happened. I could only get you out. They won't let a silver-eyes go.'

'No! No! No!' She thumped her fists against Erun's chest. 'We have to go back—'

Erun wrapped his arms around Arisa and held her to

him. 'I'm sorry, little one, but you have to believe she'll be alright.'

She pulled away from her guardian. 'No! Believing in impossibilities is how Rea ended up on that ship. There's no hope. And there's no Water Catcher to save them.'

'The Water Catcher will come, Arisa. You have to believe that.'

'No. The Water Catcher can't be real. If they were, they would never let terrible things like this happen.'

Erun's brow crinkled. 'There's always hope,' he said with certainty.

'Not for Rea or people like us.'

'And that is why no one will ever know the *real* us, or we will end up like Rea. As you have seen, it's too dangerous.'

Arisa's next words were bitter in her mouth. 'Not as dangerous as waiting for a hero that will never arrive.'


ARISA DIDN'T CRY that day. She couldn't let anyone see her cry. But she did make a promise to herself. From that day on, she wouldn't rely on hope. She would do whatever she could to protect those who couldn't protect themselves. Maybe it might help wipe her conscience clean for not being able to save Rea, and for knowing her secrets were the only thing that had kept her safe.

At eleven-and-three-quarters, Arisa replaced stolen hope with a grim determination to never let anyone – to never let *them* – get the better of her again. They would pay for what they had done. And she would be ready the next time they came for her or anyone she loved.

# CHAPTER 1

*Six years later*

*A*risa walked alongside the towering wall of stone and wood that surrounded Obira City, separating it from the rest of Lamore. It was the same wall that divided Lamore's capital from the all-seeing castle on the headland above.

It was a wall she yearned to escape beyond.

She tried to force herself to forget the fact that she was trapped in this place. She let her thoughts wander to the Nymoi Alps and their snowy peaks in the distance, the glittering sun hovering above them. For the millionth time, Arisa imagined what it would be like to cross the mountain range and visit the long-lost land of Kengia that lay on the other side.

It was that fleeting time of day when dusk and twilight met. When the silvery hues of the afternoon sun gave way to pearly roses and purples, and the first evening stars pierced their way through the sky's blanket. When anything seemed possible and she could forget, if only for a few magical minutes, that everything she wished for was in fact impossible. At this time of day, she could forget the darkness; a darkness that only intensified with the coming of night – and right now was setting in fast. She must have stayed back at school much later than she thought.

Arisa quickened her pace along the cobblestone streets, jostling through the end-of-day crowds. She screwed up her nose as the city's stench came to her on the wind. She was overly familiar with the smell: a mixture of raw sewage and sickness. Obira's foul air was something you couldn't easily forget or become accustomed to, but tonight the odour was worse, amplified by the yowling wind tunnelling its way through the city. Arisa shuddered as the temperature dropped. She pulled the boy's cap further down over her ears and wrapped her cloak a little tighter. It was frightfully cool, even for a winter's night. The kind of cold that burrowed into the core of your bones.

Another blast of the unfamiliar wind came, howling as it startled a flock of pigeons. She shielded her face as they hurtled toward her. But just as abruptly, the birds turned skywards. The flock tracked across the sky, silhouetted by an immense full moon. The sight reminded her of Erun and his steadfast belief that the strangest things always occurred when the moon was full. She smiled at the thought of her guardian and his fantastical mind. But her smile faded as she registered again how quickly the light was disappearing around her.

She walked faster, striding easily in her boy's tunic and battered leather boots. Arisa was seventeen, but her slim build meant she could still easily pass as a boy. She need only tuck her long hair under a cap. It gave her a certain level of protection when travelling Obira's unpredictable streets at night, as she did all too often. She felt a little safer seeing the lamplighters move from one streetlight to the next, illuminating a path through the city's murk.

She passed a row of groaning stone townhouses, each as dirty and rundown as the last; shopfronts with their overhanging second stories, and lines of threadbare rags strung between the buildings. It was a sea of grey-and-brown sameness. Hollow-faced children looked out from doorways with wide eyes and outstretched hands, and scrawny women balanced screaming babies on their hips.

Arisa reached the city gates, watching enviously as lines of Lamorian citizens passed through, returning to their homes in the countryside for the night. Coming in the opposite direction were noblemen re-entering the city. A pair of Royal Guards stood outside the gatehouse, nodding deferentially to the richly dressed lords as they headed back to the safety of the castle after visiting their grand manors in the counties. Wordlessly, the nobles passed the fishermen, the villagers and the farmers whose blood, sweat and tears sustained their luxurious lifestyles.

Arisa and her lowborn compatriots stood aside as a liveried coach passed through the gates. Beside her, a merchant she recognised from a stall that sold mackerel pies struck up a conversation with another man.

'What news from your village?'

The man shook his head and sighed. 'Taxes have been raised again to make up for the shortfall in crops.'

'It's the same in ours,' the stallholder lamented. 'But it could be worse, I suppose.' He looked around surreptitiously and dropped his voice. Arisa leaned closer to hear. 'The Chancellor has enclosed the common lands near Calliope.

He's dismissed his farmer reeve, Sergei, and evicted many of his tenant farmers.'

'Sheesh,' the other man muttered under his breath. 'I guess after they managed to get the silver-eyes and Kengians under control, it was only a matter of time before they came after us.'

It unsettled Arisa, how easily each man accepted this latest act of cruelty. She wanted to physically shake them, to urge them to stand up for their rights, but the pair had moved on, rejoining the queue to leave the city.

She would usually turn away from the gates now and head into the labyrinth of alleyways that weaved through the city, but a sudden darkness fell around her, swallowing everything in her path.

She looked up, a little hesitantly. The full moon, which had filled the sky just minutes before, was gone, completely obscured by clouds. The glowing line of lamplights that had stretched out ahead was now a series of dull, disconnected dots in the distance. Obira had been reduced to a mass of sinister shadows.

A heaviness formed in the pit of her stomach. Arisa was thankful when one of the guards lit extra torches outside the gatehouse and along the wall.

The remaining guard kept a watchful eye on the Lamorians leaving the city. 'Don't we know you lot?' he interrogated one family, a man and a woman who were attempting to lead an old workhorse and a rickety cart through the gates. A boy who looked to be seven or eight years old – it was hard to tell from his thin frame – was sitting in the cart among small piles of rejected vegetables. He caught Arisa's eye and gave a shy smile. She smiled back.

'We do. We do know them.' The other guard pointed a stubby finger at the family.

The father shook his head and gave an apologetic smile.

'They're some of those grubby Kengian farmers we booted off the Chancellor's land,' Stubby Fingers persisted.

His offsider gave a menacing smirk. 'I think you're right. A little hard to tell, though – Kengian filth all looks the same to me.'

Arisa watched nervously as the boy stood up, as if to challenge the two guards, but his mother reached out to still him.

The first guard picked up an undersized potato from the cart and examined it. 'Where did you grow this?'

'In a village near Iveness.' The mother spoke with downcast eyes.

'You wouldn't be sneaking back onto the Chancellor's lands and taking things that don't belong to you?'

'You accuse us of being thieves?' The father stepped forward, his shoulders squared.

Stubby Fingers surveyed the man with a sneer.

The woman grasped her husband's arm. 'Please be assured, we would never steal from the Chancellor. These were grown on a small allotment a villager was kind enough to share with us.'

There was a moment of silence while the guards stared at the family and their cart. Finally, Stubby Fingers grunted, 'I think I believe the Kengian wench. Take a look at this.' He picked up a spotty-looking squash. 'You'd never find produce like this on the Chancellor's lands.'

Stubby Fingers' friend wandered over. He took the squash with a smirk, before dropping it to the ground and smashing it under his foot. Arisa's face burned in anger.

'Not even fit for pigs.' The pair laughed heartily.

She heard the woman urge her husband in Kengian to forget about it. But Arisa couldn't. She bit her lip, trying to avoid drawing attention to herself.

In the years since Rea had been taken, she'd let the darkness grow inside her, fuelled by hatred of the injustices she saw every day, but she'd been careful not to speak out. She knew where speaking out in Lamore got you. But every inch of Arisa's being urged her to do something now; to stand up for what was right. She couldn't fail to protect these people, like she'd failed Rea.

She stepped toward the guards, not knowing what she would say – but she needn't have bothered, for the guards' attention was elsewhere. Their eyes were fixed on the sky above.

Arisa followed their gaze upwards, catching sight of the moon as the clouds parted. It transformed from darkness into grey, into shades of yellow and orange, before finally turning a bright, fiery red.

'It can't be,' she whispered to herself.

'A blood moon,' came the Kengian woman's unbelieving voice beside her.

The guards pointed at the moon, their mouths agape.

A buzz started around the gates as everyone stopped what they were doing. People came out of nearby houses to watch as the sky morphed from black all the way to crimson, until it matched the flaming red of the moon. The air was full of wonder for a few moments – before it thickened with fear.

'A blood moon…I haven't seen one of those since the year the Prince was born.' Stubby Fingers' voice was shaking. 'It's a bad omen, it is.'

Arisa shuddered at the truth in his words. The last blood moon had brought death to her doorstep, as well as many others.

'Mother, does this mean the Water Catcher is coming?' came the boy's small voice.

'Shush, Hyando.'

'It does!' He clapped his hands with glee. 'The blood moon is the first sign. It means the Water Catcher will come and save us. And defeat the mean King.'

'What's that?' Stubby Fingers spun around to face the boy.

The father stepped in front of the cart, waving his hands pleadingly. 'Nothing. The boy said nothing.'

'It didn't sound like nothing. It sounded like treason to me.'

The boy jumped up and down on the cart, and began shouting at the top of his lungs. 'The blood moon is here. The Water Catcher is coming. The Water Catcher is coming!'

His cries elicited a mixed chorus of whoops and hisses from the crowd.

'Listen here, brat—' Stubby Fingers manoeuvred his bulky frame up onto the cart and tried to grab the boy.

'Leave him. He's just a boy.' The mother struggled against the other guard as he pinned her arms behind her back, and the father tried futilely to pull Stubby Fingers away.

Arisa watched on, frozen, as the guard clambered toward the boy and slipped on a stack of hessian sacks. The cart wobbled heavily and the horse bolted forward. It happened so quickly, yet time seemed to slow as the sudden movement propelled the boy into the air, momentarily suspending him.

Then everything quickened again, and he plummeted to the ground.

His head connected with the cobblestones with a sickening crack. And then there was nothing but silence. Silence and blood. The ground, the sky, this night; they were all stained with blood.

And Arisa had done nothing to stop it.

# CHAPTER 2

$\mathcal{P}$rince Takai had been back at the castle for two days, and other than at supper in the Great Hall among all the other nobles, he still hadn't spoken to his father.

For the many years he had spent under the stewardship of the Duke of Lakeford at his property in Lamore's north, Takai had only seen his father a handful of times. He had seen his mother even less. They were practically strangers to him, but now that he was back, he expected things to be different. He was nearly eighteen, so it was time he took his rightful place at court, and become involved in ruling the kingdom that he would one day inherit – but he seemed invisible to the court's decision-makers.

He was intent on putting a stop to that.

Takai left his apartments and was heading toward his father's private rooms when the King's chief adviser, Chancellor Horace, emerged through the privy chamber doors. The Chancellor was one of the people – if not the only person – who had unchecked access to the King. His position was at odds with his humble origins; Horace had ascended to power far beyond someone of his lowly birth. He was elevated at court because he had been the King's childhood companion, and was now married to the King's distant cousin, Countess Datanya. Yet, from what Takai knew, Horace had his sights set even higher.

Judging by what the Duke of Lakeford had told Takai, being the King's chief adviser and strategist wasn't enough for Horace. These, after all, were just job titles. Positions that could be easily taken from him at the smallest slip-up or sign of the King's displeasure. Horace needed to shore up his and his family's power. He wanted the kinds of titles that could never be taken from them – and he would do anything to get closer to the crown.

'Your Highness.' The Chancellor greeted him with half a bow.

'Chancellor,' Takai grunted, and made to go around him, but Horace blocked his path. Takai gritted his teeth, knowing the Chancellor took his role as the 'voice' of the King seriously and wouldn't be in a hurry to allow anyone else access to the monarch. 'I'm just calling on my father.'

Horace clicked his jaw and grimaced. 'Apologies – the King has just retired for the evening. But please, come and speak to me a moment.' He indicated the way to his own rooms, and Takai resigned himself to another day without speaking to his father.

The Chancellor occupied the grandest rooms at the castle, second only to the King's apartments next door. It was a testament to his position and influence at court. There, Horace pontificated for some minutes about how glad he was to have the Prince back at court, and invited him to join the King's council at its next meeting. He went on to highlight his son Guthrie's achievements in Ette and how much Guthrie had impressed the Governor-General, Sir Marcus. Finally, he droned on about the virtues of his daughter, Theodora – a pretty enough girl whom Takai had gladly re-acquainted himself with; but he had no interest in discussing her with her scheming father.

As Horace's speech seemed about to draw to a close, Takai nodded politely and was about to excuse himself when a howling sound outside silenced their conversation.

'That sounded like a—'

'A wolf,' Horace said, eyes wide as they both went to the window and opened the shutters.

Takai peered out into the darkness, convinced his ears had deceived him. He couldn't remember the last time a wolf had been sighted in the kingdom. But there it was again. An unmistakable howl – and it sounded close.

He tried to make out the animal in the darkness of the castle grounds. And that was when he saw it.

Not the wolf. The moon.

Takai rubbed his eyes and looked again to confirm his mind wasn't playing tricks on him. But the moon was undoubtedly blood-red.

Lamore had gone almost two hundred years without a blood moon – until around eighteen years ago, the year of his birth, when one had appeared. And now there was another.

Horace frowned. 'Two blood moons in as many decades – both in the King's reign. The King will see it as a bad sign.'

'Surely he doesn't still believe in the Water Catcher prophecy?' Takai said. 'I thought there was no way of it coming to pass. That the firstborn Kengian line no longer exists.'

'Yes, any hope of a Kengian with the power to catch water – whatever that means – died with the last blood moon.

I made sure of it. But your father is superstitious. Especially after—'

Takai's hand curled into a fist. 'After the Kengian Prince tried to bewitch him. No wonder Lamore turned on all the Kengians and silver-eyes.'

Horace clicked his jaw again from side to side. His lower jaw was permanently misaligned. Takai had heard that the Kengian Prince himself had given the Chancellor the injury, not long before the Prince had been killed in a riot when the people of Obira rose up against the Kengians.

'That kind of magic doesn't have a place here,' Takai spat.

Horace raised a curious brow, but Takai wasn't about to divulge the reasons for his dislike of Kengians. It would bring back painful memories of his time in Lakeford. Even as a child, he had been singled out by the Kengian farmers, distrustful of the King's son. Some had been rude, some outright abusive – terrifying for a young boy far from home.

Takai looked out at the fiery moon with a new sense of satisfaction. Perhaps the blood moon *was* a sign – not of a prophecy coming to pass, but a sign that Lamore was on the rise, and that Kengians would soon learn their place in the kingdom he would rule...even if they had to be taught the same lesson all over again.

# CHAPTER 3

'Can you save him?' The father's voice was pinched with fear.

Arisa cast her eyes across the room to Hyando, the boy's broken body disturbingly small in the makeshift cot set up at the back of Erun's apothecary. Soft dawn light broke through the cracks in the shutters; the blood moon was long gone, but had left its devastating mark.

Hyando's mother, Lina, hovered over her son, murmuring words of comfort into his unhearing ears. Arisa stared at his mop of red curls – matted with blood, clumps sticking to his ashen forehead. She desperately wanted to assure Hyando's parents that their son would be fine, but something in Erun's manner told her otherwise. She watched as her guardian carefully applied gauze to Hyando's head. There was a nervous energy in his overly precise movements. Erun examined the boy's chest and stomach, his expert hands gauging the extent of the injuries beneath.

He pushed his eyeglasses up his nose and his lips thinned

momentarily. A lump formed in Arisa's throat as Erun walked slowly back to his workstation.

'Can you? Can you save him?' the father repeated, more urgently.

Arisa turned to meet the man's intense gaze. '*Te elli wuru sou rotse,*' she replied in Kengian. *We will do our best.*

The father nodded and gave her a grateful smile. Arisa had to look away. She balled her fists, longing to surrender to her anger. Anger at the unnecessary violence that had brought Hyando here. Anger that an innocent boy had been targeted for his harmless beliefs. Anger that she hadn't prevented it. She could barely contain the fury churning in her stomach.

She handed the father, who introduced himself as Cynfor, a fresh flannel to place on the boy's hot forehead. She hoped it would give him a distraction from pacing the floor and wringing his beaten hands. By the cot, Lina clutched Hyando's small hand in both of hers, as if willing him through touch alone to come back to her. Her red curls were wild and untamed, dark rings inscribed under her hazel eyes.

Arisa scrutinised the boy's ghostly face. It was strange-ly serene. Erun had given him a herbal sedative to help with the pain, and Hyando had slipped in and out of conscious-ness throughout the night.

He was a handsome boy, with perfect rosebud lips. Lips that suddenly contorted with pain.

'*Kom iko koelt non. Onmy musi iko,*' Lina whispered. *I'm here, little one. Mama is here.*

'He's moving. It's a good sign, isn't it?' Cynfor gave Arisa a hopeful look.

She glanced over to Erun, appealing to him for an answer, but he was preoccupied compounding more medicine. 'Let me speak to my guardian.'

Erun was surrounded by hundreds of vials of colourful liquids, creating an eerie glow around him. His brow was furrowed in concentration. Arisa dropped her voice to a whisper as she approached.

'Please say you can do something.'

Erun turned to meet her gaze. His harried expression said it all.

'There must be something.'

Erun shook his head slowly. 'He has ruptured several vital organs. They're beyond repair. All we can do now is help him with the pain.'

'Surely *you* of all people can fix him? You're a Scholar. This is what you trained to do.'

Erun took off his eyeglasses and rubbed the nape of his neck. 'There is nothing more I can do. It's beyond my powers and learning. The boy's father asked me earlier to send for the Shaman, in case.'

Arisa let out a strangled gasp. 'A Shaman? Are you sure it's come to that?'

'It has. I sent word during the night. The boy's parents will take comfort from the Shaman's ritual. Hyando will be at peace then.'

'But it's not right.' Arisa clenched her fists. 'It's not fair.'

'It may not be fair, but it is the reality.'

She slumped into a chair by the fireside and looked over at Hyando again. His father was earnestly patting his forehead. The futility of it engulfed her, a great fire stoked in her belly. Her fingernails dug into her palms.

'I will not have it, Erun. I will not have it.'

Erun came to sit beside her. 'You'll not have what, exactly?'

Arisa was about to say she would have justice for Hyando, but a small voice cried out from the other side of the room.

'Mama,' Hyando croaked. 'Papa.' His head thrashed from side to side, as if he were having a bad dream. Erun and Arisa raced to his side.

'Hyando!' Lina reached out to touch her son's brow.

Cynfor leant over the boy. 'We're right here.'

Hyando's eyes flung open. And that was when Arisa realised the boy's fate had been decided long before this night.

She stood frozen as she stared into Hyando's eyes. It wasn't the look of the sick and dying that struck her; she had seen that look many times before. It was something she hadn't noticed in the darkness – but now, with the arriving dawn, it was unmistakable.

Hyando's eyes were silver, like a shard of mirrored glass.

Arisa hadn't seen anyone with that eye colour since Rea. It brought a flood of emotions back to her. Emotions she'd tried hard to forget.

It didn't matter what happened here today. Hyando hadn't stood a chance in Lamore. Like Rea, he could never have escaped persecution. His eyes would always have betrayed his identity. Even if he could dress, speak and act like a Lamorian, it was useless if he bore the mark that only a Kengian with forbidden magic could possess. Arisa felt suddenly ashamed. Ashamed of the city she lived in, ashamed of her own relatively privileged and protected life. A level of shame she hadn't felt since Rea.

'Where am I?' Hyando asked.

Lina patted her son's hand. 'At a friend's.'

The boy's eyes sought out Arisa. His silver gaze locked on her amber one, but she had to look away.

Instead she watched Erun as he examined the boy. She looked up briefly to give his parents a half-smile. A smile that gave no false hope or promises. A smile that said: *Savour this. Savour this small moment in time, while you have your son back.*

Erun gave Lina a small nod and squeezed Cynfor's shoulder, then he and Arisa stepped away, back to the fireside.

'I'm cold, Mama,' Hyando squeaked.

'Here you go.' Lina pulled the blanket up over her son's shoulders, her face wet with tears. Hyando winced at her touch. 'Does it hurt a lot?'

'Not so much,' came the brave response. Lina patted his hand gently. 'Mama, tell me a story, please.'

'What would you like to hear?'

'A story about Kengia.'

'Which story?'

'The prophecy, of course.'

'No. Not that one.' She gave a pained smile. 'Not today.'

'Yes,' the boy insisted. 'That one, please.'

Like Hyando's mother, Arisa wasn't sure she wanted to hear it. The prophecy had been the trigger for last night's accident – but something about this family made her want to listen, to be part of their closeness somehow, even if she didn't believe in the story they were sharing.

Finally, Lina took a deep breath and began. She spoke in her native tongue, haltingly at first, but soon slipping into the lyrical cadence the Kengian language was known for. Even in her sadness, her storytelling had a musical tone. Hyando nestled into the cot, clearly soothed by his mother's voice.

'A long time ago – about two hundred years ago, in fact – King Alfred ruled the kingdom of Lamore. It was a golden

KYLIE FENNELL

age. Lamore's neighbour was the much larger kingdom of Kengia, our homeland. The two kingdoms were, of
course, separated by the Nymoi Alps.

'In King Alfred's time, access between the kingdoms was
possible via a narrow, winding mountain path. And despite
their vast differences, the two nations lived in peace. Trade
occurred between them, with Kengia supplementing Lamore's few natural resources. A formal alliance between the
nations was cemented when King Alfred married the Kengian King's firstborn child, Mary.'

Hyando's eyes lit up. 'And she had magic powers.'

Lina smiled. 'As the eldest royal child, Mary possessed an
unusual power over nature. Stronger powers than any Kengian, even the silver-eyes like you. She was able to control the
air and wind. While most Lamorians were scared of magic,
Mary gave them no reason to fear her. They came to love
their queen, as well as King Alfred's ability to bring peace
and prosperity to their kingdom. It wasn't an empire, back
then. King Alfred didn't rule over other lands or kingdoms.
But not everyone revelled in Lamore's peaceful existence.
Alfred's brother Emberto—'

'The Conqueror?'

Lina's brow furrowed. 'Yes, that is what the Lamorians call him. Emberto resented Lamore being reliant on the
good nature of the Kengians, and was scared of Mary's powers. He urged Alfred to invade Ivane and Ette, across
the Kyprian Sea, as they too were rich in natural
resources. King Alfred didn't agree, which made Emberto look for a reason to turn on his brother. And he
found a reason – in the prophecy.

'Emberto remembered hearing it as a boy. The prophecy
foretold that someone of Kengia's firstborn line would cause

the demise of the Lamorian regime. The prophecy said there would be a child who could—'

'Catch water.' Hyando's voice rose with excitement.

Lina laughed. 'You know this story too well.'

'Please go on, Mama.'

'Since Queen Mary possessed magical powers over nature, Emberto paid great heed to the prophecy. Alfred knew nothing of his brother's fears, which only grew with the appearance of a blood moon – the first sign the prophecy foretold. King Alfred and Queen Mary's son was born shortly after, and the child's birth was celebrated with a great display of lights in the sky.'

'Firesky!'

Lina nodded. 'The prophecy's second sign. It was all Emberto needed to be convinced the prophecy was coming to pass. He overthrew his brother, and imprisoned the King and his family, though Mary and her son were able to escape back to Kengia. Sadly, the child was not the Water Catcher, and Emberto soon invaded Ette and Ivane.

'He even imprisoned the last Firemaster, trying to force her to make great new weapons for him. Emberto may not have got his weapons, but through great determination he took Ette and Ivane as his own. It started one hundred and eighty years of Lamorian occupation, and what became the Kyprian Empire. The empire held until twenty years ago, when King Delrik's father lost Ette and Ivane.'

'But King Delrik took Ette back,' Hyando said quietly.

'Yes, he did.'

'And will he want Ivane back from King Laskar too?'

'He probably will.'

'And Kengia?'

Lina shook her head decidedly. 'No one will ever be able

to take Kengia. Not while the Kengian King continues to use his magic over the coastal and mountain borders.'

'King Leo will protect Kengia until the Water Catcher comes and saves us all,' Hyando said.

'Yes. When the Water Catcher comes, everyone will live in peace, and we will return home again. Until then, Kengia will remain shut off from the rest of the world.' Lina paused. 'I'm sorry there isn't a happier ending.'

'It's alright, Mama.' Hyando smiled up at his mother. 'There will be a happy ending. The Water Catcher will come.' He nodded to himself.

Arisa wished she could share the boy's confidence. But she knew there would never be a Water Catcher.

She swallowed the lump in her throat, and tried to distract herself by twirling the silver chain and medallion that hung around her neck. Focusing on the coldness of the chain in her hands, she traced the medallion's intricate pattern, determined to stop the tears from forming. She caught Erun's eye, and he was by her side in a moment. His arm went around her shoulders.

'Everything will be alright.'

'It will not be alright.' She glanced over at Hyando and his family. 'Nothing's alright about this.'

'Arisa…' She could see a question forming on Erun's lips. 'You said something earlier. Tell me what you meant by it.'

'Sorry?'

'You said you "will not have it". What did you mean?'

Arisa dropped her chain abruptly and clenched her jaw. She met her guardian's gaze with a defiant look. 'I meant that I will not have this grievous act and many more like it go unpunished. The King and his advisers must suffer for what they have done to their people. They are hateful. They must be stopped.'

Erun rubbed his neck before speaking in a deliberately even tone. 'Arisa, you shouldn't speak in such terms.'

'In what terms?'

'In terms of hate. Hate only leads to violence.'

'Maybe violence is the only way.'

'Nobody wins from violence. It only leads to further pain.'

'The Lamorian regime needs to hurt. Hurt like they have hurt others,' she spat. 'How can you *not* hate them for what they've done? How can *you*, of all people, forget so easily?'

Erun flinched. 'I have not forgotten, but it doesn't mean I'm full of hate. I don't advocate violence against anyone, and you shouldn't either. I thought you wanted to protect and *help* people, not hurt them. Isn't that why you wish to be a surgeon? It's the reason I'm a healer. It's the best way we can help, at least until…' His voice trailed off.

'Until what? Until a Water Catcher turns up? We both know it will never happen. It's impossible. There can never be a Water Catcher.'

Erun shook his head emphatically. 'You must have hope. You must believe.'

'I believe. But I believe in justice, not ancient prophecies.'

'Who exactly do you speak of justice for?'

'I told you. Hyando. Hyando's family. My family.'

'And…'

'*And* Rea.' Arisa's voice broke as she said the name out loud, her eyes awash with tears. 'There should be justice for her.'

Erun gave her a swift look and tilted his head toward the rear door of the shop. She knew she couldn't cry in front of Hyando and his parents.

She ran outside into the garden. At least now she didn't

have to meet the eyes of the boy she had failed – the boy they had all failed. Among the rows of herbs and medicinal plants, Arisa could be alone and cry.

She stood by the evergreen Kengian silverleaf tree. Erun said it reminded him of the sacred yew in Lochlen, the capital of his homeland: the source of all Kengian magic. There, under its silver boughs, she could shed tears for all the Kengians, for her fellow Lamorians, for her parents, and for Rea. The tears ran freely down her cheeks now as she sobbed.

At times like these, the wonder of Kengian magic seemed so far away. Every Kengian was born with some magic in their veins, and with the right training and dedication, they could become one with nature. Over time, the silver-eyes like Rea and Hyando could learn to communicate on a higher level with all the natural elements – hearing the crackling voice in a fire, the mumbling of a stone. The firstborn line of the Kengian royal family had those silver eyes, but were also gifted with elemental magic. They had the power to manipulate nature, bend it to their will, like the Water Catcher was prophesied to do...If the firstborn line existed at all. But it was lost – lost like the Firemasters, who could not only master the elements but also transform into different creatures. Now all that was left were Kengian Scholars like Erun, who learnt science and spells to harness the lifeforce known as *kira*; and the Shamans, who were the bridge between this world and the next, who could see through the eyes of those in the past, be it person or animal, and gain glimpses of possible futures.

Arisa wept. Because despite all of this magic existing in the world, none of it could save Hyando.

In her grief, she didn't notice the approach of the woman in the hooded cloak.

'Hush, child. It can't be all that bad.'

The woman appeared in front of her, as if she had materialised out of thin air. Arisa stepped backwards, seeking refuge in the shadows cast by the building's eaves. She tried to mask her face, but her gaze was drawn to the strikingly beautiful stranger.

The woman pushed back her hood to reveal a perfectly proportioned face, and long black hair that fell in waves midway to her waist. Her skin shimmered as if covered in silver dust. 'You must be Erun's ward.'

Arisa nodded, avoiding the woman's eyes.

'I came as soon as I got the message. I'm—'

'You're the Kengian Shaman.'

'I am.'

'You have taken a great risk coming to the city. Shamans are feared as much as silver-eyes.'

'We all take risks when we must.'

'But risk for what? The boy can't be saved.' Arisa kept her eyes downcast, but could feel the Shaman's gaze boring into her.

'I'm not here to save the boy, in the sense that you think. I'm here to guide his soul and help it transition into the next realm, into his next existence. There, he will be at peace.'

She snorted. 'Is that all there is to be hopeful for? That his soul will be at peace? Why can't he live? Why can't his family's life be easier in *this* world? Why can't we all be saved from this forsaken place?'

'Is that what you believe? That we can't be saved?'

'We can't. None of us can be spared from the hopelessness of this kingdom.'

Before Arisa realised it, the Shaman was standing directly before her again. She reached out and lifted Arisa's chin. Arisa tried to resist, but was overcome by the strange energy and warmth emanating from the woman's hands.

The Shaman stared right at her. She was so close that Arisa saw her pupils dilate for a split second. The Shaman continued looking into her eyes for what felt like an eternity, before smiling and releasing her chin.

'You don't believe what you're saying. You know, as well as I do, that there is hope. The blood moon has come and the Water Catcher will follow.'

'I'm well past hoping and believing in an impossible prophecy,' Arisa scoffed. 'It isn't enough.'

'You're right. It isn't enough to just hope and believe. You must *know* it. You must know with every inch of your being: better times are on the way.'

Arisa made to argue, but the Shaman put up a hand to silence her. 'Hope and believe for now, and when you're ready, you will know.'

'Know what?'

'You will know when you know.' The Shaman gave a knowing smile and one last piercing look before disappearing into the house.

Arisa was left to puzzle over the cryptic words. What did she mean, Arisa 'must *know*'? The only thing she knew was that there must be justice. It wasn't enough to try to protect others. There must be justice for Hyando, for Rea, for everyone. The hateful Lamorian regime must suffer – suffer as much as she was suffering right now.

She may not know how and when, but Arisa would make it happen.

'They will be punished,' she pledged to herself, wiping the rust-coloured tears from her cheeks. Out here, her real self was exposed for the world to see.

Arisa raised her eyes to the sky – her Kengian eyes, as

silver as the sun above. 'And I shall be the one who punishes them.'

*Get the* **The Firemaster's Legacy**.

You can find out more and purchase any of Kylie's books at **www.kyliefennell.com** or via the below QR code.

# BEGINNINGS: THE KYPRIAN PROPHECY – AN ORIGINS NOVELLA

Get it now for free!

**No Email Address Required**

*"Only a fool can't understand that there cannot be light without the darkness, and that power lies in harnessing the very thing people are scared of."*

As a silver-eyes Laha has an extraordinary ability to harness the power within nature. She is also a royal companion to the Kengian Princess Mary, and with all of Kypria finally at peace Laha should be content…but she is far from it.

Laha has lost her powers and a darkness claws away inside her. She doesn't fit in at the Lamorian court, nor does she want to. She yearns for a life of excitement and adventure, but most of all she yearns to regain her powers and understand her dark urges.

The answer arrives in the form of a mysterious fortune teller whose prophecy and presence threaten to destroy everyone Laha cares about including the Lamorian Prince Emberto. Despite this she is drawn to the fortune teller and the woman's offer to help her realise the full potential of her powers...if she's willing to embrace her darkness.

Laha's choices lead to discoveries about her own identity and her friends being caught up in a deadly showdown between the most powerful of all Kengians – the Firemasters.

*Beginnings* is a stand alone novella that also sets the scene for the Kyprian Prophecy series and Book 1 – *The Firemaster's Legacy*.

*Beginnings* is **available for FREE** on all major online book retail sites. No email address required!

# ABOUT THE AUTHOR

**Kylie Fennell** has made a 25-year career out of wrangling words, working as a journalist and editor, and more recently an author of speculative fiction. If she wasn't a writer, she'd be a superhero librarian – conquering the Dewey Decimal System by day and saving the world one book at a time by night.

As an Australian writer of European and Aboriginal (Gumbaynggirr and Bundjalung) descent she likes to explore culture and identity through her writing, as well as magic… always magic!

Kylie lives in Brisbane (Yuggera and Turrbal Country) with her husband, son and too many pets.

To find out more or to purchase Kylie's books go to _www.kyliefennell.com_.

If you want to stay up-to-date with Kylie's writing **or be part of her book review team** you can sign up to her mailing list via her website. All subscribers receive a **free book** – **_Seeds from the Story Tree_** – a collection of award-winning speculative fiction stories and other short works, exclusive to Kylie's subscribers.

You can also connect with Kylie on social media.

# THE FAE OF THE CRYSTAL PALACE – A NEW YA FANTASY ROMANCE SERIES COMING SOON!

## THE PLEDGE: AN ORIGINS SHORT STORY

A Fae Ranger sent through a portal to Victorian England to stop an assassin faces an impossible choice: save her family or the Fae Realm in a battle between the light and darkness.

This origins story sets the scene for the *Fae of the Crystal Palace* – a fantasy romance (with a touch of mystery) series. **Get the story for FREE here!**

facebook.com/kyliefennellauthor

twitter.com/kylie_fennell

instagram.com/kylie_fennell

bookbub.com/profile/kylie-fennell

goodreads.com/Kylie_Fennell

pinterest.com/kyliefennell

tiktok.com/@kyliefennellauthor

patreon.com/KylieFennell